BATTLING THE WIND AND WAVES ON THE SEA OF COMMERCE

John Xiao Zhang

Copyright © 2022 John Xiao Zhang

The moral right of the author has been asserted.

Apart from any fair dealing for the purposes of research or private study, or criticism or review, as permitted under the Copyright, Designs and Patents Act 1988, this publication may only be reproduced, stored or transmitted, in any form or by any means, with the prior permission in writing of the publishers, or in the case of reprographic reproduction in accordance with the terms of licences issued by the Copyright Licensing Agency. Enquiries concerning reproduction outside those terms should be sent to the publishers.

This is a work of fiction. Names, characters, businesses, places, events and incidents are either the products of the author's imagination or used in a fictitious manner. Any resemblance to actual persons, living or dead, or actual events is purely coincidental.

Matador
Unit E2 Airfield Business Park,
Harrison Road, Market Harborough,
Leicestershire. LE16 7UL
Tel: 0116 2792299
Email: books@troubador.co.uk
Web: www.troubador.co.uk/matador
Twitter: @matadorbooks

ISBN 978 1803131 269

British Library Cataloguing in Publication Data.
A catalogue record for this book is available from the British Library.

Printed and bound in the UK by TJ Books Limited, Padstow, Cornwall
Typeset in 11pt Adobe Garamond Pro by Troubador Publishing Ltd, Leicester, UK

Matador is an imprint of Troubador Publishing Ltd

BATTLING THE WIND AND WAVES ON THE SEA OF COMMERCE

This is a golden age, an epoch filled with hope, vitality, creativity, wisdom, tenacity and wealth.

This is also a troubled age, an epoch that witnesses dissatisfaction, inequality and the wealth gap, incredulity and lack of supervision over power.

CONTENTS

LIST OF CHARACTERS		XI
PROLOGUE		XVII
PART I	A SUCCESSFUL CONFUCIAN BUSINESSMAN IS MORE RESPECTABLE	1
CHAPTER I	A FRUSTRATED PUBLIC BIDDING	3
CHAPTER II	IT IS NOT EASY TO WORK AS A DIRECTOR IN A STATE ENTERPRISE	17
CHAPTER III	THE STOCK MARKET IS A GAMBLING HOUSE	30
CHAPTER IV	I SAVED HER	40

PART II	**THE DISTRESSING LOVE TRIANGLE CONTINUES**	**51**
CHAPTER I	WE HAVE NOT MARRIED EACH OTHER	53
CHAPTER II	LET'S DIVORCE	61
CHAPTER III	SHE IS MISSING	71
CHAPTER IV	LET'S SHARE HIM	78
PART III	**A CRISIS IN THE TRADE WAR**	**87**
CHAPTER I	A BUILDING COLLAPSE ACCIDENT	89
CHAPTER II	A HARD INVESTIGATION AND COLLECTION OF EVIDENCE	98
CHAPTER III	CEO ZHANG HAS BEEN WRONGED	107
CHAPTER IV	REVIVING THE BUSINESS	117
PART IV	**PAYING THE PRICE FOR A BETTER SOCIETY**	**127**
CHAPTER I	SHOULD WE FOLLOW THE ROAD OF SOCIALISM OR CAPITALISM?	129
CHAPTER II	A NEW STAGE TO BUILD A MODERN ENTERPRISE SYSTEM	140
CHAPTER III	THE DIFFICULT SITUATION OF THE REDUNDANT WORKERS	149
CHAPTER IV	HE IS YOUR BIOLOGICAL BROTHER	155
PART V	**2008, A YEAR OF GREAT SADNESS AND REJOICING**	**167**
CHAPTER I	CHAOS IN THE REAL ESTATE INDUSTRY	169

CHAPTER II	FACING BANKRUPTCY IN THE CRISIS	179
CHAPTER III	BUSINESS IS BOOMING AGAIN	193
CHAPTER IV	THE INSPIRING OLYMPIC GAMES	204

PART VI	A GOLDEN AGE WITH SOME SOCIAL ISSUES	**215**
CHAPTER I	THE BIG DEVELOPMENT OF URBANIZATION	217
CHAPTER II	A LIFE-AND-DEATH STRUGGLE AGAINST CORRUPTION	229
CHAPTER III	A GOLDEN AGE WITH WORRIES	239
CHAPTER IV	FOLLOWING TAOISM IN HIS RETIREMENT LIFE	253

| EPILOGUE | 262 |

LIST OF CHARACTERS

Main Characters

I. Zhang Feng, *main hero in the trilogy and in this volume. A handsome and talented man who suffers greatly during the Cultural Revolution. After the revolution, he first becomes a scholar and then later a political leader in his city. In this volume, he enters into the world of business and work hard to improve the living conditions of the people and the economy of the country. He is also called* Brother Feng *by his lovers and friends,* Xiao Feng *or* Xiao Zhang *by his family and people around him who are older than him.*

II. His close friends: in Volume 1, 2 and this volume,

  A. Wang Hai, *a factory director.*

- B. Li He, *used to be a medical doctor. Then a director of a travel agency.*
  They support Zhang Feng in his mission to carry out economic and political reforms, and his business.

III. His lovers: in Volume 1, 2 and this volume,
- A. Yu Mei, *wife of Zhang Feng, daughter of a late high ranking officer (her name means plum blossom.). She is also called Xiao Mei or Mei Mei by her family and lovers. In volume2, she is a head of a department in a city bureau. In this volume, she helps Zhang Feng in the running of his business.*
- B. Dan Dan, *ex-wife of Zhang Feng, (her name means peony). She is a scholar at a university in Volume 2, in this volume, she is a general manager in Zhang Feng's company.*
- C. Qing Lian, *a classmate of Zhang Feng and an active Red Guard in Volume 1. (Her name means lotus), a journalist in volume2. In this volume, she helps her ex-husband Li He to run a travel agency.*

IV. His personal and political enemies:
- A. Cai Wenge, *an active Red Guard in Volume 1. Prisoner in Volume 2 and an evil businessman in this volume.*
- B. Director Shen, *a high ranking official who is a rigid left-wing element set against economic and political reform, and a corrupt official.*
- C. Li Qiu, *Zhang Feng's university classmate but also an official in the government who is a political villain.*

Characters by Alphabet

Bai He, *daughter of Li He.*

Cai Wenge, *an ambitious villain, enemy to Zhang Feng in this trilogy. In this volume, he is an evil businessman.*

Chang Zheng, *rival of Zhang Feng and a Red Guard in Volume I, son of General Zhao Wu. In volume 2 and 3, he is a friend to Zhang Feng, discharged from the army who becomes a civil officer to support Zhang Feng*

Chen Tao, *an university classmate of Zhang Feng in the past, , an officer in city council who supports Zhang Feng in Volume 2. He is a manager in Zhang Feng's company. in this Volume.*

Dan Dan, *Zhang Feng's lover and ex-wife, a beautiful and talented girl. a lecturer at a university in Volume2 and general manager in Zhang Feng's company in this volume.*

Dan Feng, *Son of Zhang Feng and Dan Dan.*

Du Shan, *a businessman from Taiwan.*

Captain Fan Wei, *police captain who supports the main character Zhang Feng*

Hai Jing, Master, *Dan Dan's father, he used to be a Taoist monk who taught Zhang Feng martial arts in Volume I, with a secret identity. In volume 2and 3, he is Zhang Feng's father-in-law.*

He Hua, *a younger girl in the countryside where Zhang Feng and his friends worked as 'Educated youth' in Volume I. In volume 2, she enacts economic reform in the countryside by conducting a land contract scheme. In this volume, she runs supermarkets in the city.*

Helen, *an overseas Chinese lady who works for Volkswagen. She loves Wang Hai.*

He, Secretary, *a secretary of the party committee of Hua Dan County.*

Huang Lei, *a lecturer of Jili University and a friend to Zhang Feng. He runs a company in this Volume.*

Jian Jun, *son of Chang Zheng.*

Lan Hua, *daughter of Qing Lian.*

Liang Fu, *a businessman in Hong Kong.*

Liang Hua, *a professor at the London School of Economics, supervisor to Dan Dan. He loves Dan Dan and tries to marry her.*

Li He, *a close friend to Zhang Feng, a doctor of Chinese medicine in Volume 1 and a company director in Volume 2 and 3.*

Lin Jianguo, *a savior of Zhang Feng in Volume I. an officer in the government who always supports Zhang Feng in Voilume2, He is a manager in Zhang Feng's company in this volume.*

Li Qiu, *a university classmate of Zhang Feng in the past, an officer who follows the evil leaders in the government.*

Lv Guohao, *director of the Jiang Cheng Daily Newspaper.*

Qing Lian, *an active Red Guard who loves the main hero Zhang Feng secretly in Volume I. She is a journalist in volume2. She run a travel agency with her ex-husband Li He in this volume.*

Wang Hai, *a close friend of the main hero Zhang Feng*

Wang Li, *a university student who works in a government department after graduation in Volume 2. She loves the main character Zhang Feng secretly. She is a manager in a hotel in this volume.*

Yu Mei, *Zhang Feng's lover and wife. Daughter of the late party secretary of the province. An officer in a local government department in Volume 2 and a manager in Zhang Feng's company in this volume.*

Zhang Feng, *the main hero in the story. A handsome and talented man.*

Zhang Lin, *Zhang Fen*g's younger sister.

PROLOGUE

This is the last volume of the historical fiction trilogy, *Sailing across the Red Storm Trilogy,* representing modern Chinese history, following volume one: *Sailing across the Red Storm* and volume two: *Floating and Sinking on the Sea of Officialdom.* The time span of this trilogy covers over half a century from the 1960s to 2010s – a significant period of time, reflecting the darkest and brightest moments in modern Chinese history.

In volume one: *Sailing across the Red Storm*, the whole country and its people suffer from hardship and unprecedented calamity during the Cultural Revolution. In volume two: *Floating and Sinking on the Sea of Officialdom*, drawing lessons from the Cultural Revolution and learning from the suffering caused by the dictatorship and poverty of the old Stalinism, the country begins economic and political reforms and tries to build an open, free, democratic and prosperous society. In this volume, we will see that China has entered a commercial and free marketing society with rapid economic development and a continuous rise in living standards. China has integrated into the international community and become an economic super power although the country still has a lot of social issues to resolve such as democracy, corruption and the gulf between the rich and poor.

If we use the changing seasons to describe these three periods in the trilogy, they look like chilly winter, warm spring and hot summer.

This last volume is set against the historical background of the third period of time described above. Our main character, his lovers, friends and family, are struggling against the commercial tide, with some plain sails and some battling with the wind and waves. Yet, like the voyage of their country, they have bravely sailed to a peaceful and happy harbour.

It is spring, 1997. In the beautiful North Mountain Park of Jili City, Northeast China, our main character in this trilogy, Zhang Feng, is taking a spring outing. He was already a middle-aged man with the scars left by many vicissitudes on his handsome face. After suffering political persecution and the threat of death during the Cultural Revolution, he had finished his Higher Education and became a successful scholar. Then he entered political circles to help carry out economic and political reforms to build his country into a democratic and prosperous society. Yet, he had experienced what it was like to float and sink on the sea of officialdom.

When free marketing was legalized in the country in the 1990s, he left official circles, creating his own, real estate company. He became a 'Confucian Businessman', striving for economic development and the improvement of living standards. Like Zhang Feng, numerous members of the social elite changed their careers and went into business in 1992. They became known as '1992 Businessmen'.

Holding his wife's hand, they walked slowly up to the top of the mountain. Yu Mei was his second wife but she had actually been his first girlfriend. Like Romeo and Juliet, they were life-death lovers. They had suffered many ordeals during the Cultural Revolution, experiencing many partings and reunions, but they had to finally part from each other because of the deception of a wicked man. When the Cultural Revolution ended, Yu Mei felt hopeless and gave up her secular life to became a Taoist nun in the Taoist temple of North Mountain. Then Zhang Feng married his close childhood friend, Dan Dan, who was a clever and beautiful girl.

Yet, at the beginning of economic reform, after Zhang Feng had worked for the Government as a high ranking official, Yu Mei unexpectedly reappeared as the Director of the Foreign Trade Department in Shenzhen City. So they fell in love again, deeply. Soon their love was noticed by Dan Dan. In order to resolve this difficult love triangle, Dan Dan married her PhD supervisor, Professor Liang Hua at the LSE and moved to the UK with their son, leaving Zhang Feng free to marry Yu Mei.

Four years after Zheng Feng had left politics, Dan Dan returned home with her son, helping Zhang Feng and Yu Mei to open a real estate company. Her husband, Liang Hua, did not return with her but occasionally visited. This made Zhang Feng feel awkward, as it seemed like doing business together was affecting her family life.

Reaching the top of the mountain, Zhang Feng and Yu Mei

sat on a huge rock: their favourite place to enjoy the beautiful scenery. From this point, they could see the great river flowing to the East and a bright sun shining over the lofty mountains. It was a view which made people admire the magnificence of Nature and sigh with emotion about the vicissitudes of life and the rapid passing of time. The rock was hidden by dense woods so no visitor could see them. Resting against Zhang Feng's broad chest, Yu Mei enjoyed his caresses with her eyes shut.

Stroking her hair, Zhang Feng sighed with emotion,

"Yu Mei, time has passed so rapidly. Looking back at the ups and downs in our life, our hearts are filled with many emotions. We climbed up from hell to the happy human world, from harsh winter to vital spring. I used to be a prisoner, then became a successful scholar, then a high ranking official, able to carry out reforms. Now I am a millionaire, a successful Confucian Businessman!"

Holding his hand, Yu Mei said, "I always take all your achievements for granted. Even 30 years ago, when I first knew you, I realized that you would be successful, whatever you did, because you are a talented and hard working person, with strong will power and bravery."

"All women like to praise their husbands!" Zhang Feng smiled.

"It depends on whether their husbands are worth praising!"

Zhang Feng gazed at the beautiful scenery before his eyes, thought for a while, and said,

"After the main leader, Deng Xiaoping, died at the beginning of this year, China had a peaceful power transition for the first time in its modern history, restoring collective leadership and renouncing dictatorship. Although Deng was responsible for Tiananmen Square event, he made great contributions to bring order out of chaos after the Cultural Revolution and carry out the economic and political reforms which have improved our economy and living standards so much. Our business also benefits greatly from his policy."

"People's attitudes towards social status have also changed. They respect you more now as a CEO than when you were Mayor of the city. Brother Feng, will the handover of Hong Kong at the end of this year benefit the economy of the mainland?" Yu Mei asked.

"Of course! Hong Kong will join the huge market of the mainland and bring in more funds and technology. Dan Dan's husband, Liang Hua, and his brother in Hong Kong all believe Hong Kong citizens should welcome the handover rather than emigrate abroad. It seems that some of them still have an impression of the old China, during the Cultural Revolution."

Both of them were concentrating on their talk and did not notice the foot steps behind them.

"Daddy!" a child's voice cried.

Turning round, Zhang Feng and Yu Mei saw Dann Feng, the son of Zhang Feng and Dan Dan, running towards them, followed by Zhang Feng's ex-wife, Dan Dan. Dan Feng was already twelve years old and was studying at the best middle school in the city. Inheriting good genes from Zhang Feng, he was both handsome and taller than boys of the same age.

A few years earlier, Zhang Feng and Dan Dan told him about their divorce which did not upset him too much as he and Dan Dan lived on the same street and the two families met quite often. Dan Dan worked in Zhang Feng's company as the General Manager and she had a very good relationship with Yu Mei. They were like sisters. People around them did not feel uncomfortable because attitudes towards love and marriage changed greatly after the Cultural Revolution. Dan Dan's husband, Liang Hua, just visited them occasionally. He said he was too busy with his teaching and research in the UK but Dang Feng always called him 'Uncle Liang', not 'Daddy', which made Zhang Feng and Yu Mei feel awkward.

Dan Dan explained that Dan Feng had called Liang Hua 'Uncle Liang' before Dan Dan married him so he had got used to it and could not change now. Dan Feng always affectionately called Zhang Feng 'Daddy', and called Yu Mei his 'second mother'. Yu Mei had lost her fertility following a miscarriage from her deceptive marriage with the villain, Cai Wenge. She loved and cared for Dan Feng like her own son.

Dan Dan walked up and sat down beside them.

Zhang Feng said to Dan Dan, "Our villa project is nearly finished. Most of them are already sold. I did not realize that the free market surge in 1992 had created so many rich people so quickly! I have reserved two villas with riverside scenery, one for me and Yu Mei, and the other for you and Dan Feng. When Liang Hua returns, he can live together with you and Dan Feng. It is not easy to find luxury property in England so maybe, he would prefer to stay here after he has seen this villa."

"Not really," Dan Dan said. "He is writing a three volume economics book. He might feel distracted if he stayed here."

Dan Feng suddenly asked Dan Dan, "Mum, why do Daddy and second mother always live together but you and Uncle Liang do not?"

Dan Dan flushed and replied sharply, "You are a child and do not understand how different couples live in different situations."

Zhang Feng and Yu Mei stopped talking about the relationship between Dan Dan and Liang Hua as both of them, especially Yu Mei, suspected that the main reason for Dan Dan divorcing Zhang Feng and marrying Liang Hua nine years ago had been to resolve the painful love triangle between them at that time. She sacrificed herself in order to give Zhang Feng back to Yu Mei; she did not really want to marry Liang Hua. That was why she returned home with Dan Feng after four years to help with Zhang Feng's business. Originally, she had said she would return to the UK after Zhang Feng's company was established but four years had passed and Zhang Feng's business was very successful and yet she remained, showing no inclination to return to England. She always gave reasons as to why she would like to remain. It seemed that Liang Hua did not care what she decided to do.

Zhang Feng quickly changed the topic and discussed the expansion of their business to other provinces with Dan Dan. Suddenly, a female voice was heard behind them,

"Do not talk about business during the spring outing! Just relax and enjoy the sightseeing!"

Looking back, they saw Qing Lian, the ex-wife of their good friend, Li He, and her daughter, Lan Hua. Qing Lian was in a green coat and jeans and looked beautiful. Just like Yu Mei and Dan Dan, she did not look like she was in her forties. Qing Lian used to love Zhang Feng secretly when they were at middle school but became a fanatical Red Guard during the Cultural Revolution. She only realized that she was, herself, a victim of the revolution later and tried to commit suicide as a result. Miraculously, she was saved by Zhang Feng. She went to university after the Cultural Revolution, working for a city newspaper as a journalist and married Li He, a friend of Zhang Feng, although she still loved Zhang Feng.

Ten years ago, when Zhang Feng was in the middle of his

difficult love triangle and very upset, he unintentionally had sex with Qing Lian. He mistakenly identified her as Yu Mei when he was drunk. Since then, she had divorced Li He and moved to Dalian city where she had married another man and had a little girl. Just as Zhang Feng started his business, she returned to Jili City and began running a travel agency with her ex-husband, Li He. Her daughter, Lan Hua, was now nine years old and was very pretty.

"Aunt Qing Lian! Sister Lan Hua! Are you also having a spring outing?" Dan Feng warmly greeted them.

Dan Feng was very dear to them as Qing Lian had looked after him often when he was a small child. He once asked his father whether he could call Qing Lian his 'third mother' but he was firmly told he could not by Zhang Feng who still remembered the 'accidental' affair. Although he had always tried to help her in life and business, secretly, he still felt guilty.

Dan Feng liked to play with Lan Hua. Holding her hand, they tried to catch a dragon fly together, leaving behind the three women, who all loved Zhang Feng deeply. Both Yu Mei and Dan Dan knew Qing Lian loved Zhang Feng but their life experience and maturity made them more tolerant. They were not on guard but treated her more like a sister. She was still single and because of this, they, together with Zhang Feng, cared about her private life.

Zhang Feng asked her, "Qing Lian, Huang Lei has visited you quite often recently but he isn't only asking you to arrange a holiday, is he?"

Huang Lei was a good friend of Zhang Feng and used to be the Director of the Department of Chemistry at Jili University. His wife had died in a road accident two years ago. He left his academic career in 1992 and had opened a fine chemical company. At that time, Zhang Feng helped him with the funding to create his company and so he felt deep gratitude towards Zhang Feng. As a result of his friendship, he was also familiar with Qing Lian and had tried to woo her recently.

Qing Lian looked rather shy as she answered Zhang Feng.

"I regard him as just a good friend. I have got used to being single and living with my daughter. When I have any problems at home, I always get help from you and my ex-husband, Li He."

Both Dan Dan and Yu Mei tried to persuade Qing Lian to accept Huang Lei's advances, saying that he was a reliable and responsible man. Qing Lian said she would consider the matter again.

It was lunch time and Dan Dan suggested going back down the mountain to have something to eat. There were a lot of restaurants and food stands at the entrance to the park. As they left the park, they saw many brand new cars lining up on the square, colourful flags fluttering in the wind and music playing.

A deep and familiar male voice announced, "Dear citizens! Please take a look at our newly designed cars, including our 'Red Flag' cars which you could only dream about owning before because they were reserved for top state leaders! You will also see a new Audi model which is both fast and smooth to drive…"

"Wang Hai? Is he promoting his new cars as the Director of his factory?" asked Zhang Feng.

Wang Hai was both Zhang Feng's loyal friend and his brother-in-law. He was the Director of the Jili Motor Vehicle Factory which was the largest in the country at that time. Walking up to the promotion site, Zhang Feng and his ladies saw that Wang Hai was talking to Li He, Qing Lian's ex-husband, and his wife and daughter. The two groups greeted each other warmly. Li He's daughter, Bai He, was the same age as Qing

Lian's daughter, Lan Hua. The two girls were both beautiful and liked each other. They all liked handsome Dan Feng. Sometimes, when these families got together, Li He told Zhang Feng that in the future, they might be related by marriage. Seeing that Qing Lian looked unhappy, Li He said he would give priority to Qing Lian's daughter, Lan Hua to have Dan Feng ,but not his daughter Bai He, but Qing Lian quickly changed the topic.

Wang Hai drew Zhang Feng aside and pointed to a stand at the other side of the entrance.

"Can you see? Your sworn enemy, Cai Wenge, is there, promoting his properties. He really over-estimates his abilities. His real estate company is very small but he dares to compete with your, much larger company."

Looking in the direction Wang Hai pointed to, Zhang Feng saw that a thin, weak man, with some grey hair, was handing out promotion leaflets. Yes, he was Zhang Feng's personal and political enemy, Cai Wenge. Cai had been Zhang Feng's middle school classmate, an ugly and stupid person but he was ambitious and had always tried to compete with Zhang Feng in all areas of life.

During the Cultural Revolution, he had been a fanatical Red Guard who madly sought revenge on Zhang Feng. He plotted to send Zhang Feng to prison and then to the execution ground. He also destroyed the relationship between Zhang Feng and Yu Mei, deceived and then married her but abandoned her later. Cai was punished at the end of the Cultural Revolution and sentenced to imprisonment for eleven years but after he was released, he opened a real estate company. Two years earlier, during a spring outing in the North Mountain, he came across Zhang Feng and his friends. He showed no regret. Quite the reverse; he challenged Zhang Feng once again saying he would beat Zhang Feng in the business world.

"He really is a villain!" Zhang Feng said, angrily. "He is also an unscrupulous businessman. I hear he uses poor quality materials to build houses and cheats his customers when he sells them. He lost to me politically and he will be defeated in business as well."

"Be careful, brother – he never acts in normal ways. People have said he tries to find business partners from outside provinces in order to grab more shares in our local market," Wang Hai said.

Not wanting to annoy Yu Mei, Zhang Feng and Wang Hai did not go any further. After talking for a while, they decided to all have lunch in a meat pie restaurant. Wang Hai drew Zhang Feng aside after the others had entered the restaurant.

Seeing the secretive expression on Wang Hai's face, Zhang Feng asked, "What other matter do you still have on your mind, my Director?"

"Brother, it looks like that fortune-telling picture will control all of your life. You see, the seven people on the picture are all here today. Remember? In the picture, the tall peak is you, the lower peaks on each side are your loyal friends, me and Li He. The three flowers at the foot of the peaks are your lovers Yu Mei, Dan Dan and Qing Lian, and the ivy around you, symbolizing a poisonous snake, is Cai Wenge."

It was really true, Zhang Feng thought. He would have liked to argue that Qing Lian used to be Li He's wife and had nothing to do with him but he remembered his unintentional affair with her so he said nothing.

He entered the restaurant with Wang Hai to join the others for lunch.

PART I

A Successful Confucian Businessman Is More Respectable

Chapter I

A Frustrated Public Bidding

One week after the spring outing, a senior management meeting was held in the newly built, four storey building of Zhang Feng's company. As the Chairman of the Board of Directors and CEO, Zhang Feng was sitting in the host's position. Dan Dan, as the General Manager, was sitting on his left side and Chen Tao, the Manager of the Marketing Department, was sitting on his right. The Manager of the Sales Department, Yu Mei, and the Manager of the Construction Department, Lin Jianguo, and other senior managers were all in the meeting. Zhang Feng explained that Chen Tao would tell them about an important project planned by the City Council.

"Jili City Council proposes building a huge, modern shopping mall, containing different services like shopping, hospitality and health care, a bit like those in Singapore. It will improve the appearance of the City and make things convenient for the citizens. The City Council will hold a bidding meeting next week. As the number one real estate company in our province, we should bid for this project."

"I agree with Manager Chen. We have achieved a lot, building thousands of good quality apartments and houses but we should also expand into commercial buildings," Zhang Feng said.

"Along with the handover of Hong Kong and joining the WTO, China will soon become a huge commercial society and there will be numerous demands for commercial real estate, such as offices, finance, insurance and exhibitions so we should take this public bidding seriously," Dan Dan added.

Lin Jianguo, Manager of the Construction Department, said,

"My department has recently prepared for commercial building. We have employed two experienced architects from the Provincial Architecture Academy, and an overseas Chinese architect of commercial buildings. This will enhance our human resources for the bidding."

Yu Mei said Dan Dan and Lin Jianguo could go to the bidding meeting but Zhang Feng said he should go, together with all his senior managers, as this would be the first commercial project for their company and would give them good experience.

A week later, Zhang Feng and his senior managers drove to the City Construction and Planning Department in three Mercedes-Benz cars. There were several officers at the entrance and it seemed that they were waiting for some VIPs. Just getting out of his car, Zhang Feng saw Director Li of the Department and his assistants who greeted him, respectfully.

"Welcome Mayor Zhang! Oh, no! I mean CEO Zhang!"

Li had been the Deputy Director of the Department when Zhang Feng was Mayor of the City but at that time, they did not specially respect each other. It looked like nowadays, attitudes towards social status had changed greatly. People respected you more if you were rich but, as Dan Dan and Yu Mei said, it used to be very dangerous if you were a wealthy person like a landlord or a businessman before and during the Cultural Revolution. You were an enemy of the Communist Party and its people and could even be put into jail or killed.

After China gave up on rigid socialism and started political and economic reforms, living standards were much improved and more people became rich. Attitudes towards wealth were totally the opposite: to be rich was more prestigious now and to be poor was shameful. People respected successful businessmen more than high ranking officials.

When Zhang Feng was Mayor, he lived in a small house, allocated by the City Council, used a small car given to him by the City and earned a modest salary. Now, he was the CEO of the biggest real estate company in the province, a millionaire, living in a luxury apartment and driving prestigious cars. As a result, the high ranking officials always respected him greatly because he had money with which to help the City Council and he contributed to charities as well.

Director Li also warmly welcomed Zhang Feng's senior managers. He accompanied Zhang Feng and the others into the building. He said he was very pleased that Zhang Feng's company would be bidding for the project and thought that the project should be given to them. Following Confucian teachings about life, Zhang Feng was never arrogant, in the political arena or in business. He told Director Li that he would seriously prepare for the bidding and compete fairly with other companies, even though he knew his company was good enough to carry out the project.

Director Li said,

"Yes, yes, I will support your company."

Near the entrance of the conference hall, there were a few people smoking and chatting. A thin guy with grey hair and an ugly, triangular face turned back. Seeing him, Yu Mei suddenly hid behind Zhang Feng, her body shaking.

Seeing Director Li, this man made a deep bow and said, "How do you do, Director Li."

Then he said to Zhang Feng, with a faint sneer,

"Hello, CEO Zhang. I know your company is a powerful one but as small companies, we also have the right to enter a bid, don't we?"

Zhang Feng tried to ignore Cai Wenge, his personal and political enemy, but Cai had overestimated his ability to compete with Zhang Feng in commercial circles. Cai had a very bad reputation in real estate business. He just occasionally got some small project by bribing officials.

Watching Zhang Feng and his senior managers entering the conference hall, Cai said to himself: Zhang Feng, do not assume that you will get the project automatically. Let's wait to see what will happen.

This project attracted the interest of many local and outside companies. They all regarded it as a very profitable project.

Before the introduction meeting, Dan Dan said to Zhang Feng, "Can you see that Cai is sitting on the back row and talking to his friends? People say he found a few business partners from outside provinces to help him enter a bid. Recently, he has also quite often visited the corrupt Deputy Province Director, Shen, who always made you suffer when you were the Mayor. We should be careful – Cai is very sinister."

"Do not worry. The members of the bidding review committee are all professional experts so it will not be easy for Cai to influence their decision."

The introduction meeting started and Director Wang, of the bidding review committee, explained the details of this large project. Because this was a major project in the City, it had to be built to a high standard. At the same time, the bid should be reasonable as the City only had limited funding for this project. After his introduction, he handed out the details to the interested companies and answered questions from representatives. There was one month to prepare a bid.

Back at his company, Zhang Feng held a meeting to discuss the bidding process. He reminded his senior managers that they should concentrate on the quality of the project and make sure to use the best materials; a profit was needed but they did not have to be too greedy. More opportunities would follow if they did a good job now.

In the next few weeks, the team prepared the bid and worked very hard to make it as attractive as possible but Cai Wenge spent his time trying to find 'back doors' to get the project. He tried to bribe the members of the review committee and other related, high ranking officials. He knew that, along with the progress of free marketing, corruption had also become more widespread and serious and some corrupt officials used their power to obtain money illegally. Deputy Governor Shen was in charge of the economy of the province so if Cai could buy him off, there would be some hope of securing the project. Cai had actually bribed Shen a few years ago for some small project.

One weekend, Cai secretly knocked at the door of Shen's home and entered the sitting room behind Shen's housemaid.

After a few minutes, Shen walked in and said to Cai, with a smile, "Do you want to get your teeth into the shopping mall project? The problem is, your mouth is too small to swallow this big piece of meat."

Cai obsequiously replied,

"That's true, as you say, but this time, I have two business partners from Shandong and Shenzhen, so we are just as powerful as Zhang Feng's company."

"I always feel angry when somebody mentions Zhang Feng. He sometimes acted against me when he was in politics and he is even more arrogant now that he is a prosperous businessman. I will teach him a lesson this time and let him know that this project is not necessarily his, even though his company is the most powerful one in the province," Shen said, angrily.

Cai felt very happy. His company might get this project after all if Shen did something to suppress Zhang Feng's efforts to make a successful bid.

Looking at Cai, Shen said, "But your other problem is you have a criminal record so the other leaders might worry about you getting this project."

Cai knew it was time to bribe Shen. He showed him a housing promotion leaflet saying,

"Please look at these pictures of some villas we built recently. They are all luxury villas with big gardens, a fish pond, double garages with a nearby golf court, supermarket and theme park."

Noticing Shen's happy expression, Cai continued,

"I will give you one of these villas if you like, either for yourself or one of your relatives."

"Thank you very much. I can at least guarantee that you will be on the bidding short list."

Cai knew it was time to add more to his offer. He put a heavy bag on the table.

"Here are some local specialities for you."

Shen knew bribers would normally put cash in boxes or bags and gently unzipping the bag, he saw piles and piles of money.

"All right. I will arrange for you to get the project. Just wait for the good news."

One month later, all companies interested in the project started to hand in their bids. On behalf of the Songjiang Real Estate Company, Dan Dan described the architectural plans to build this huge shopping mall, the expected time it would take and the funding needed to finish it. Her tender and confident voice, clear explanation and informative photos and pictures were praised by all the members of the review committee. After she had finished, Zhang Feng, Yu Mei, Lin Jianguo and Chen Tao all commended her presentation.

As they were leaving the room, Zhang Feng and Dan Dan were behind the others when Zhang Feng kissed Dan Dan suddenly and said,

"You are excellent Dan Dan!"

"Stop doing this! Somebody might see us!" she said, shyly.

When they were married, Dan Dan always enjoyed Zhang Feng's caresses but they could no longer do this in public as they were divorced. Yet Dan Dan felt happy because she knew Zhang Feng still loved her. Zhang Feng's kiss was actually noticed by Yu Mei but she pretended not to have seen them; Yu Mei always felt that she owed Dan Dan. Dan Dan had only divorced Zhang Feng because she wanted to give him back to Yu Mei.

After two weeks, the bidding review committee declared that three companies were on their short list, including Zhang Feng's company and another major company in the province.

Surprisingly, Cai's united company was also on the list. In Zhang Feng's company, everybody was talking about this strange situation. Lin Jianguo said, even with two partners, Cai was still not qualified to build the shopping mall. Chen Tao suspected that Cai had bribed some high ranking officials to get on the shortlist for the tender. Dan Dan and Yu Mei thought that it would be better to check the decision making process of the bidding.

Just like the speculation between Zhang Feng and his colleagues, there was a fierce argument within the bidding review committee. Some members, who had been influenced by Shen, were in favour of Cai's company. They said Cai's offer was cheaper and would save money for the City Council. But other, more professional members believed that although the offer from Zhang Feng's company was dearer, it would guarantee the quality of the building for the long-term benefit of the City. It was a more reliable bid. Because supporters of both bids were equal in number, the final decision was difficult to make.

The delay of the final decision made Zhang Feng suspicious. His assistants also thought that they should find out what was going on so Zhang Feng decided to ask his friend, the current City Mayor, Chang Zheng. Chang Zheng had been Zhang Feng's rival during the Cultural Revolution and both of them had loved Yu Mei at that time. After some shared, complex experiences, they became friends. When Chang Zheng left the army, he worked as Zhang Feng's colleague in the City Council and now he was the top leader in the City. He was an honest and incorruptible official with a very good reputation.

In Chang Zheng's home, the two good friends inquired about each other's well-being. Chang Zheng already knew the purpose of Zhang Feng's visit and revealed how the members of the bidding review committee were arguing over whether to give the project to Zhang Feng or Cai Wenge. He himself believed Zhang Feng should get the project as Zhang Feng's company had a good reputation which was very important for the quality of the project yet he could not interfere directly with the work of the committee. He guessed that Cai had bribed Shen who used to be a left-wing activist and was now corrupt although Chang Zheng had no evidence of this. Chang Zheng suggested that Zhang Feng should investigate the other two companies who had co-operated with Cai to see whether they were reputable or not.

Yu Mei brought back similar information from Director Li who also believed Zhang Feng should get the project but because some powerful leaders had tried to interfere with the decision making, the situation had become more complicated. Zhang Feng and his colleagues decided to investigate the two companies working with Cai to see whether they had performed well.

Lin Jianguo said he would like to investigate the company based in Shandong Province because he had some friends working for the Construction Department there. Yu Mei said she would go to Shenzhen to investigate the second partner company as she had a good relationship with quite a few high ranking officers there but Zhang Feng suggested that it would be better to have somebody to accompany her. The Deputy Manager of the Construction Department, Mr. Xiao, offered to go with Yu Mei. He was a qualified architect and a tall, strong young man.

On the way to Shenzhen, Xiao looked after Yu Mei very well. Like Zhang Feng, Xiao was clever and handsome so his colleagues had given him the nickname 'Junior Zhang Feng'. Yu Mei also liked him and regarded him as her little brother.

In Shenzhen, Yu Mei made several phone calls to her old friends in local government and made appointments to see them the following day. Her friends told her that it would be easy to investigate the company which made Yu Mei feel more confident.

In the evening, Yu Mei and Xiao had dinner together. Yu Mei asked Xiao why he still did not have a girlfriend since he was 38 years old and Xiao replied that he'd had a girlfriend in the past but they had split up after two years.

"You are both talented and handsome so it should be easy for you to find a pretty girlfriend."

"Yes, it would have been easy before I worked in your company!" Xiao said.

"You mean finding a girlfriend is hampered by working in our company?" Yu Mei asked.

Xiao flushed and said shyly,

"Since I saw you, I have found no girl as beautiful as you. You look like a fairy from Heaven."

"You are joking! I am already an old woman! Nearly 50! Listen to me, my little brother, try to find a good girl as soon as possible. I will introduce some pretty girls to you."

"It is impossible! You look like a mature lady in her 30s! Ah, a fairy would never get old!" Xiao laughed.

"Please do not flatter me. Save your compliments for your future girlfriend! Go to your bed! We have hard work to do tomorrow," Yu Mei said.

Two days after Lin and Yu Mei had left, Zhang Feng's company suddenly received a phone call from the bidding review committee, saying that there would be a press conference to announce the decision at 2.00pm the following day which greatly surprised Zhang Feng and Dan Dan. The conference was originally scheduled to take place in a week's time.

"It seems that Cai has realized that we might look into his business partners so he has taken the initiative to push the committee into announcing their decision before we get the outcome of the investigation," Dan Dan said.

"Both Lin and Yu Mei contacted me yesterday and told me they have made some progress but they still need some official evidence. I am going to call Chang Zheng to find out more about the situation." Zhang Feng said.

A few minutes later, Zhang Feng told Dan Dan that Chang Zheng had guessed that Cai might bribe one more member of the committee to get a majority of members to support him. If Zhang Feng could not produce evidence of the investigation tomorrow, Cai would win. Zhang Feng could appeal later but the procedure would take a very long time.

At 2.00 o'clock the next day, the conference hall of the bidding review committee was packed with people, not just the representatives of the companies involved but also, journalists and the media. Zhang Feng, Dan Dan, Chen Tao and other senior managers in the company were restless in their seats. Right at that moment, in a smart suit and with shiny hair, Cai cheerfully walked in with his partners.

He stopped as he was passing Zhang Feng's seat and said,

"Hi, Mayor Zhang! No, CEO Zhang! Are you waiting for the good news? I am afraid you will be disappointed today. I have some tissues here for you to wipe away your tears later."

Zhang Feng responded to his words angrily.

"Cai Wenge, you are social scum. You caused a lot of trouble during the Cultural Revolution and now you run a crooked business. You might gain something temporarily but you will bring shame and ruin upon yourself sooner or later."

Cai pretended not to hear Zhang Feng's curse and walked to the front row of seats to show he was the winner of this competition. Zhang Feng heard the discussion from people around him who believed the project should be given to Zhang Feng's company. Zhang Feng prepared himself for a bad result.

At 2.00pm sharp, Director Wang, of the bidding review committee, walked to the middle of the platform. He looked unhappy which signalled a bad result for Zhang Feng as he was his supporter. He announced, in a weak voice, that the project would be given to Cai's co-operative company.

The hall was in uproar as he finished the declaration. A few journalists asked him why Zhang Feng's company had not got the project and Director Wang answered that this was the decision of the committee. Cai's design was acceptable. The key point was his costing was low and therefore, good for the City's finances. A journalist asked whether Cai was able to guarantee the quality of the project but Wang did not answer his question. Cai stood up, waving his hands at the audience and walked to the platform.

He said, excitedly, "My dear leaders and journalists. Thank you to the committee for giving me the project. It means our local council has broken the marketing monopoly of the big companies and is giving fair opportunities to other competitive companies. Ha, ha!"

He arrogantly waved his hand at Zhang Feng.

But suddenly, an official quickly walked up onto the stage and said a few words to Director Wang. Then Director Wang announced loudly,

"Ladies and Gentlemen, I have just received an urgent notice from the City Council to stop the declaration of the bidding. The result I have just announced is invalid. The review committee is going to have an urgent meeting. We will announce the final decision in about one hour's time."

The audience burst into further uproar. Those who supported Zhang Feng felt very happy and saw hope for his company. Zhang Feng and Dan Dan also felt optimistic as they thought the outcome of the investigation had arrived at last. In an extremely awkward position, Cai returned to his seat.

One hour later, Director Wang and all the members of the committee entered the hall. He spoke loudly to the nervous audience.

"Directors of companies, journalists, I now announce the final decision made by the committee. According to the official evidence we have just received, the performance and achievement of the two companies co-operating with Cai Wenge do not reach the commercial and technical standards required. Some of the documents they submitted to the committee are spurious. Their local authorities have removed their business licenses. Our City Council will also stop Cai's license. Therefore, the project has been given to…" He purposely stopped for a few seconds, then continued, "The project has been given to the Song Jiang Real Estate Company!"

The hall burst into thunderous applause. Standing up, Zhang Feng and his colleagues saluted the committee members and the audience.

Cai and his partners secretly left the hall as Director Wang pointed to the entrance and said,

"Look! The heroes who helped to reveal the truth have come!"

Zhang Feng, Dan Dan and the audience turned to look at the entrance and saw Lin Jianguo, Yu Mei and their assistants entering the hall briskly and saluting them. Everyone in the hall stood up and applauded them warmly.

A journalist hailed them excitedly, saying, "This great project, which will benefit generations to come, is now in safe hands!"

Chapter II

It Is not Easy to Work as a Director in a State Enterprise

Getting the bid, Zhang Feng and his colleagues all felt very happy. They said Lin and Yu Mei had made great contributions and revealed the dirty tricks of Cai Wenge.

"It seems that in this turbulent sea of commerce, we not only have to compete with our business opponents but also, fight against unscrupulous merchants and corrupt officials. Seeing more people getting richer, some officials are envious so they want to use their power to get money illegally. It is a worrying situation," said Zhang Feng.

"The Party and Central Government should establish organizations to combat corruption, like Singapore does. But China is a huge country. It is more difficult to maintain an honest government," Dan Dan added.

Zhang Feng and his colleagues were preparing the plans for the construction of the shopping mall when Wang Hai visited one day. Having tea with Zhang Feng, Wang Hai said, unhappily,

"Brother Feng, I envy you that you are your own boss and do not need to obey the instructions of others but it is very difficult to work as a director in a state owned enterprise. The shareholding system has not expanded to Northeast China yet so we have to get final decisions from the Mechanical Engineer Ministry for all major projects. At the moment, both German and Japanese motor vehicle companies want to invest in our factory to produce new makes of cars in large quantities. It would be wonderful as ordinary people still can't afford to buy their own cars, even though housing is much better now. If we can absorb foreign capital and increase production, private cars will soon be owned by the families of ordinary people."

"It sounds good. You should negotiate with these companies," Zhang Feng said.

Wang Hai said he preferred to negotiate with Volkswagen because his factory had bought some equipment from them a few years ago and also, there was a Chinese lady in the Volkswagen delegation who was an investment expert and a fellow-townswoman which made communication easy.

"Then negotiate with Volkswagen! Is this lady very pretty? Be careful! It may be a love trap!"

"I dare not fall into that kind of trap! Your sister always watches me. She looked unhappy when some pretty female engineers visited our home once. Also, your Pili boxing skills are still waiting for me!"

Zhang Feng laughed loudly.

A week later, agreed by the Mechanical Engineering Department, a deputy director of the factory went to Beijing and negotiated with Toyota. Wang Hai stayed in River City to negotiate with Volkswagen, then they would decide which company they would co-operate with, according to the outcome. To prepare for the negotiations, Wang Hai bought a smart suit. Zhang Lin was knotting his tie, and said,

"My husband looks quite handsome in this suit!"

She did not forget to remind Wang Hai not to get too close to the ladies.

"Do not worry! No any other woman could ever be as beautiful as my wife!"

One sunny morning, the negotiations between the Jili Motor Vehicle Factory and Volkswagen started in the meeting room of the factory. Wang Hai, other deputy directors and the general engineer were sitting on one side of the long table. The Asian CEO of Volkswagen and his assistants were on the other side and, among them, was a beautiful Chinese lady in a red suit who looked very smart. She was both a member of the delegation and the interpreter.

Initially, the meeting went smoothly. Both sides explained their plans for collaboration. Volkswagen planned to construct a huge branch to build a hundred thousand new cars each year. The Chinese side needed to provide the site, sales, after-sales service and part of the funding. The German businessmen were very interested in the huge Chinese market and their Chinese counterparts were interested in the Germans' advanced technology and efficient management.

The factory provided a tasty lunch for their German guests and near the end of the meal, Helen, the Chinese lady, approached Wang Hai.

"Director Wang, do you have time to have a cup of tea with me?"

Wondering about the background of this lady, Wang Hai invited her into his office. Sitting on the sofa and drinking tea, she looked like a fascinating and charming mature lady but not a serious negotiator.

She said to Wang Hai, shyly,

"Director Wang, we are destined to be together. You know, not only are we fellow townsmen, you are also my idol."

She took a newspaper cutting from her handbag and showed it to Wang Hai. He was surprised to see his photo in this cutting, showing him looking strong and fit in swimming trunks. It was taken by a journalist after Wang Hai had become champion of the cross river competition in the summer of 1966.

"Why do you have this photo?" Wang Hai asked.

Helen explained that she had been just seven years old when she went to watch the competition. Noticing Wang Hai's tall, strong figure, she felt he would win the challenge. In the end, Wang Hai did actually win. She then cut out the article containing Wang Hai's photo in a local newspaper the next day and kept it for many years, treating him as her idol.

She went to Jili Industrial University in 1977 and studied in a German University in 1987. Later, she married a German engineer but divorced him after three years of marriage. She worked for Volkswagen for a few years but because she missed her country and family, she asked if she could get involved in investment work in China. She was an excellent investment expert and was able to speak many different languages and so, the Asian CEO of Volkswagen thought highly of her and had asked her to play an important role in this negotiation.

After knowing something about her background and position in the delegation, Wang Hai felt happy as this special relationship with Helen could easily help him find out more details on the German side. Wang Hai couldn't help noticing that there was an element of hero worship involved.

But just when they were about to talk more, Deputy Director Song, who was in charge of the after-service department, entered the office. He did not have a good relationship with Wang Hai because Wang Hai always gave more after-service contracts to external contractors which reduced his power.

Song said, mysteriously, "Sorry to disturb your talk." then he left the room before Wang Hai could explain about Helen.

Seeing Wang Hai look unhappy, Helen asked him whether their talk would cause him trouble. Normally, members of both sides should not have private conversations before the negotiation was finished. Wang Hai said he was not worried as they were fellow townsmen and keen to talk about their past experiences. Helen said farewell to him and left the room quickly.

That weekend, Wang Hai visited Zhang Feng's home and told him about the negotiations. He also asked about the construction of the villas by Zhang Feng's company because these houses were more spacious than his own apartment. The only reason for him to keep his apartment was that it was quite close to his factory. Zhang Feng suggested that it would be better for Wang Hai to wait a while as he would be very busy after the new investment scheme started and it would be more convenient to live closer to his factory.

Leaving Zhang Feng's home, Wang Hai walked to the riverside port where the cross river swimming competition had taken place over thirty years ago. Suddenly, he saw a lady in white leaning on the rail and watching the flowing river.

He was walking closer to her when the lady turned her head, and both of them said, "It is you!" at the same time.

It was Helen.

"Director Wang, fate has brought us together again. My parents' house is very near here and I like to walk near this old port which always brings back memories of your manly physique in the swimming competition."

Graceful and charming, Helen was very attractive to men but then, why had her German husband divorced her? She guessed Wang Hai wanted to know more about her private life.

"Brother Hai… may I call you that? I worship you but I also know you have your own family. Can we at least be good friends?"

Wang Hai agreed to that. She said she always missed the food in her home town and especially liked the meat pie in a restaurant nearby so she invited him to join her. Wang Hai said he would like to go with her but he actually wanted to know more about her private life and the details of the Volkswagen investment scheme.

They enjoyed the delicious pies together at the restaurant. Wang Hai normally looked down on Chinese women who chose to marry foreigners but he felt Helen was not that kind of woman. Just as he thought, Helen told him that when she studied in Germany, her boyfriend back in China terminated their relationship which upset her greatly. A German boy in her class tried to comfort her and possibly, in order to heal her empty heart, she married him. Yet the different cultural background and life style ruined their relationship and they parted in the end.

She had tears in her eyes as she was talking about this unfortunate marriage and Wang Hai gave her some tissues. Just by chance at that moment, a department director from Wang Hai's factory walked into the restaurant and saw what looked like an intimate moment between them. He quickly left.

Wang Hai comforted Helen and said she would find a good man easily because she was a pretty female professional. Looking at Wang Hai affectionately, she said,

"Not really. I have realized that Chinese men have changed their attitude towards love and marriage greatly. It is not easy to find a man with a successful career who cares for his family at the same time, like you."

Wang Hai said that he could help her find a decent man if she decided to stay in China. Shaking her head, she said she would feel happy if she had a close male friend like Wang Hai. Seeing that nobody was looking at them, she told Wang Hai quietly that the Germans tended to be honest when they did business, having a long-term vision. Her boss and colleagues were satisfied with the condition of Wang Hai's factory but they also needed to consider the possibility of investing in factories in Beijing, Shanghai and Guangzhou. She suggested that Wang Hai should be more flexible in the negotiations.

After their meal, they sat by the riverside and talked about many things they liked. Wang Hai felt that he was starting to fall in love with Helen; he had endless things to talk to her about. It was only when the glow of sunset appeared on the horizon that he remembered his wife had asked him to return earlier that evening to make dumplings. He said goodbye to Helen and returned home in a hurry but he did not realize at the time that his meeting with Helen would bring him trouble.

The German side of the negotiations suddenly made new demands over the next few days, asking the Chinese side to invest five million dollars which made Wang Hai and his colleagues unhappy because they had to get the money from the Mechanical Engineering Department. Wang Hai asked Helen about the reasons behind this demand. Helen said their CEO wanted to prepare for the future expansion of production. The funding was to be part of the shares for Wang Hai's factory when China began its shareholding system in the near future and his factory would be the controlling shareholder which would benefit his factory. Wang Hai agreed with her and started to apply to the MED for the funding.

Surprisingly, the MED did not approve the application. Quite the opposite – it sent an investigation team to check on the behaviour of Wang Hai during the negotiations. The MED had received a letter of accusation, implying that Wang Hai had betrayed the interests of the country by giving unnecessary funding to the German side. Also, it claimed he'd had an affair with the Chinese lady in the German delegation. So Wang Hai's role was temporarily stopped by the department and the negotiation was suspended as well.

Wang Hai knew who had informed against him. It must have been Deputy Director Song as he had seen Wang Hai talking to Helen in his office that day but Wang Hai did not know that his meal in the restaurant with Helen had also been seen by a director who was an assistant of Song.

Wang Hai returned home in a deep depression. Just as he was entering the hall way, his wife, Zhang Lin, rushed up to him, crying, and started beating him with her fists.

"You are so ungrateful! Beautiful women give you nose bleeds and now you are suffering your punishment! You lost your post and I feel ashamed!"

Wang Hai understood that Zhang Lin already knew about the incident and the investigation but he had not betrayed his country nor his family. It was the jockeying for power in his factory which had caused him grief.

Somebody knocked at the door. Zhang Feng and Yu Mei

entered the sitting room and thinking that Zhang Feng might punish him on behalf of his sister, Wang Hai said to Zhang Feng, incoherently,

"Brother Feng…brother-in-law…Please listen to me first! You can punish me if I really have done something wrong."

Zhang Feng asked Yu Mei to comfort his sister and then went into another room with Wang Hai. Seeing Zhang Feng was very calm, Wang Hai explained to him what had happened in the last few days.

Thinking for a while, Zhang Feng said,

"It seems that the personal connections in state companies are quite complex, similar to the situation I was in when I was in politics. Tell me, is Helen very beautiful? You have fallen in love with her?"

Wang Hai quickly explained that he just regarded her as his little sister and nothing more.

Zhang Feng said with a smile,

"I know how guys, like you, like pretty ladies but you just fantasize, without taking action. I trust you. You would not betray your country and family. Fine, let's discuss how to cope with this matter."

They moved back to the sitting room where Zhang Feng comforted Zhang Lin and then discussed with Yu Mei how to help Wang Hai. Wang Hai said he was not worried about the investigation but was more concerned about the delay in the negotiations which might end in a bad result for the factory.

Wang Hai said the leader of the investigation team was Director Wen who had helped him to get some funding ten years ago. Yu Mei said happily that she knew Director Wen well. He was a subordinate of her father's old friend in the state council so she would visit him to get some more information.

Dan Dan could visit Helen and ask her for the truth about her relationship with Wang Hai. After all these efforts, Wang Hai would hopefully regain his post and return to the negotiations soon.

After Dan Dan's visit to Helen, Helen talked to the investigation team and the leaders of the factory. She strongly criticized the informer and said someone had tried to smear her and Wang Hai. Their relation was purely one between fellow townsmen and friends and nothing to do with an affair or business and their second meeting had been purely accidental. Director Wen very politely comforted her and said the team would not accuse an innocent person. Regarding the additional funding applied for by Wang Hai, experts would be checking whether or not it would damage the interests of the country.

After Yu Mei's visit to Director Wen, Wang Hai received a phone call from the team, asking him to meet. Wang Hai went to the factory and walked into the meeting room where he saw Deputy Director Song just leaving. Seeing Wang Hai, Song said that the team was investigating Wang Hai's performance and personal relations. He hypocritically told Wang Hai that he regarded him highly and then he reminded Wang Hai that he already had a pretty wife and it was not worth chasing other women.

Wang Hai said to him, angrily,

"Somebody is seeking personal revenge on me and is keen to remove me from my post. Unfortunately, it will not be that easy."

Song knew Wang Hai was condemning him and hurriedly left. Entering the room, Wang Hai met Director Wen and the two men shook hands warmly. Wen said they had not met each other for a long time. Then Director Wen and his assistants listened carefully to Wang Hai's explanation about his relationship with Helen and the benefits of the additional funding requested by Volkswagen and also, about the power struggles within the factory.

At the end of the meeting, Director Wen told Wang Hai that he did not need to worry about the situation. The team had received a lot of background information and there would be a conclusion to the matter soon.

A few days later, the investigation team held a meeting with all the staff and workers in the factory. On behalf of the MED, Director Wen announced that after the detailed investigation, the accusation against Wang Hai had been found to be false. He had not had an immoral affair and had never betrayed the interests of the country so the MED decided to restore his post and allowed him to still be in charge of the negotiations. The good news was that the MED had approved the funding for the co-operation. His speech drew loud applause from the audience and some officials and workers who had supported Wang Hai even had tears in their eyes.

Bidding farewell to Director Wen, Wang Hai held his hands warmly and said,

"Director Wen, do you still remember that ten years ago, when I saw you in the MED, I promised to help you buy a nice car. Please tell me, which car would you like?"

"Wait until you have the new make of German cars in production, then I will tell you," Wen answered with a smile.

The negotiations restarted the next day but what made Wang Hai feel uncomfortable was that Helen was absent. There was a new interpreter working for the German side. The Asian CEO of Volkswagen explained that Helen had been called back to the headquarters of Volkswagen for a meeting. Yet Wang Hai and his colleagues understood that the German side worried that they might have further possible troubles if Helen still got involved in the negotiation.

The negotiations reached agreement over the next few weeks. Volkswagen would build a huge branch to produce fifty thousand new make cars which would increase to a hundred thousand in the next few years. The news made people in the city and province feel very excited as it meant private cars would be available for the families of ordinary people and not only rich businessmen and high ranking officials.

Spring had come. A huge celebration meeting was held in Wang Hai's factory with high ranking officials and business leaders all attending, including Zhang Feng, Dan Dan, Yu Mei and other senior managers along with Li He and Qing Lian, Chang Zheng and other officials. The meeting was held in the big hall of the factory. Director Wen attended on behalf of the MED. Volkswagen also sent its senior representatives.

After the speeches of both sides, the cocktail party started. The bosses from both private companies and state companies made the most of business opportunities and exchanged information about the economic reforms. They all felt very optimistic about the shareholding system and they believed a modern, commercial society would soon emerge.

After drinking a lot of alcohol, Wang Hai felt slightly dizzy. He walked out from the hall and into a small, nearby wood to enjoy the fresh air. In this happy atmosphere, he was thinking of Helen who had made such a great contribution to the success of the negotiations but she was not here which made Wang Hai feel rather sad.

Suddenly, a tender voice behind him said,

"Brother Hai, are you ok? Did you have too much to drink?"

Turning his head, Wang Hai saw slim and graceful Helen, dressed in white, just standing there behind him which made him very excited.

Watching him with affection, she said,

"I am very glad the co-operation was successful. We did not work hard for nothing and the accusations were also proved false. We will meet again later. I still work for Volkswagen's Asian headquarters in Singapore and I miss you. Maybe, one day, I will swim with you in the Songhua River."

Seeing that nobody was around, Wang Hai plucked up his courage and said,

"I will miss you as well. I hope you find a good man to live with."

"But the man I love already has his family." Helen said with sorrow and affection. Finally, she continued,

"Brother Hai, may I say farewell to you in the Western way?"

Before Wang Hai could react to her request, she had stood up on her toes and kissed him on his face. She then ran to a taxi. In his confusion, he rubbed his face to remove the lipstick left by her kiss. He heard the voices of two men nearby.

"A tall and athletic man is always attractive to some ladies!"

"A pretty lady is also attractive to some men!"

Looking back, Wang Hai saw both Zhang Feng and Chang Zheng standing under a tree, watching him and smiling.

"It is not my fault! She wanted to say goodbye to me in the Western way."

"Do not worry! I will not tell my sister," Zhang Feng laughed.

Chapter III

The Stock Market Is a Gambling House

The success in establishing a joint venture with Volkswagen put Wang Hai in raptures. He and Zhang Lin held a big party, inviting all of their friends including Zhang Feng, Dan Dan, Yu Mei, Li He and Qing Lian. They cheerfully congratulated him on his success.

"My factory will soon become a shareholding company, and I will be CEO Wang!" said Wang Hai.

But Zhang Lin replied, "Don't get dizzy with your success. Be careful! Keep away from pretty ladies!"

"That was a misunderstanding," Zhang Feng said immediately.

Yu Mei changed the topic.

"Do you know, the first stock market transaction service just opened in our city? That is a huge milestone for our economy. In the past, we believed that the stock market was one of the main evils of capitalism. Yet now we know that it can help raise money for business enterprises and then they do not need funding from the Government."

Hearing what Yu Mei said, depressed Li He was suddenly excited again. He had been stressed recently because market competition had become fiercer. More than twenty new travel agencies had started up last year so the profits of his company had decreased sharply.

He asked Yu Mei about the details of the stock market transactions as she had witnessed the opening of the first stock market in China in Shenzhen. Yu Mei said, in 1992, she saw over ten thousand people queue up overnight to buy shares. Li He asked if all of them earned good money from buying shares and Yu Mei said it was risky. If they bought houses using the money from share transactions straight away, or they stopped at the right time, then they would gain but if they became greedy, they would lose. Li He became more and more excited and started to drink heavily.

The next day, Li He told Qing Lian he needed to go to a nursing home to arrange a travel package with them but instead, he drove to the stock market hall in the city centre. He was surprised by the scene in front of him: the hall was at full capacity. Some people stared at the figures on the big screen, some were shouting to the traders to buy shares, some were waiting in the long queue to open accounts. Li He was very excited but he did not know how to start. He saw a lot of people surrounding a man with a beard, talking endlessly about how to buy shares. Li He asked a short man what the bearded man was talking about.

"He is the famous share-buying expert, Mr. Lv, nick named 'Big Beard', from Shanghai. He is very experienced in dealing with shares."

Li He did not understand what Big Beard was talking about so he waited until he had finished and asked him, with respect, whether Big Beard could teach him to buy shares.

"No problem! You will get rich if you learn from me but you will need to pay me a tuition fee." Big Beard said.

Li He gave him five hundred Yuan willingly. Big Beard then told him how to open an account and which shares he needed to purchase first. He suggested that Li He should buy a small amount of shares initially, to practise, then buy larger amounts after he had built up some experience. Feeling the advice from Big Beard was very reasonable, Li returned home to get ten thousand Yuan which the couple had planned to use for purchasing a bigger house, then he returned to the stock market hall and opened an account, buying one thousand shares from a company recommended by Big Beard.

A week later, Li He arrived at his travel agency, singing a folk song and greeting every member of staff cheerfully. Qing Lian knew he must be happy as this had always been his habit.

"What do you think? I have just bought ten thousand Yuan shares which have doubled in just one week!" said Li He.

"Ah, you have been lucky but be careful! The stock market is very changeable. Do it just for fun but do not take it too seriously," Qing Lian replied.

"I have an adviser, an experienced share-buying expert who supports me so I will definitely make more profit. I am fed up with our travel business which is tiring and hard but it is really easy to buy shares. You just look at the screen and talk to the stock traders," Li He said, cheerfully.

Qing Lian thought Li He was dabbling in shares for fun, like the way people bought lottery tickets. Many people just spent a very small amount each week so it did not matter if they lost.

Yet something happened at last. A few weeks later, Li He's wife came to Qing Lian nervously. She told Qing Lian that Li He had used their savings to buy a lot of shares, without her agreement. This amount was actually for them to purchase a bigger house. As they were arguing, Li He insisted that this amount would be doubled in the next few weeks and then they could buy a new house straight away.

Qing Lian tried to comfort her by saying Li was a cautious man who would not go to extremes. Yet Qing Lian was still worried about Li's situation and she decided to consult Zhang Feng and Yu Mei. She would take this opportunity to see Zhang Feng because she still missed him, even though Huang Lei was wooing her.

When Qing Lian arrived at Zhang Feng's house, Yu Mei, Dan Dan and Dan Feng were all there, cooking their dinner. Seeing Qing Lian, Dan Feng ran to her and held her hands saying, "How are you? Aunt Qing Lian, is sister Lan Hua well?"

Qing Lian kissed Dan Feng, saying that although he was just 13 years old, he was already quite tall. Like his father, he would be a handsome and tall young man when he grew up. Qing Lian knew Yu Mei and Dan Dan had a good relationship with each other, like sisters, even though they were Zhang Feng's wife and ex-wife. They had shared a very complex, emotional experience during the Cultural Revolution. They gathered together like one family quite often which was good for Dan Feng as he did not feel that he was a child from a single parent family.

Not wanting to disturb their dinner, Qing Lian told them about the problem of Li He buying so many shares.

Yu Mei said, "Oh my God! Please tell Li that this Big Beard is a swindler! He pretended to be a share-buying expert in Shenzhen and cheated a lot of people. After he was condemned, he escaped to Shanghai and now he has come here! Please warn Li He not to follow Big Beard who might earn you some money but in the long term, you will lose miserably. Nowadays, people say that 70% of share buyers will lose money, 20% will break even but only 10% will make a profit."

Qing Lian was quite worried and she left to find Li He.

In the stock market hall, Li He anxiously asked Big Beard why the stock market had been so changeable recently but he replied that this was actually a good time to buy and he suggested Li should buy even more shares. Li He went to his friends and relatives to borrow more money.

It seemed that Li had become addicted to share buying. He did not go to his business and did not return home very often. Qing Lian went to the stock market hall to see him. He looked very tired, sitting on a bench and eating dry bread. Qing Lian felt sorry for him and tried to persuade him to stop. She told him Big Beard was a swindler but Li said he could not withdraw his purchases as he had put in a lot of money already. He said the shares he had bought looked promising and he might make a huge profit. Qing Lian warned him that the stock market was a gambling house and he might be sucked in more and more but Li said he would only stop once he had made a good amount of money.

One week later, a group of truculent men came to Li's company and asked him to repay his debts. Qing Lian realized that Li must have borrowed a lot of money from different places and she told them to wait a few days. Li's wife also phoned Qing Lian and told her that some men had come to their house demanding that Li pay back his debts. Li was now in hiding somewhere for a few days, trying to avoid his creditors.

Just then, the company accountant rushed to Qing Lian and told her that Li had asked for a large amount of money a few days ago and just ignored her warning that the money should be used to repay the interest on their bank loans. Because he was the CEO of the company, the accountant had to give the money to him. Qing Lian was shocked at him using their business accounts to buy shares. This meant he was an addicted gambler now.

She went to the stock market hall in a hurry. As she got nearer the hall, she saw a crowd of people standing outside the building, watching a ledge near the top of the roof and shouting to a man standing there. Looking carefully, she saw that the man was the missing Li He who was crying and about to commit suicide by jumping from the building. Qing Lian rang Zhang Feng and Wang Hai, using her new mobile phone, and asked them to come immediately. She also asked Zhang Feng to pick up Li's wife and daughter. A man next to her told her that the stock market had crashed yesterday and many people had lost their entire life savings as a result. Two people had already jumped from the building: Le He would be the third. Qing Lian felt even more anxious. Li was her ex-husband and her business partner and she had to do something to save him.

She pushed through to the very front and shouted loudly,

"Li He! It's me! Qing Lian! You cannot do this! You have a wife and daughter and many friends! You can still earn back the money you lost! You could even go back to your hospital job! Zhang Feng, Wang Hai and your wife and daughter will arrive very soon. At least you should say farewell to them."

Qing Lian said these words because she was stalling for time. Seeing Qing Lian, Li began crying even more. Qing Lian knew Li was reliable but he was not resolute and manly and that was why she loved Zhang Feng more. Her words made Li hesitate and he did not know whether he should jump or not.

Less than ten minutes later, Zhang Feng, Wang Hai and Li's wife and daughter arrived. Asking Li's wife and daughter to talk to him, Zhang Feng, Wang Hai and Qing Lian quickly climbed up to the top platform. In order not to shock him, they walked up quietly and heard Li talking to his wife and daughter.

"Shu Lan and Bai He, I have nothing now. The stock market rose sharply the day before yesterday and I wanted to sell my shares but that bastard Big Beard asked me to wait and I trusted him. The market fell greatly yesterday, losing 2000 points and all my investment of two million Yuan was gone! I lost our savings and I cannot pay the mortgage! I cannot repay the money I have borrowed and I cannot avoid the creditors! I lost the money I took from the business and I am facing bankruptcy! I cannot support you anymore. Two others have already jumped from the building. Let me follow them!"

Listening to Li's painful words, Wang Hai became very angry.

"You are so stubborn! Li He, you did not listen to our warnings and you ended up being sucked into the clutches of a mad gambler!"

Li turned back and saw Zhang Feng, Wang Hai and Yu Mei, which frightened him so much he almost fell.

Gesturing to Wang Hai to stop, Zhang Feng said to Li He, calmly,

"Li He, we have been good friends for many years. We even survived the red storm of the Cultural Revolution. It is normal to lose money in business. We can still earn the money back if we learn the lesson and concentrate on our business. It doesn't need to be a dead end!"

Crying, Li replied,

"Brother Feng, I do not want to commit suicide but the

creditors are surrounding my home and company every day, asking me to pay back the debts. I have let my family and all my colleagues down!"

Then he started to cry more fiercely. Zhang Feng made a gesture to Wang Hai, telling him to move to the left side of Li He. At the same time, he moved more to Li He's right side and attracted his attention which gave Wang Hai the chance to get hold of Li He. Zhang Feng then spoke to Li He firmly.

"Li He, we are good friends so we must do something to help you. We will lend you money to repay your debts and keep your company afloat."

Li He was in a daze at Zhang Feng's suggestion. He did not know whether he should accept the help of his friends or not. Thinking of what he had done in the past, he said to Zhang Feng,

"Brother Feng, I once let you down during the Cultural Revolution and now I will be the cause of you losing money again. Oh, I am not a decent person."

While he wiped away his tears with his hand, Wang Hai quickly grabbed him and they both fell to the floor. Zhang Feng helped to drag Li He away from the edge of the platform just as Li He's wife and daughter arrived. Seeing that Li had been controlled by Zhang Feng and Wang Hai, everybody felt calmer. Li He stood up, hugged and cried with his wife and daughter.

After Li had calmed down, his friends discussed further how to help him. Zhang Feng said he could lend one and a half million Yuan to Li He. Wang Hai said he would lend Li three hundred thousand: that was his end of year bonus. Qing Lian would give two hundred thousand which was the money she had saved to buy a new house. Li He was moved by their generous help and knelt down to honour them.

"Thank you all, my loyal friends, I will try to repay your money as soon as possible, with interest."

"Do not talk about interest. We have been faithful friends for so many years," Zhang Feng said.

They all told Li He that there would be no pressure on him to repay the money in a certain time. In their minds, they were willing to just give him the money if it meant saving his life.

A week later, with the help of his friends, Li He repaid all his private debts and paid the mortgage on his house on time. His company also repaid the interest on the bank loan and proceeded with business once again. He vowed that he would never play the stock market again. He started to concentrate more on his job, together with Qing Lian, trying to improve their service and providing more travel destinations to their customers, such as the beautiful, remote areas of Tibet, Xingjiang and Inner Mongolia. Their business became better and better.

One summer weekend, Li He and his wife invited his good friends Zhang Feng, Wang Hai, Dan Dan, Yu Mei, Qing Lian and Zhang Lin, to a party in their home.

Holding his glass of wine, Li He said,

"Thank you very much, my dear brothers and sisters. Without your generous help towards my family and company, I would be in another world today. I have learnt a bitter lesson this time. We should not be too keen to make a quick profit. We should do our own work, patiently and steadily."

Wang Hai said carelessly, "In the past, we always said that evil capitalism would ruin families. When the stock market crashed, millionaires suddenly became poor men and a lot of them jumped from buildings to kill themselves. It nearly happened right here, beside us."

Seeing how awkward Li He felt, Dan Dan said,

"Do not mention this again. It seems that we are having the same social issues as Western countries. Our people were so poor in the past and they wanted to get rich overnight. Our Government should draw lessons from the West in the past, building welfare systems to stabilize society, with policies to encourage the rich and help the poor."

Everyone agreed with her.

Holding up his glass, Zhang Feng said, "I used to float and sink on the sea of officialdom but now, I realize that the sea of commerce is also turbulent. Our three families have all experienced hardship but fortunately, our ships did not overturn! Let's battle with the wind and waves and continue on our brave voyage! Cheers!"

They all stood up and drank their wine.

Chapter IV

I Saved Her

The school summer vacation had started in Jili City. Apart from holiday homework, schools also organized summer camps for students, offering military style, physical and entertainment activities which were enjoyed very much by children. Without the restraints of the classroom, children were able to express their natural characteristics and vitality.

On the first day of camp, Zhang Feng drove Dan Feng to the assembly point in the city centre. Having inherited his father's genes, Dan Feng was tall and handsome. They got out of the car and walked up to the waiting buses.

"Dan Feng! Wait for me!" a boy called out to Dan Feng.

It was Chang Zheng's son, Jian Jun, arriving with his father. They had studied in the same school, the Second Middle School, although Jian Jun was one year older than Dan Feng: tall and strong, like his father. Both of them were class captains in their class.

As the two boys were talking about the summer camp, two girls ran up to them from behind a big tree. One of them was Qing Lian's daughter, Lan Hua, and the other was Li He's daughter, Bai He. Both of them were nine years old and studying in the same class in the attached first school of Jili Normal University. Like their mothers, they were both pretty and clever. They played together often, like sisters, due to the special relationship between their families. Zhang Feng liked Lan Hua, partly because he sympathized with Qing Lian's experience and partly because he did not have a daughter of his own. Strangely, Qing Lian always found some reason to deflect his involvement.

The two boys and two girls joined their parents. Seeing how they got along together so happily, Chang Zheng said they could all be relatives by marriage when they grew up. Zhang Feng said why not and only Qing Lian looked hesitant, saying it would be their own choice. Zhang Feng, Chang Zheng and Qing Lian reminded their children to be safe and to enjoy their camping activities.

Both schools had good links and organized the same camp for their students so they could take any bus. Dan Feng and Jian Jun got on a bus first and asked the two girls to sit behind them so they could chat together on the journey. The two boys said this camp would offer field survival training and students would learn how to cook and live in tents. They said they would help the two girls if they had any problems and the girls said they would be very happy to get help from their 'big brothers'.

At about 3.00pm, the students arrived at an open space near the Songhua Lake where some of their teachers and army officers were waiting for the children. The first task was to set up the tents and a few of the army officers helped the students with this. Both Dan Feng and Jian Jun were good at doing physical things and they quickly set up their tents with the help of their classmates. Then they visited the site where the girls were camping and found that they did not know how to put up a tent. The two girls were very happy to have help from their 'brothers'.

Dan Feng helped Lan Hua and Jian Jun helped Bai He to set up two different tents and competed with each other to see who would finish first. Teenage boys have always been attracted to pretty girls and they wanted to show off their strength and capability in front of them. They all worked together and in the end, Jian Jun's tent was up first and Dan Feng's was up five minutes later. Jian Jun boasted that he had learnt this skill from his father who used to serve in the army. Dan Feng said he quite often helped his mother to set up tents when they had holidays in England. This time, because a pole had been put in the wrong place by one of the girls, he had finished second. Seeing that the two boys were reluctant to accept the result, the girls told them both how capable they were which helped to calm things down.

In the late afternoon, the adults started to teach the children how to cook which was one of the elements of field survival training. They needed to dig a small hole in the ground, then put a pot across the top and set fire to dry wood underneath to cook the food. Dan Feng and Jian Jun were still racing to finish the work and cooked up some rice. Dan Feng went over to the girls' site again to help them because he was good at cooking but this time, Jian Jun did not go because he did not know how to cook. His father was a high ranking official and they had a housemaid to cook for them so he never had a chance to learn.

Dan Feng could see that the girls were having difficulty starting a fire. He used some paper and thin, dry twigs to make a small fire first and then added bigger branches. The girls cheered up. Dan Feng asked whether they could cook or not. Lan Hua said she was able to cook as she had only lived with her mother and she needed to do a lot of the housework. When Dan Feng returned from the girls' site, Jian Jun felt unhappy as he knew he had lost to Dan Feng in this activity.

Later that evening, Jian Jun went over to show the two girls how to arrange their sleeping bags inside the tents. The two girls thanked him for his help which made him feel a lot happier. The two girls laughed secretly at how seriously the boys were taking this 'competition'.

On the second day, the activities started, including military, physical and entertainment activities and competitions. The two boys were keen to see who would get the upper hand in these competitions and the two girls also wanted to see which of their two 'brothers' was the more capable.

After a few days of 'military' training, there was a competition between Dan Feng's class, the defenders, and Jian Jun's class, the attackers. In an open field, surrounded by woods, Dang Feng's group had to defend a red flag planted in the ground. If Jian Jun's team could seize the flag, then they would win. Dan Feng thought it was very likely Jian Jun's team would attack through a break in the woods, so he, with another ten strong classmates, kept monitoring this direction.

As he predicted, a group of Jian Jun's classmates rushed through the break and Dan Feng led most of his classmates to block them. Jian Jun and a large group emerged from the back of the woods and pushed away the few boys who were defending the flag and seized it. Losing the 'battle' like this made Dan Feng feel very disappointed.

Hearing the warm applause from the two girls, Jian Jun said,

"I am the younger generation of the army. My father used to be a division commander and he told me about a military tactic called 'make a feint to the east and attack in the west', which is what I used today."

The company commander standing by his side was surprised.

"My God! Are you the son of Commander Chang? That is why you are so capable in military operations."

The two girls came up to disappointed Dan Feng and tried to comfort him.

"Do not worry, Brother Feng, there are still plenty of other competitions!"

"Yes, I will win in the other competitions." Dan Feng said.

In the next day's 1000 metre race, Dan Feng and Jian Jun were ahead of all the other boys at the half way point. In the last 100 metres, they sprinted towards the tape, neck and neck. Both Lan Hua and Bai He applauded loudly. Lan Hua said she was sure that Dan Feng touched the tape first but Bai He said no, it was Jian Jun and they started to argue with each other.

After a brief discussion, the camp leaders declared a tie for both Dan Feng and Jian Jun. The two girls ran to them with bunches of wild flowers picked from the field. Taking the flowers and patting each other on the shoulder, the two boys wondered who would win in the wrestling competition.

Two days later, both Dan Feng and Jian Jun were in the finals of the wrestling. The result surprised the teachers, students and army officers. The principal of the Second Middle School told the army officers and teachers about the interesting backgrounds behind these two boys. One of their parents was the previous Mayor and the other's father was the existing Mayor but both of them were good friends.

Before the final match, Bai He believed Jian Jun would win

because his father had been an army officer in the past but Lan Hua was sure that Dan Feng would win as he had learnt martial arts from his father. The two girls bet on the winner for a hair ribbon.

The final started and the two boys fought against each other fiercely. Dan Feng seemed to have less strength than Jian Jun so he lost the first game. Bai He was happy and asked Lan Hua to give her the ribbon but Lan Hua said the match had not finished yet.

Jian Jun helped Dan Feng up.

"Please give up little brother."

"You haven't won yet! Let's see what happens in the next game," Dan Feng answered.

Dan Feng was a clever boy. He knew he was not as strong as Jian Jun but he could win at martial arts because he had learnt from his father.

The second competition began. Having just won the first, Jian Jun underestimated his enemy. When Dan Feng stepped back a few paces, Jian Jun thought he had run out of strength but Dan Feng suddenly used the skill of Pili boxing to kick Jian Jun's leg while attacking him with his fist. Without warning, Jian Jun fell to the ground and everyone watching applauded. The army commander said it looked like Dan Feng already knew martial arts and the principal said Dan Feng's grandfather had been a Taoist martial arts master.

Jian Jun stood up angrily.

"So you already have some martial arts skills! Well, let's see what will happen in the last game."

The last competition was win or lose so both boys acted cautiously. At one point, Dan Feng was almost beaten down by Jian Jun but stood back up on his feet again after doing a backward somersault which inspired applause. In the end, Jian Jun was impatient and kept attacking. Dan Feng used the skills of Wu Dang boxing, learnt from his grandfather, to kick the back of Jian Jun's leg, making him fall down to the ground. Dan Feng won and the spectators applauded them warmly for their brilliant skill.

The two girls walked up to the two boys and Bai He said, "I lost a hair ribbon to Lan Hua. She bet that Dan Feng would win. Bother Jian Jun, you should do better next time."

Dan Feng patted Jian Jun's shoulder and said, "Brother, this was only for fun. It does not matter who wins! I can learn from you to improve my strength and do better in games."

"Ok. You can teach me some martial arts when you have time," Jian Jun said after calming down.

The children were eating their 'poor meal', specially made to recall the past suffering of the people at lunch time but both Lan Hua and Bai He could not swallow the food because the taste was so bad.

Their teacher said,

"Do you know, your parents even did not have enough such food to fill their stomachs at the end of the 1950s, during the famine? You are so lucky to have meat, egg, seafood, rice and flour every day now."

His words really surprised the children.

After lunch, Lan Hua asked Bai He, "Whose class will win first place after all these competitions? I believe it will be Dan Feng's class."

"Why?"

"Because the last competition is all about entertainment. Dang Feng has a musical talent. I once listened to his accordion performance and singing which were really wonderful."

Just as Lan Hua said, the last time he was in a talent competition, Dang Feng won prizes for his accordion performance and his vocal solo and his class won the award.

A lot of the girls found Lan Hua and Bai He and asked them about the two boys. The two girls answered proudly that the two boys were their 'brothers', although they were not actually related. Those girls left with jealous expressions in their eyes.

The last day in the camp was a free day. In the morning, the two boys asked the two girls to go swimming in the lake. The girls said they did not swim but they would pick flowers by the lakeside and watch their two brothers swimming.

After changing into their swimming trunks, the two boys jumped into the lake and knowing the two girls were watching, they began to show off their swimming skills.

Watching their two big brothers in the water, Lan Hua suddenly asked Bai He, "Ah, Sister Bai He, who do you like more between our two big brothers?"

"I like both of them," Bai He answered, shyly.

"Which one do you like more?"

"I feel I like Brother Dan Feng more as he is both handsome and talented."

"You cannot do this! I also prefer Brother Dan Feng! You should let me choose first as I am your elder sister!"

"Leave it! Leave it! They may not even like us! There are a lot of girls who like them. Did you see the expression in those girls' eyes when they watched them in the sports competitions? We are still little girls in our brothers' eyes. Our teachers said we should not love boys too soon because we are still so young. We should not think too much about our brothers."

Just then, a huge fish jumped out of the water and the two girls quickly walked out onto a wooden jetty to watch the fish.

They actually saw quite a few big fish swimming in the clean water but Lan Hua became too excited and forgot to watch her steps. She suddenly fell into the water.

Bai He was frightened and shouted, "Help! Help! Lan Hua is in the water!"

Luckily, the two boys were very close. They swam over quickly to rescue Lan Hua and caught her at almost the same time to bring her ashore. Spitting out some water, Lan Hua opened her eyes slowly.

"Thank you very much for saving me."

The two boys both held her close and said at the same time, "I saved you!"

Bai He explained that she saw the two boys gently cradling her in their arms at the same time.

Lan Hua said, in that case, all of them had saved her.

The two boys felt guilty about the incident as they had asked the two girls to go to the lake in the first place. They sent the two girls back to their tent and told Lan Hua to change out of her wet clothes and get some rest before tomorrow's return journey.

The next day, on the way back to the River City, the two boys and girls travelled on the same bus again. Seeing Lan Hua talking and laughing, the two boys felt reassured and began to discuss how to improve their skills for the next summer camp.

Noticing the two girls were unable to hear them, Jian Jun said to Dan Feng quietly,

"Little brother, do you think the girls will become very pretty when they grow up?"

"Of course!" Dan Feng replied.

Jian Jun winked secretly and said,

"If possible, I mean if it is possible, which you would prefer? Lan Hua or Bai He?"

Dan Feng made a gesture to Jian Jun, telling him to be quiet.

"You are only 14 years old. Too young to think about girls. They are still little girls but if I had to say, I like both of them, especially Lan Hua because she is pure and pretty, like her mother."

"You cannot compete with me in everything! I also prefer Lan Hua. I am your elder brother and I should have priority!"

Jian Jun looked a bit anxious but Dan Feng smiled.

"I am just joking. Do not take it too seriously. They might not even like us when they grow up."

"That's true! They are only nine years old now and it will be another ten years before they are grown up. We may already have other girlfriends by then."

The two boys started to talk about other things, not realizing that they would really fall in love with these two girls in the future and just like their parents, it would once again become a complex love triangle.

PART II

The Distressing Love Triangle Continues

Chapter I

We Have Not Married Each Other

After the students returned to the city, their parents came to pick them up. Dan Feng was a bit anxious as his parents were not there, but in the end, Zhang Feng's assistant arrived. He told Dan Feng that his parents were busy with moving to the new villas.

The assistant drove for over twenty minutes to a small, residential area by the riverside. There were over twenty stylish villas here, built by Zhang Feng's company. Their car stopped in front of two villas, next to each other. The assistant told him that the one on the left was his new home but he entered the right one first as he wanted to tell his father about his achievements in the camp.

Inside the villa, Dang Feng felt amazed. It was a huge house. Seeing his busy father and second mother, he ran to them.

"Daddy! After all the competitions in camp, my class won the first prize. I beat Jian Jun in the wrestling match and won the first prize for my solo singing and accordion performance!"

"Great! We did not train you for nothing!" Zhang Feng replied, happily.

"Second Mother! I saved Lan Hua from drowning!"

"Really?" asked Yu Mei, caressing Dan Feng's hair. She regarded him as her own son.

"Like your father, you are ready to take action for a just cause. Your father saved me from a group of hooligans when we were teenagers."

"Really? Father, can you tell me this story?"

Not wanting his son to know too much about the complex relationship between Dan Dan, Yu Mei and himself, Zhang Feng asked Dan Feng to go and help Dan Dan unpack. Zhang Feng also told Dang Feng that his stepfather, Liang Hua, was back home now. Dan Feng was a kind boy and liked his stepfather but he had got used to calling him 'Uncle Liang'.

Back in his house, he told Dan Dan and Liang Hua about his achievements in the camp. Liang Hua said it seemed that Dan Feng had inherited his father's talent. Dan Dan showed her son around their new home and Dan Feng excitedly saw there were six bedrooms, three bathrooms and a spacious balcony where you could enjoy the beautiful riverside scenery. Seeing there was also a large back garden, he said he would cut the grass regularly because he still remembered how people cared for their gardens when he lived in England.

In the evening, Zhang Feng and Yu Mei invited Dan Dan's family over for dinner. It was so convenient for them to get together as they were next door neighbours now. They enjoyed their meal and celebrated their move into these luxury villas.

"Do not forget, there are still a lot of people struggling to get properties in a good condition. We need to build more cheap but high quality properties, just like the Singapore Government is doing," said Zhang Feng.

Zhang Feng and Yu Mei were trying to persuade Liang Hua to stay but he looked hesitant and said little. He felt that China had changed greatly in the last decade since economic reforms had begun and living standards were much higher now. Only millionaires in London could afford to buy luxury villas such as these but he still needed to concentrate on his research. He could only go into business if he stayed here but he was not a businessman so it would be better to still act like a 'seasonal bird'.

When he said this, both Zhang Feng and Yu Mei noticed the worried expression in his eyes. Dan Dan also looked awkward so Yu Mei quickly changed the topic.

The next morning, at about 7.00, Zhang Feng received a phone call from Lin Jianguo. Lin told Zhang Feng that there would be a dragon boat race today on the Songhua River which would be worth watching. Yu Mei said Liang Hua should go as he had never seen such a wonderful sight.

She knocked on the door of Dan Dan's house. Probably it was too early and Yu Mei had to wait for a few minutes before the door was opened. Liang Hua opened the door in his pyjamas but on seeing Yu Mei, he quickly said he needed to change and ran into a downstairs guest bedroom. At the same moment, Dan Dan walked down the stairs, also in her pyjamas, and said good morning to Yu Mei. It was clear that they had not slept together! Yu Mei felt strange. Seeing Yu Mei was puzzled, Dan Dan explained that Dang Feng had a cold last night so she had also slept upstairs to look after him. Dan Feng came running down the stairs in his pyjamas and Yu Mei asked about his cold.

"I never catch colds! I am a strong boy!"

Yu Mei was going to explain that his mother had said he had a cold but Dan Dan interrupted and asked Yu Mei what she had come round for. Yu Mei told them about the dragon boat race. Liang Hua and Dan Feng were excited and said they must go to watch it.

Leaving Dan Dan's house, Yu Mei was suspicious. Why did Dan Dan and Liang Hua not share the same bedroom? It happened with some married couples for different reasons of course but why did Dan Dan lie to her and say Dan Feng had a cold? Was she not sleeping with Liang Hua? Was it possible they had a sham marriage? Maybe Dan Dan really had sacrificed herself nine years ago to divorce Zhang Feng and give him back to Yu Mei because they were life-death lovers. Yu Mei felt quite anxious as she still remembered the letter she wrote to Dan Dan at that time. In her letter, she said that if Dan Dan was unable to marry Liang Hua in the end, she would give Zhang Feng back to her. With all this worry and anxiety, she could not concentrate on the race at all.

In the evening, noticing Yu Mei was upset, Zhang Feng asked her what had happened. She should be feeling happy in this new, luxury villa. After a moment's hesitation, she told him of her suspicions about Dan Dan's marriage.

Zhang Feng thought for a while and then said,

"It is impossible. Even though Dan Dan could bear the suffering, Liang Hua could not, as a man. Maybe they just cohabit and never had a formal marriage."

"But why is Dan Dan reluctant to return to England and so willing to work with you here? When we started our company, she said she would go back to the UK once the business was on the right track. Yet now, our business is very successful and she still tries to find different reasons to stay here. My instinct tells me she still loves you deeply and her relationship with Liang Hua does not look like one between real lovers," Yu Mei pondered.

Holding and kissing her, Zhang Feng said, "My little fairy! Are you jealous? I treat her as a family member, like it was during the Cultural Revolution when I regarded her as my elder sister."

"Brother Feng, I am not so touchy. I always think of her as my sister. I said before, I would have shared you with her if polygyny was still allowed but now the law will not allow us to do this which creates an awkward situation for us. I feel I owe her too much if she has really sacrificed herself for the sake of our marriage."

Zhang Feng pointed out that they did not have evidence for her sacrifice and it would be rude to ask them directly. It was better to wait and observe.

Originally, Liang Hua had intended to stay for one week but Dan Dan asked him to stay a few more weeks after Yu Mei noticed that they did not sleep together in order to ease her suspicions. He was rather bored and decided to look at the changes which had taken place in the River City.

China had changed a lot in the last decade: there were high-rise buildings, huge new airports, train stations and high speed motorways. Walking along the riverside, Liang Hua saw the beautiful, five star Songjiang Hotel. He still remembered the pretty girl, Wang Li, the manager of the hotel, who had been introduced to him by Zhang Feng.

Getting close to the hotel, he saw some foreign tourists getting out of their taxis and entering the hotel. A pretty, plump lady was welcoming them and she looked familiar to Liang Hua. It was indeed Wang Li. Liang Hua had not seen her for almost ten years but she was still beautiful, with all the charm of a mature lady. Wang Li also saw Liang Hua and recognized him immediately. She greeted him warmly and invited him to go into the hotel.

Nearly ten years ago, Zhang Feng and Dan Dan had tried to introduce them for a relation, but had failed. Yet they still regarded each other as normal friends. Wang Li led him to a luxury guest room and offered him tea and Dim Sum. Wang Li asked him how his marriage to Dan Dan was going and he replied simply that it was fine. Wang Li guessed that their relationship was probably not very good as Dan Dan was still living here with her son, Dan Feng, and had never returned to England. Maybe Dan Dan still loved Zhang Feng even though they had divorced.

Liang Hua asked Wang Li whether she was married. Heaving a sigh, she said she had just parted from her boyfriend after three years. She told him the attitude of the younger generation in China towards love and marriage was totally different now. Young people were now very independent and would not make efforts to compromise so the divorce rate was quite high.

Liang Hua tried to comfort her and said it should be easy for her to find a nice young man because she was young, charming and well educated. Wang Li said she was no longer young at thirty years old but Liang Hua felt that women in their thirties were more attractive to men who preferred more mature ladies. Wang Li suddenly remembered that Liang Hua was once attracted to Dan Dan more than her because Dan Dan was an older, charming woman at that time. She was happy that Liang Hua thought of her as a mature woman now.

It was evening and Wang Li invited him to stay for dinner and feeling happy, he accepted. Knowing Liang Hua used to be a Hong Kong resident, the hotel chef cooked some delicious

Cantonese dishes and the popular Chinese liquor, Mao Tai, was also on the table. Wang Li urged Liang Hua to drink and said today they could drink as much as they liked because both of them wanted to drown their sorrows. Wang Li had just lost her boyfriend and Liang Hua was upset with his lukewarm relationship with Dan Dan.

Wang Li was able to drink a lot but Liang Hua became tipsy very easily. Wang Li asked him for his address but he could not give it clearly. Wang Li knew Zhang Feng and Dan Dan had moved house recently so she tried to call him. Yu Mei answered the phone call. She told Wang Li that Zhang Feng had gone out and that Dan Dan was at a university classmate's party. She would drive to the hotel herself to pick up Liang Hua.

Arriving at the hotel, Yu Mei saw Liang Hua lying on a sofa, unconscious, and Wang Li suggested waiting a while until he was more sober. A member of the hotel staff wanted Wang Li to deal with a fussy customer at the counter so she left the room.

Yu Mei moved up more closely to see whether Liang Hua was awake and suddenly, he opened his eyes, looked at Yu Mei and murmured,

"Dan Dan, you… are coming?"

"No, I am Yu Mei. Dan Dan is at a party."

"No. No. You… You… cheat me. You… have cheated me… for so many… years."

Yu Mei felt a bit nervous as he might reveal the truth about his relationship with Dan Dan.

With his eyes half opened, he murmured, slowly,

"Nine years ago, when you left Zhang Feng, you said you would… marry me. But you kept asking me… to wait… Then you said… you could not marry me… we could only live together… Then you said you had difficulty with that as well…"

They did not marry! Yu Mei felt her heart beating very fast.

"I know… you still love Zhang Feng. So you prefer to live here and work with him. You said, you are happy just to be his sister… even though you cannot marry him again."

Yu Mei tried to wake him up, but he still carried on,

"You asked me to… find another woman but I cannot… find a woman as charming as you!"

Tears covered his whole face now and Yu Mei gave him a tissue. Just then, Wang Li entered the room. She had actually been listening to him outside the room for a few minutes and understood the real relationship between them which made her feel quite shocked.

She realized that when she had visited Liang Hua and Dan Dan in London, this was why Dan Dan behaved in a very intimate way with him. Dan Dan was performing and wanted Wang Li to report back to Zhang Feng and persuade him to believe she was in love with Liang Hua. This woman had sacrificed her own happiness to benefit other lovers and this man had patiently waited for impossible love!

Yu Mei did not know Wang Li had been listening. She asked Wang Li to find a servant to help them put Liang Hua into the car.

Driving back home, Yu Mei saw a light on in Dan Dan's house so she knocked at the door. Dan Dan and Dan Feng were shocked to see Liang Hua so drunk. Yu Mei told Dan Dan that Liang Hua had met Wang Li that day and had a drink with her. Dan Dan looked a bit nervous and quickly put him to bed.

Yu Mei returned home but she did not sleep well that night.

Chapter II

Let's Divorce

The next day was Sunday and everyone was relaxing at home. Yu Mei did not sleep well as she kept thinking what Liang Hua had said. Zhang Feng was still in bed because he had drunk too much the previous evening with his business friends.

Up on the balcony, Yu Mei tried to clear her head: what should she do? The two families could maintain the existing relationship if Yu Mei and Zhang Feng did not know the truth about the marriage of Dan Dan and Liang Hua. But now, Yu Mei knew the truth so she could not just ignore it. What if it was just wild talk from Liang Hua? She was unable to wait and decided to ask Dan Dan directly.

Knocking at the door, Yu Mei saw Dan Dan in her pyjamas and she apologized for disturbing her so early and asked whether they could talk. Dan Dan said it was fine and asked Yu Mei to go up to the balcony first to wait for her. She needed to change her clothes. After a few minutes, Dan Dan appeared with two cups of coffee. It was not only Dan Dan who had got used to drinking coffee in England. Drinking coffee had become fashionable in China recently as well.

Noticing that Yu Mei seemed to have something on her mind, Dan Dan was a bit nervous because she knew it must relate to Liang Hua's drunkenness last night. She and Yu Mei loved the same man. They had gone through all the disasters of the red storm during the Cultural Revolution with him and his floating and sinking on the sea of officialdom. Now they were battling with the winds and waves on the sea of commerce. Their shared experience meant they understood each other. They chatted for a few minutes.

"Dan Dan, sister, are you getting along with Liang Hua?"

"Yes. We have gotten used to living in two places."

"Sorry to ask about private things but why do you not sleep in the same room, considering that you only meet each other a few times a year?"

Hesitating for a few seconds, Dan Dan said,

"We have been married for nearly ten years now and are no longer attracted to each other. Also, he has a bad habit of snoring. Not sleeping together for couples is not only popular in the UK but also in China now."

Seeing that Dan Dan was reluctant to give her the truth, Yu Mei became impatient.

"Sister Dan Dan, I have always regarded you as my blood sister. Please tell me the truth right now. Liang Hua revealed the reality of your marriage completely yesterday."

"Really?" Dan Dan flushed. "Do not believe his wild talk when he is drunk."

"But drunken talk can also be the truth. As a scholar, his words were quite logical even though he was drunk. It seemed that he was quite depressed about your relationship. He said you never got married and that you do not really live together either. You always asked him to wait. Yet he knew that you still loved Zhang Feng and that is why you do not want to return to England. It is just what Brother Feng and I guessed at that time. You sacrificed yourself in order to give him back to me."

Yu Mei started to cry. Dan Dan passed her a tissue.

"Sister Yu Mei, I love Liang Hua and we may marry later. Even if we do not marry, I am still content with the existing situation. I work with you and Brother Feng and we all get together often to eat and play, like a family. To be honest, I feel happy to be his sister."

"No! Being a wife and a sister are very different things! You used to have a happy family which was ruined by me!" said Yu Mei with tears in her eyes.

She reminded Dan Dan of the promise Yu Mei made her. Dan Dan remembered clearly that when she decided to divorce Zhang Feng, Yu Mei had said that if Dan Dan was unable to marry Liang Hua, she would return Zhang Feng to her. Yet Dan Dan did not want to cause further trouble to the two families and she wanted to forget the promise and asked Yu Mei to ignore the relationship between herself and Liang Hua.

Returning home very upset, Yu Mei thought she should not ignore Dan Dan's sacrifice and it would be better to discuss this matter with her husband. Zhang Feng had just woken up and was drinking fruit juice in the sitting room. Seeing Yu Mei so upset, he wanted to know what had happened. She leaned on his shoulder and cried, telling him about what had taken place that morning.

Zhang Feng felt it would be difficult to resolve this issue. In the past, he had also suspected that Dan Dan had sacrificed herself for the benefit of Yu Mei and him but if he divorced Yu Mei and remarried Dan Dan, Yu Mei would suffer again and would feel very lonely without her own child. Zhang Feng said he would discuss all of this with Dan Dan. If she was really content with the existing situation, then all should be well.

To avoid seeing Liang Hua, Zhang Feng asked Dan Dan to come to his house. Yu Mei stayed out of sight and only he and Dan Dan spoke on the balcony. Dan Dan knew what Zhang Feng was going to talk about.

"Xiao Feng, are you going to ask about my relationship with Liang Hua? Yu Mei has been thinking too much. Although I have not married Liang Hua, we have still lived together for many years, like an ordinary couple."

Zhang Feng frowned.

"In that case, you do not love him like a wife. Please tell me, would you prefer to live with me? Do you hate me or still love me?"

Lowering her head, she said,

"How can I hate you? I am pleased to see you and Yu Mei living together happily. Like during the Cultural Revolution, I was happy to care about you as a 'sister'. Now we still work, eat and play together, like one big family. Liang Hua does not disturb us as he only visits occasionally."

Zhang Feng thought for a while and said,

"No, a sister and a wife are different things. During the red storm, I was foolish to think of your love as the love of a sister. As Yu Mei said, I have poor emotional intelligence! She has noticed that when you watch me, the expression in your eyes is still filled with the love of a wife. Yet, I have not noticed it. I feel terribly sorry that I have let you live in loneliness and sorrow."

His words broke Dan Dan's heart. She began to cry and threw herself into his arms.

"Xiao Feng...no, Brother Feng!"

Her reaction showed how much she wanted to be his wife again. Zhang Feng was moved to tears, remembering her deep love for him over so many years. He was in extreme grief. Ignoring the fact that Yu Mei might see them both, he embraced and kissed her with deep emotion. After a few minutes, she became aware of what they were doing.

In the tone of a sister, she said to him,

"Xiao Feng, it is impossible for everything to be perfect. Even though I want to be your wife again, I would not do it, as it would ruin your love and marriage with Yu Mei. Let's keep things as they are. I am happy enough to see you every day, working with you and having family gatherings with you, Yu Mei and Dan Feng."

Then she left the balcony and did not forget to say,

"Sister Yu Mei, I am leaving, the problem has been resolved!"

It seemed like Yu Mei did not hear her but actually, Yu Mei had heard their conversation and had seen them embracing and kissing. She felt very bad and hid in the bathroom to cry which was not because of jealousy but because she blamed herself. She had ruined Dan Dan's happiness and taken away her husband.

Zhang Feng tried to find Yu Mei and found her sitting on the floor of the bathroom, crying. He thought she was jealous and had seen him and Dan Dan kissing so he quickly explained that he just wanted to comfort Dan Dan.

"It is not because I saw your embracing her that I feel so unhappy. I would actually prefer if you embraced her forever."

Looking at him, she said, seriously, "Brother Feng, let's divorce!"

Zhang Feng was shocked by her suggestion. He led her to the sitting room and made her sit on the sofa while he made some tea.

"Do not mention divorce! It is not the right way to resolve this problem."

Yu Mei replied in a husky voice,

"I promised Dan Dan before we married that I would give you back to her if she was unable to marry Liang Hua. I should keep my promise although I know it will hurt. I have lived happily with you for ten years now which should keep me satisfied. I cannot be too selfish. It will be good for both Dan Dan and Dan Feng if you remarry her. You told me once that I was your turbulent sea and Dan Dan was your peaceful lake. You are probably tired after swimming in the turbulent sea for ten years. Now it is time to return to your peaceful lake."

Just like ten years ago, Zhang Feng felt it was almost impossible to deal with this complex love triangle. He loved both of them but he could only have one of them. He felt unable to divorce Yu Mei as she would leave secular society again so it would be better to keep the existing situation as it was. However, Yu Mei said it would be easy for her to find another man, even if she was nearly 50 years old, as she still looked so young and beautiful. She remembered that handsome Manager Xiao who loved her so she said, even in their circle, there was somebody who loved her.

Zhang Feng said, "No! We are life-death lovers! We cannot part with each other in this life."

They argued and could not persuade each other which annoyed Yu Mei and she slept in a different bed room that night.

Liang Hua had caused the trouble for Dan Dan this time but she felt sorry for him as she had delayed their marriage for many years. He could have found other women willing to marry him in that time. Whenever she tried to persuade him to find other women, he always said he did not mind just having a platonic relationship with her.

After this upset, Dan Dan seriously wanted him to terminate their relationship and suggested that Wang Li could be his choice. Seeing Wang Li had become more mature, Liang Hua started to show an interest in her. He said to Dan Dan that he would think about it.

Yu Mei tried to avoid Zhang Feng over the next few days which was noticed by their friends and colleagues. Manager Xiao asked Yu Mei whether she'd had a quarrel with her husband. Yu Mei said it was just a family matter.

One morning, Yu Mei told Zhang Feng she was going to take him to the hospital to check his liver function as he had been drinking too much recently. Zhang Feng had indeed felt a bit unwell recently and Yu Mei said she had already contacted the company secretary to say he would be late.

Yu Mei drove the car to the city centre and stopped in a car park. Zhang Feng felt worried as this car park was a long way from the hospital. Yu Mei led him to a street where the city registration office was situated.

"Why have you brought me here?"

"Let's see if there are any changes to the divorce regulations."

Zhang Feng was worried that Yu Mei might force him to divorce her so he did not want to enter the building. Yu Mei persuaded him to go into the office and said they would just make some enquiries.

Surprisingly, when it was their turn, Yu Mei said to the girl behind the counter,

"We want to divorce."

"What? You said we were only going to get some advice. Also, we did not bring any documents with us." Zhang Feng said.

While taking registration cards and their certificate of marriage out from her hand bag, Yu Mei said to the girl,

"They are all here!"

Seeing the expression on Zhang Feng's face, the girl said,

"It looks like you have not discussed this matter fully. You are a wonderful match! Why are you going to get divorced?"

Filling in the form, Yu Mei told the girl they had to divorce because of emotional problems. She persuaded Zhang Feng to go through the divorce procedure and have a few happy years with Dan Dan and Dan Feng. Then she asked the girl to put the seal on the application form.

Holding the seal, the girl hesitated. Suddenly, a hand seized the seal. Looking back, they saw Dan Dan was standing next to them, breathing heavily.

Yu Mei grabbed Dan Dan's hand and said to her,

"Sister Dan Dan, I have deprived you of your happy marriage for almost ten years and I feel very guilty! Why will you not let me keep my promise to give Brother Feng back to you?"

The girl at the counter did not want this nice couple to get divorced so she asked them to go back home to think about it again. Zhang Feng and Dan Dan dragged Yu Mei out of the office.

Walking and crying, Yu Mei said to Dan Dan,

"Sister Dan Dan, you should not prevent us from getting a divorce."

That morning, when the secretary told Dan Dan that Zhang Feng and Yu Mei were going to the hospital to check his liver function, Dan Dan was suspicious because Zhang Feng did not have any symptoms. She wondered whether Yu Mei would force him to get divorced and so she rushed to the registration office and witnessed the scene as it happened.

Feeling annoyed, Zhang Feng took Yu Mei back home and asked her to have a rest. She fell asleep straight away as she had not slept well for a few days now. Looking at her wan and sallow face, he felt very sad. It was worrying to be back in the love triangle again.

Liang Hua had also been upset. It looked like just being there brought trouble to these two families so maybe it was time to say goodbye to Dan Dan. Meeting Wang Li on this visit had given him a better impression of her. She was a charming and mature lady now, not a pure and simple girl. Should he meet her again to say farewell before he left in a few days' time?

He hesitantly went to her hotel and sat on a bench at the riverside to watch the entrance of the hotel. Suddenly, somebody patted him on his shoulder. Turning round, he saw Wang Li in a formal uniform, looking very smart.

Wang Li asked him, with a smile,

"Professor Liang, have you come to see me or do you want to stay in our hotel?"

"I have come to see… another person… but also, I want to say farewell to you because I will be returning to England soon."

"Why wait? Come in!"

After finding out that he had never married Dan Dan but he still loved her deeply, Wang Li had a better impression of him. He was a man with affection and faith. Wang Li knew that Dan Dan had tried to persuade him to find another woman. Maybe he would consider her.

Entering the hotel and finding a quiet room, she asked the waiter to bring Dum Sum and beer. With ten years of experiences, both of them had changed their attitude towards love and marriage. Wang Li was more mature now and had given up her unrealistic secret love of Zhang Feng. Parting with her boyfriend had made her more appreciative of men like Liang Hua. Liang Hua had also finally woken up from his platonic love and wanted to find a woman who would enjoy a family life with him. Their looks and warm conversation showed they were interested in each other.

Before he left, Liang Hua carefully asked whether he could have her contact details and she agreed. Her hotel had recently installed the internet and they could send emails to each other rapidly and did not need to wait for one week or ten days to receive letters. They reluctantly said goodbye to each other. Liang Hua said he would invite her to visit him in England very soon.

Chapter III

She Is Missing

One week later, Zhang Feng visited an architecture academy for the design of the shopping mall. He stayed there the whole day but when he returned home, he could not find Yu Mei. He saw a few papers on his desk and picked them up and became very agitated when he saw they were a divorce agreement and a letter she had written to him.

'Dear Brother Feng, I would like to give you back to Dan Dan. Your original happy family was ruined by me. I let both Dan Dan and Dan Feng down. Having had ten happy years with you, I am satisfied. It will be easy to divorce you as we do not have children. Just sign the divorce agreement and send it to the registration office. Then remarry Dan Dan. Do not worry about me. I will not go the Taoist temple again. I might even come back after you have married Dan Dan and become your sister again.'

Zhang Feng started to sweat. What should he do? Should he talk to Dan Dan first? He asked Dan Dan over and showed her Yu Mei's letter. Reading it, Dan Dan was crying instead of showing happiness.

"Yu Mei, my dear sister, why have you done this stupid thing? It is not only Brother Feng who needs you in his life, I will also miss you if you leave us. We will not be happy without you, even if we are remarried."

Dan Dan knew Yu Mei was Zhang Feng's spiritual partner. Without her, he would not have real contentment, even if he regained his happy family with Dan Dan and Dan Feng.

"Xiao Feng, this is not the time to talk about our marriage. The most important thing is to find Yu Mei, bring her back and persuade her not to divorce you. It will be enough to keep the existing situation as it is and we can still live together as one big family."

Zhang Feng agreed with Dan Dan but how would they ever find Yu Mei? It was not wise to report this to the police and better not to disturb the company staff as well. Zhang Feng thought of his loyal assistants, Lin Jianguo and Chen Tao.

The next day, they discussed how to find Yu Mei. She had said she would not go to the Taoist temple again so she might travel to Beijing or Shenzhen. In the end, they decided to send Lin Jianguo to Shenzhen and Chen Tao to Beijing to search for her. Zhang Feng and Dan Dan would search the River City. However, they all knew it could be very difficult to find her.

Zhang Feng was sick with worry. Dan Dan looked after him and tried to comfort him. One day, Qing Lian visited him when Dan Dan was not at home. She told him that their business was improving and Li He was behaving himself as well. Hopefully, he would soon be able to repay some money to Zhang Feng and

Wang Hai. Zhang Feng said Li He did not need to repay him so soon as he and Wang Hai were not short of money.

Noticing Zhang Feng was upset, Qing Lian guessed that something must have happened. She asked why Yu Mei was not at home and after a moment's hesitation, he told her about Yu Mei's running away from home.

Heaving a sigh, she said,

"Brother Feng, the love triangle has upset you again. The monogyny law should make an exception to allow you to marry both Yu Mei and Dan Dan as you are all life-death lovers."

Zhang Feng shook his head and said it was impossible. Qing Lian wanted to look after him, cooking and tidying his home but he declined politely. He remembered the 'accidental' sex he'd had with Qing Lian ten years ago when he was facing the same difficult love triangle.

Yu Mei did not leave the city. She went to the Fengman District where she had enjoyed a lovely holiday with Zhang Feng thirty years ago. She stayed in a small hotel and prepared to stay there a few weeks until Zhang Feng and Dan Dan married. She even wanted to attend their wedding. She informed Manager Xiao (who secretly loved her) about leaving the company for a while and told him to wait for her call if she needed to contact him.

Although she was 48 years old now, she was still fairy-like and charming, like a beautiful mature lady in her thirties. Almost every man passing her would turn back to look at her again. She did not want to attract the attention of local people, so every day, she would walk up to Songhua Lake and have a relaxing walk there. She walked to the place where she used to date Zhang Feng and noticed that some villas had been built nearby. She did not realize that a pair of lascivious eyes were watching her.

Two days later, she rang Manager Xiao who told her everything was fine and both Lin Jianguo and Chen Tao were on business trips. She knew that they must be trying to find her. She walked to the lakeside and sat under the tree where she had kissed Zhang Feng. Suddenly, she heard a male voice behind her.

"Pretty lady, would you like a cup of tea?"

Turning back, she saw an old man holding a large teapot. Feeling a little thirsty, she bought a cup of tea from him and drank it but after a few minutes, she started to feel dizzy and passed out.

When she woke up, she found she was sleeping in a large bed in a comfortable room but she wondered why she was there. She felt strange. Just then, the door opened and she saw a familiar and ugly face: Cai Wenge! She was shaken with fear. Cai was her ex-husband and the sworn enemy of Zhang Feng. As a fanatical Red Guard, Cai had ruined her relationship with Zhang Feng, marrying her and then abandoning her. He was sentenced to eleven years in prison after the red storm and following his release some years ago, he opened a company and continued to challenge Zhang Feng.

"Ha, ha! You cannot live with Zhang Feng now but do not worry! You can live with me again! I am also a millionaire now!"

"You have kidnapped me! I will go to the police!" Yu Mei shouted.

"It is useless to report this to police. You are my ex-wife. You have walked around my house and I have the photos as evidence to show how you are enjoying a few days with me. Somebody will bring food to you."

He left the room and locked the door. Yu Mei realized that the old man was Cai's assistant. He had given her the tea with the drug in it and she was taken to Cai's villa after she had lost consciousness.

In the evening, a woman in her forties came to give Yu Mei some food. She looked like a kind country woman and Yu Mei asked who she was. She told Yu Mei that she was Cai's wife. Cai had found it difficult to find a partner after being released from jail and had to find a wife in the countryside. To get city registration, she had agreed to marry him but after Cai had launched his company and had some money, he started to treat her badly, cursing her and beating her. He said he would divorce her and find another woman. He even brought some women home for sex, often in front of her.

She asked Yu Mei, "Sister, Cai said you are his ex-wife. You are such a pretty lady. Why did you marry this ugly man?"

Yu Mei explained how she had been cheated by Cai in the past. He was a villain and this time, he had kidnapped her. Yu Mei quietly asked her whether she could help her escape from this house. Cai's wife said it would be very difficult as Cai always locked the house from outside when he left.

Thinking for a while, Yu Mei gave her a piece of paper with Zhang Feng's phone number on it and asked her to call Zhang Feng. Cai's wife said there was no landline here as Cai only used a mobile phone but she could try to call Zhang Feng using a public telephone when she went to town shopping the day after tomorrow. Yu Mei kept thanking her and worried about whether Cai might punish her when he knew she had helped Yu Mei to escape. She said she was already fed up with Cai's bad treatment and she would definitely divorce him.

Cai came to Yu Mei's room every night to harass her, saying she was more sexy than ever and wanting to have sex with her. She cursed him and pushed him out of the room.

Both Lin Jianguo and Chen Tao returned to the city without finding Yu Mei. Zhang Feng also visited the Taoist temple in the

North Mountain but did not find her either. Dan Dan said Yu Mei might not have gone too far away from the city. She would contact them if she got into trouble.

Cai did not trust his wife and did not allow her to see Yu Mei again so Yu Mei did not know whether she had contacted Zhang Feng or not and she felt very anxious.

On the fifth evening, he entered her room again after drinking. He said he had been too patient with her, waiting for her consent, and he must have sex with her this night. If she still refused, he would rape her. Yu Mei tried to defend herself but she did not have a weapon because Cai had hidden all the knives and scissors. She tried to escape him inside the room but she soon lost her strength as she was weak and tired.

At last, Cai threw her to the bed and started to strip her. She struggled against him and bit his hand. Seeing blood on his hand, he became angry and started to squeeze her neck which made it difficult to breathe. She had to use her remaining strength to shout loudly.

"Brother Feng, help me!"

A miracle occurred! Zhang Feng's voice could be heard outside the door.

"I am coming to save you, Yu Mei!"

Zhang Feng and Lin Jianguo broke down the door and entered the room. Zhang Feng grabbed hold of Cai's clothes and threw him to the floor and Lin Jianguo kicked him.

Zhang Feng held Yu Mei and helped her tidy her clothes, shouting to Lin Jianguo, "Jianguo, beat him!"

Embracing Zhang Feng, Yu Mei cried with emotion. Facing Cai, his sworn enemy who had once sent him to the execution ground and ruined his relationship with Yu Mei, he started to beat Cai together with Lin Jianguo. Being beaten by two strong men, Cai was rolling on the floor. Yu Mei reminded them just to punish Cai, not beat him to death so they stopped.

Zhang Feng said to the shaken Cai,

"Cai Wenge, you have done so many evil things in the past. Now you kidnap and rape women. We will report you to the police and send you to jail again."

Helping Yu Mei get into the car, Lin Jianguo drove them back home. On the way, she cried for a while and then fell asleep in Zhang Feng's arms.

Cai's wife had successfully passed on Yu Mei's note to her relatives in the town but because the public telephone was out of order, they had only been able to ring Zhang Feng that afternoon, telling him to go to that address.

Zhang Feng realized immediately that it was Yu Mei in trouble so he drove to the Fengman District with Lin Jianguo. Cai's wife had opened the door for them and knew they had come to rescue Yu Mei so she pointed the direction out to them.

Hearing Yu Mei scream, they had broken the door down and saved her from the evil Cai.

Back home, Lin said goodbye to Zhang Feng and left. Zhang Feng carried Yu Mei to the bedroom and left her to sleep. At midnight, Yu Mei woke up from her nightmare and cried again. Zhang Feng tried to comfort and caress her and finding herself in Zhang Feng's arms, she felt reassured and fell asleep again. Holding and embracing her the whole night, he did not sleep at all, fearing she might run away again.

Chapter IV

Let's Share Him

Waking up the next morning, Yu Mei saw she was sleeping in Zhang Feng's arms and he was watching her closely, with affection. Seeing he was tired, she worried,

"Brother Feng, did you not sleep all night?"

"No, because I was worrying about you running away again. I will watch you every minute," Zhang Feng said, seriously.

Yu Mei apologized.

"I am terribly sorry, Brother Feng. I will not run away again."

Zhang Feng felt he could not relax until this love triangle had been finally resolved. Yu Mei also felt it would be very difficult to resolve this situation. If she did not divorce Zhang Feng, he could not remarry Dan Dan and they could not have a family reunion. Yet, it was so difficult to divorce him! Even running away from him had not worked.

Just then, the doorbell rang. It was Dan Dan. Seeing how haggard Yu Mei looked, Dan Dan held her and cried like a child. Yu Mei also cried. Seeing how much these two women cared about each other moved Zhang Feng deeply. He gave them tissues and after five minutes, they stopped crying.

Dan Dan blamed Yu Mei for running away from home and making everybody worry so much. She told Yu Mei to never do such a stupid thing again. From Lin Jianguo, Dan Dan knew how Yu Mei had been rescued yesterday. Dan Dan felt that Cai Wenge ought to be severely punished this time and Zhang Feng said he was going to the police to report Cai's crime and give Cai some more years in jail. Dan Dan said she would go to the office to deal with business and asked Zhang Feng to stay home to look after Yu Mei.

After Dan Dan left, Yu Mei said that Dan Dan was a very open-minded and magnanimous woman and she would always regard her as her own sister. In the past, two sisters were able to marry the same man. She suddenly had an idea in her mind. She asked Zheng Feng to go up to the balcony with her to have some tea. The warm sunshine made them feel more relaxed.

"Brother Feng, you told me before that Dan Dan thinks we are life-death lovers. She regards me as her blood sister. She said if China still allowed polygyny, she would like for both of us to be married to you at the same time."

Zhang Feng felt confused.

"Yes, she said this when we got married because she noticed that I always missed you but the existing law does not allow us to do this."

Yu Mei's idea was to share Zhang Feng with Dan Dan secretly so they did not break the law. She knew she was the only person to make this proposal. Dan Dan would not suggest it. It looked like she wanted to fight for Zhang Feng. Zhang Feng was also not the right person to make this suggestion. It looked as if he wanted to get Dan Dan back. Then Yu Mei told Zhang Feng that if she did not divorce him, he must agree to live with Dan Dan three days a week and live with her three days a week. On Sundays, the two families would join together.

By doing this, they could resolve this difficult love triangle without any violation of the law because bigamy had not been committed. Chinese people were more open-minded towards love, sex and marriage these days. As long as a love affair outside marriage did not affect family relationships, people did not care about it very much and anyway, Dan Dan was Zhang Feng's ex-wife and they had a son as well. Nobody would be suspicious if Zhang Feng and Dan Dan were seen by people as a couple. With a higher divorce rate, it was very common for men to visit their ex-wives and children and it was more convenient for Zhang Feng to visit as the two families were next door neighbours.

Thinking about Yu Mei's suggestion, Zhang Feng believed it was a workable way to resolve their problem, better than divorcing Yu Mei. When he stayed with Dan Dan and Dan Feng, they could have dinner, chat and watch TV together, like a real family but he told Yu Mei that he would not sleep with Dan Dan in the same bed. Yu Mei did not need to worry.

Yu Mei was unhappy with the sleeping arrangements and said, "No, you must sleep with Dan Dan. You did when you were married so you should not feel shy now."

"Ok, ok, I promise, but Dan Dan might not like it as she does not want to upset you. We are not a legal couple anyway."

Seeing he agreed with her, Yu Mei felt happy. She knew if

both he and Dan Dan agreed to live together a few days a week, then gradually, they could develop intimate relations.

On Sunday afternoon, Yu Mei and Zhang Feng invited Dan Dan to have a cup of tea in their house. On a table on their balcony, they laid out Cantonese Dim Sum which Dan Dan liked, with beer and cola. Dan Dan felt that they might have an important issue to discuss with her. Seeing Yu Mei looking so well made Dan Dan happy.

They were all happy to eat and drink and when the atmosphere was right, Yu Mei held up her glass and said to Dan Dan,

"Sister Dan Dan, many thanks for caring about me for so many years. You have sacrificed yourself to benefit Brother Feng and me. We are going to sort out our problems. I seriously planned to divorce him and give him back to you, and even ran away from home but this just caused more trouble for you. Now, I have a compromise and suggest that we share Brother Feng. Each week, he stays with you for three days and three days with me. On Sundays, our two families will get together. Where we live is quite convenient and nobody will see him moving between the two houses. Even if he is seen by somebody, it is still perfectly normal for a man to visit his ex-wife and child. What do you think about my proposal?"

Dan Dan flushed. She did not think Yu Mei would suggest such a thing.

"It is not very good for you, Yu Mei. Even if we do have a good relationship, like sisters, love is selfish. I should not take Brother Feng away from you for half the time."

Both Yu Mei and Zhang Feng guessed that Dan Dan would not accept this proposal directly, or at least, she would be hesitant.

Yu Mei said, with a smile,

"Dear Sister, I understand that you do not want me to suffer emotionally by giving half of my husband to another woman yet I am willing to do this, as originally Brother Feng was yours. He told me that you'd had the same idea to share him with me if the law had allowed it. But times are changing. Chinese people are more tolerant about things to do with sex and marriage such as one night stands, love affairs outside marriage and sex before marriage. Many rich or powerful men have mistresses, which could damage their marriages, but our case is different, we are willing to share what we both love."

Dan Dan thought for a while and said,

"It sounds like an alternative way to sort out this problem although I do not want to take Brother Feng away from you. Ok, let's try it for a while. We do not need to do half and half. It is enough for me to have one or two days a week with him. I can arrange for him to have a different bedroom, like a guest."

Yu Mei thought it was good that Dan Dan had agreed to have him in her house for a few days a week. Gradually, they would behave like a real couple as they still loved each other. Zhang Feng also felt happy keeping the two women he loved so deeply.

"Yes, it will be just like I am a guest, visiting Dan Dan and Dan Feng."

In the end they decided on every Monday, Wednesday, Friday and Saturday, Zhang Feng would stay with Yu Mei; on every Tuesday and Thursday, he would stay with Dan Dan. After a short period of time, if things went smoothly, he would stay with Dan Dan on Saturday as well. On Sundays, the two families would do something together.

After she returned home, Dan Dan was quite happy as she

would have time to enjoy the atmosphere of a happy family, even if she was unable to remarry Zhang Feng. They would not have to worry about their difficult love triangle any more but how would she be able to explain this to Dan Feng? In the evening she cooked the fried chicken wings that Dan Feng liked and went to his bedroom after he had finished his homework.

"Dan Feng, your Uncle Liang does not visit us often which might make you feel lonely. How about if your father stays with us two nights a week? Would that be alright?"

"That's wonderful! Daddy can teach me singing, instruments and martial arts."

Seeing her pure and innocent son so happy, she kissed him but she also reminded him not to tell other people about this.

He blinked his eyes and asked,

"Is it because you are divorced? But he is still my father. He has a right to see me."

Dan Dan just nodded her head.

A few days later, it was the first time for Zhang Feng to stay overnight in Dan Dan's house. Yu Mei bought a Beijing roast duck which both Dan Dan and Dan Feng liked and asked Zhang Feng to take it. He was worried that Yu Mei might feel lonely so he bought a CD of Canton music for her and reminded her to stay safe.

She could tell he did not want to show he was very keen to go to Dan Dan's so she said,

"Go quickly! Please treat Dan Dan warmly and enjoy your happy family time together!"

Then she pushed him out of the door.

Zhang Feng had not been alone with Dan Dan and his son since he divorced her. He cooked some tasty pancakes, with spring onions and fried soybean sauce, making delicious roast duck rolls. Dan Dan also cooked a few dishes and the whole family sat down together for a very tasty dinner. Dan Feng said it was the best dinner he had had for many years.

Dan Dan treated Zhang Feng politely and felt extremely happy because at last, she could live together with the man she loved so deeply, even though it was not every day. Dan Feng needed to go to school the next morning so he went to bed early at eight o'clock. Zhang Feng and Dan Dan sat on the sofa to chat and watch TV.

When it was time for bed, both of them looked a bit nervous. Dan Dan said she had made up a bed for him in a guest room and led him there. He was surprised that all the furniture and the decorations were the same as when they lived together in the past. He did not know what to say.

"Sorry Dan Dan, thank you."

But she left immediately.

The next day, Yu Mei asked Zhang Feng whether he had had a nice evening with Dan Dan and Dang Feng. He said yes but explained straight away that he had slept in a different bedroom. Yu Mei understood that he did not want her to feel jealous.

"There will be a transitional period of time but don't wait too long. You must be intimate with her, like a husband."

He just stood there, humming and hawing.

The second time he stayed with Dan Dan she entered his bed room with him and made his bed carefully. Remembering what Yu Mei had asked him to do, he asked Dan Dan to stay for a chat. She sat on his bed, shyly. He talked about their happy life in the past which made her flush. He knew this was the sign for more intimate relations and he raised his arms. She threw herself into his arms, closing her eyes and enjoying his kisses but when he tried to take her to bed, she struggled to stand up and said,

"No! I cannot let Yu Mei down!"

Then she left the room.

Knowing Zhang Feng had failed the second time, Yu Mei felt unhappy. She complained that he did not understand women's psychology. She said Dan Dan actually wanted to have sex with him but was just worried it might upset Yu Mei. Dan Dan had not had a sex life for over ten years which was very hard for most women. She told him that women in their forties have strong sexual desires so he should try to please her. They had made her suffer for nearly ten years. Yu Mei warned him that she would run away again if he did not have sex with Dan Dan.

"Alright, alright, I will… do it."

The third time in Dan Dan's house, they still chatted for a while after Dan Feng had gone to bed. Looking at her pretty face and the emotional expression in her eyes, Zhang Feng was unable to control himself. He held Dan Dan's hands and took her into the bed room, embracing and kissing her. But again, when Zhang Feng wanted to take her to bed, she started to struggle.

Zhang Feng said to her gently,

"Honey, I have let you suffer for ten years. I cannot do it anymore."

"I do not want to upset Yu Mei." Dan Dan said quietly.

"Do not worry. It is she who asked me to give you pleasure as a husband."

Listening to him, she stopped struggling and allowed him to take off her clothes. She was very excited and enjoyed having sex with him.

Not wanting Dan Feng to see them sleeping in the same room, Dan Dan got up early to cook breakfast. Zhang Feng also got up and walked up to her back, embracing and kissing her.

Thinking of their exciting sex last night, she felt a bit shy.

"Be careful. Dan Feng may see us."

Zhang Feng said with a smile,

"He will know the truth sooner or later. He is a smart and naughty boy sometimes."

Part III

A Crisis in the Trade War

Chapter I

A Building Collapse Accident

The next day, Dan Dan met Yu Mei in an elevator. Blushing, she said to Yu Mei,

"Thank you, Sister Yu Mei." Yu Mei understood that Dan Dan was thanking her for her kindness in persuading Zhang Feng to sleep with her. The two ladies did not say more, but their looks showed their happiness at sharing the same man they both loved deeply. Zhang Feng and his two ladies looked very happy that day, which confused their staff because business remained the same, nothing different had happened. Only Lin Jianguo and Chen Tao knew that the difficult love triangle had been resolved. But Manager Xiao was disappointed. He wanted to marry Yu Mei if she divorced Zhang Feng. Yu Mei noticed his anxiety and told him about her heart-breaking love affair with Zhang Feng during the Cultural Revolution. Manager Xiao was moved by her story and said he now understood why their relationship was unbreakable. Yu Mei offered to help him to find a good girlfriend but he said it was very difficult to find another fairy-like woman like Yu Mei.

The friends and relatives were also happy about their new relationship. Qing Lian visited Zhang Feng more frequently as she thought she had been upgraded to Zhang Feng's 'sister' since both Yu Mei and Dan Dan were his wives now.

When Wang Hai came to Zhang Feng's house for dinner, he whispered to Zhang Feng,

"Brother Feng, you are really lucky to have good fortune in love affairs. One concubine in the east chamber and another in the west chamber."

"Nonsense! I just occasionally stay overnight in Dan Dan's house if I finish coaching Dan Fang too late," Zhang Feng hastened to explain.

"Stop your excuses! Can you control yourself to sit next to beautiful Dan Dan?" Wang Hai said.

Zhang Feng deliberately changed the topic and asked Wang Hai whether he had contacted Helen recently. Worried that his wife might hear the name Helen, Wang Hai made a gesture to Zhang Feng. They stopped talking about women.

Liang Hua and Wang Li had become lovers. One day, Wang Li rang Zhang Feng. Over fifteen years ago, when Zhang Feng was working at Jili University, he had played Hamlet and Wang Li, Ophelia, in a performance of Hamlet during the First Chinese Shakespeare Festival in Beijing. Ever since, they still mentioned their roles when teasing each other. Wang Li said,

"CEO Hamlet, Ophelia has loved the Prince of Norway. He is a gentleman with true affection."

"Hamlet is a man of foresight. Even ten years ago I believed you would be a nice couple," Zhang Feng smiled. Wang Li said she would invite Zhang Feng and his two wives to her wedding. Zhang Feng immediately said he did not want to commit bigamy. She guffawed on other side of phone.

Cai Wenge was punished. He was charged with attempted rape. He argued that he missed his ex-wife and could not control himself. He also showed the photos of Yu Mei passing his house, and said she was the one who wanted to see him. Cai's backstage supporter Shen, the deputy governor of the province, tried to influence the court to give Cai a light sentence.

Zhang Feng's business was going smoothly. The shopping mall was nearly finished, and projects for residential buildings also kept expanding.

But the good days did not last long. A few months later, Zhang Feng received an urgent call from a sales manager. A recently built block of flats had collapsed, injuring some residents. The fire brigade, ambulance, city management bureau and police were all already on the site.

Zhang Feng was quite nervous after hearing this. He called Dan Dan, Yu Mei, Lin Jianguo and Chen Tao, and they drove to the scene of the accident, where many people had gathered. Pushing through the crowd to get close to the block, they were surprised by the terrible scene: part of this four-storey building had collapsed, with broken precast concrete panels, damaged furniture and personal belongings everywhere. Lin Jianguo was speechless, as he was in charge of construction work.

Zhang Feng found the chief police officer who used to be Zhang Feng's subordinate when Zhang Feng was the mayor of the city. The officer had a good impression of Zhang Feng, so he tried to comfort Zhang Feng, saying that fortunately, nobody had died. But there were eight injured residents from three families, with two serious cases among them. Some experts from the City Construction Bureau were investigating the cause of the collapse.

Dan Dan and Yu Mei said the most important thing now was to treat the injured residents, especially the seriously injured ones. If they died, the consequences would be far more severe. Zhang Feng asked Dan Dan and Yu Mei to go to the hospital to express sympathy and solicitude to the injured residents. They would also talk to the director of the hospital, asking for his help to treat the injured residents with all his resources. Zhang Feng said that Li He knew more people in the medical professions and they should ask him to find better doctors. Zhang Feng would return to the company to control the situation. At the same time, he asked Lin Jianguo and Chen Tao to investigate the cause of the collapse, checking the construction work and the source of the construction materials.

The following morning, the director and the general engineer of the City Construction Bureau visited Zhang Feng's company. Both of them used to be his subordinates so they respected him. Zhang Feng received them politely. The director said that the preliminary investigation found the precast concrete panels had used defective steel bars which made the panels unable to bear the load of the walls, resulting in the collapse. Dan Dan said,

"Our company is very strict about checking the quality of all construction materials. So it is strange these defective steel bars were used in the construction."

At this moment, Lin Jianguo and Chen Tao entered the meeting room in a rush. They told Zhang Feng and the director that they had checked the warehouse that morning, but the warehouse director was not there. His assistant said that one of the director's family members had fallen seriously ill. The deputy director of the warehouse led them into the warehouse and eventually they found some defective steel bars in a small unused room. The deputy director said he had never known there were such defective steel bars in the warehouse nor who accepted them. Lin and Chen also visited the precast concrete panel factory to talk to the team head who had made these defective panels. Yet strangely, this head had left the factory the previous evening, saying he needed to return to his hometown for some family issues.

That the two key persons were missing at the same time was a suspicious sign. These two men had been working for some years for the company and had good records. So had the incidents been caused by carelessness or deliberately? The director of the City Construction Bureau said it was up to the company to investigate the real cause of the collapse. He hinted that a lot of jerry-built projects had been uncovered recently, arousing popular indignation, and the central government had asked the local authorities to investigate and deal with them strictly.

After the officers from the City Construction Bureau left, Zhang Feng was stressed and tired, without an appetite for lunch. Dan Dan brought McDonald's and Yu Mei brought Kentucky Fried Chicken for him. The two ladies knew he liked to eat Western fast food when he was under stress. Western fast foods were very popular at that time, with over 2,000 restaurants in the country. He was moved by the care from his beloved ladies. When he had just started to eat, they heard a loud noise outside the building. The receptionist called him and said several hundred people had gathered outside demanding compensation for their damaged flats. Zhang Feng and the two ladies thought this was strange as the collapse had only affected ten households, why were so many people coming to ask for compensation?

They walked down to the entrance of the building and saw an angry crowd shouting,

"Compensate us for our property! Compensate us for our property!"

Zhang Feng waved his hand and spoke to the crowd calmly,

"Dear proprietors, I am the CEO of this company. I apologise to you for the damage to your properties caused by the collapse. We will provide temporary accommodation for you and demolish and rebuild Block Number Three."

About thirty residents were living in Block Number Three who started to applaud after hearing Zhang Feng's speech. But the remaining two hundred demonstrators still looked unhappy and shouted,

"Don't you care about the people living in other blocks in the same residential area? Have you built only one jerry-built apartment?"

Lin Jianguo had noticed a man wearing a peaked cap inciting the other people to shout at Zhang Feng. His figure looked like Cai Wenge. After discussing things with his colleagues, Zhang Feng said to the crowd,

"You do not need to worry if you live in the same area. Block Number Three was built very recently and the number of defective steel bars is limited. It is unlikely they were used to build other blocks. But we will still ask experts to check every building in the same area with a metal detector. We will inform the residents if we find potential problems."

A few old people persuaded the others to trust Zhang Feng. They said he was an honest Confucian businessman. He had done a lot of good things for the citizens when he was the mayor of the River City. Yet the man wearing a peaked cap still incited the other people to make trouble. Lin Jianguo called out to him,

"The gentleman wearing a peaked cap, which block do you live in in this area? If you still feel unhappy, please come in, we can discuss the issue with you."

The man ran away quickly. Lin said to his colleagues,

"Don't you think that man looks like Cai Wenge?"

Zhang Feng and Dan Dan agreed. Yu Mei said she was shaken when she saw the man. Dan Dan said Cai should be locked in prison. Chen Tao said that a friend working in the court told him that Cai had only been sentenced to one and half years in prison because somebody in a high position pleaded for leniency for him. He then got a medical exemption and was released after a few months in jail. Lin said it was terrible that corruption occurred even in the legal system. Zhang Feng said,

"It looks this accident was deliberately plotted by somebody who intends to take revenge against us and destroy our company. We should quickly find the evidence to clear our name. Let's try to find the warehouse director and the team head of the factory, and then find the person behind the scenes."

The next day, the city's financial investigation inspector and secretary of the discipline inspection visited the company. They told Zhang Feng the city council was going to investigate this accident as a criminal case. It was such a serious construction accident because of using defective materials. So the legal representative of the company was responsible for the accident and would be punished according to the law. Lin Jianguo said he was the person in charge of construction work, so he was responsible for the case. Yet Zhang Feng insisted that he was the person responsible.

After mentioning that two key workers were missing, and the riot of the proprietors, Yu Mei said,

"There are signs that somebody caused this accident to sabotage our company."

The secretary nodded his head as he trusted Zhang Feng. But the inspector, who was a subordinate of Shen's, said arrogantly,

"Even if somebody wants to damage your reputation, the defective steel bars were in your warehouse and the precast concrete panels were made in your factory, which means you cannot shirk your responsibility."

"Can you give us a bit time to investigate the accident and find evidence that this is a conspiracy?" Zhang Feng asked.

The secretary agreed, but the inspector said he could only give Zhang Feng one week as the city council had urged the police to conclude this case quickly to calm the indignation of the citizens.

Zhang Feng and his colleagues realised that some powerful officials intended to destroy his company. It was very likely that his old enemies, Governor Shen and Director Li, had put pressure on the judicial system. So his company had to find the evidence as soon as possible.

Relatives and friends all came to give Zhang Feng their support. Wang Hai, Li He, Qing Lian and Huang Lei visited his house one evening to ask for details of the accident. They also tried to help him find the evidence. Wang Hai remembered he used to buy some steel bars from some village and township enterprises, but their products were often substandard. He said he could check these companies to find the source of these defective steel bars. Li He said he would like to help Wang Hai to investigate, leaving Qing Lian to run his business. Before they left, Wang Hai said, Zhang Feng's advice for doing business was really true: the commercial sea was not calm but turbulent. But if we consolidated together, being steadily at the helm and holding the sails, we would sail successfully to our destination. Zhang Feng thanked these loyal friends for their support. Li He said with emotion,

"Brother Feng, you saved me when I was facing bankruptcy. How can I relax when you are facing trouble?"

Chang Zheng visited Zhang Feng as well and expressed his sympathy. He also believed this was a conspiracy, as he knew Zhang Feng was an honest Confucian businessman. He said he was unable to interfere with the case directly, but he would try to help Zhang Feng to have more time to find evidence. The two old loyal friends embraced each other when they said farewell.

Chapter II

A Hard Investigation and Collection of Evidence

The collapse of Zhang Feng's building quickly attracted the attention of the media. At the end of the 1990s, China had started large-scale construction of basic infrastructure. Huge airports, train stations, city squares, shopping malls, offices, colleges and hospitals sprang up. Many residential properties were also built, so housing was greatly improved, and citizens did not need to wait for five to ten years to get their council flats. However, to make more money easily, some greedy businessmen tried to save on costs by using substandard materials, which caused a lot of jerry-built projects. But Zhang Feng always followed Confucian moral standards, putting the customers' interests first and profits second. This time, he had been framed by his commercial and political enemies.

Some media reported the accident objectively, like the River City Daily where Qing Lian used to work. Its report just gave the details of the accident, saying Zhang Feng's company normally had a good reputation. But other media, controlled by Shen's associates vigorously propagated that this accident was a typical case of jerry-built projects, with collusion between government officials and businessmen. Governor Shen intended to attack Chang Zheng as well as other honest officials who might disclose his corruption because he knew Zhang Feng and Chang Zheng were close friends. He put pressure on the city court and asked them to try this case and pronounce the sentence as soon as possible.

Three days later, the economic crime investigation inspector, with over ten policemen, stormed into Zhang Feng's office and arrested him. Lin Jianguo stood up and protested, reminding the inspector that he had given them one week to find evidence of a possible conspiracy. The inspector said,

"There is no need to wait. The evidence for your crime is very clear: the collapsed building, injured residents, defective steel bars in your warehouse. To arrest him is best, to avoid possible collusion." Then he handcuffed Zhang Feng.

Zhang Feng was very calm as he knew this day would come. He had just arranged all the work for his colleagues in case he was arrested. To Dan Dan and Yu Mei, who were crying and angry, and to Lin Jianguo and Chen Tao, Zhang Feng said,

"Do not worry. Sooner or later we will find the people who framed us. If we cannot find them, I do not mind staying in jail for a few years. I will feel reassured if you can stick to your posts and run our company steadily."

His staff lined up at the entrance of the company to send him off, and a lot of them had tears in their eyes. Holding his head high, Zhang Feng said farewell to them.

Dan Dan held a meeting after Zhang Feng left. She said to her colleagues,

"It is very clear that our enemies intend to reach a verdict soon, so they did not give us time to find any evidence of a conspiracy. So we need to speed up the investigation. We should have one group to find the team head of the panel factory, and the other group to find the warehouse director who knew the seller of the defective steel bars. Wang Hai and Li He can help us find the factory which made these defective steel bars and then we will know who bought these bars from them."

At the same time, Dan Dan arranged to send somebody to go to the detention centre to see Zhang Feng.

Zhang Feng was locked up in the detention centre of the City Police Bureau. The economic crime investigation inspector deliberately locked him in with thieves and rapists, some of whom bullied him. A recidivist recognised Zhang Feng and said with a loud laugh,

"Ha! Ha! This is our previous Mayor Zhang. Now he is in here with us! My buddies, let him have a taste of our power!" The other suspects were happy to vent their anger by beating a weak person. They swarmed up and surrounded Zhang Feng without knowing he was a martial arts master. Zhang Feng was depressed and did not want to fight against them, but the suspects believed he was frightened and began to attack him. Zhang Feng warned them he would defend himself if they did not stop. These hooligans thought the officers were weak physically and continued to attack him until he took off his coat and fought against them with his Pili boxing. In less than one minute, he had beaten them and they were lying on the floor. The recidivist hid behind a table.

"What are you doing here?" A scolding voice was heard at the door. A police officer entered with two policemen.

"He… he hit us!" The suspects on the floor pointed at Zhang Feng. The officer said,

"Nonsense! I saw you insulted him first." Then he saluted Zhang Feng and said,

"CEO Zhang, you have been wronged. I am criminal police Captain Fan Wei. They should not lock you in with these hooligans. I will find a better place for you."

He led Zhang Feng to a cell for a single person. After asking his assistants to leave, he whispered to Zhang Feng,

"I was transferred to this city from another province last year. Lin Jianguo was my comrade-in-arms when we were in the army. He asked me to look after you in the centre, saying that you have been wronged. I can also help to find the criminals who framed you as this case is a criminal case as well. CEO Zhang, I did not realise that as a professor and mayor in the past and CEO now, you have such wonderful skills in martial arts. I almost applauded you when I saw you beating those hooligans."

Zhang Feng modestly said it was a pity that he did not have enough time to practise his martial arts now. He thanked Captain Fan for his care and help and asked him to tell Lin Jianguo that he was fine in the detention centre.

The next day at lunchtime, the door of his cell was opened. Zhang Feng was surprised to see Dan Dan and Yu Mei walk in. After the guard shut the door, they sat down, one on each side of him, and started to cry. Zhang Feng caresses their shoulders and comforted them, saying,

"Do not cry, I am fine."

"We recalled the situation thirty years ago," Yu Mei said while crying. Zhang Feng understood and said,

"I see, you remember the scene when you met me in the jail during the Cultural Revolution. I was facing the death penalty at that time." Hearing his words, the two ladies started crying even harder. He tried to calm them down,

"Yes, we did not realise that running a business can land you in jail as well. But at least, there's no death threat this time. Maybe just a few years in jail."

Dan Dan and Yu Mei stopped crying. They only had ten minutes for this visit, so Dan Dan quickly told him about the arrangement of their urgent investigation. She mentioned Captain Fan as well, who would help them to investigate this case. Zhang Feng said with emotion that there were more good people in this world. Dan Dan and Yu Mei told him that they knew the evil Governor Shen intended to sentence Zhang Feng as soon as possible, so they had to hurry to find the evidence to clear his name.

Chen Tao, with his assistant, tried to find the missing team Head Chen. His neighbours said Chen's hometown was in Hua Dan County. Chen Tao remembered He Hua's hometown was also in the same county, so he then visited her supermarket in the city. He Hua knew Zhang Feng was in trouble and promised to help Chen Tao to find Head Chen. She telephoned her husband Li Yong first and asked him to search for the address of Head Chen. Then she travelled to Hua Dan County with Chen Tao and his assistant.

They arrived at the county and phoned Li Yong. They were pleased that Li had found Chen's home in Ba Dao Town. They continued to drive for another half an hour to get to the town. When they knocked on the door, Chen's family members looked nervous and told them Chen was not at home. They obviously knew Chen was in trouble and did not want to tell them where he was. Chen Tao suddenly remembered Chen's hobby was fishing, particularly when he was stressed.

Chen Tao asked the local people where they could find lakes or rivers nearby, and they told him there was a river outside the town. Chen Tao, his assistant and He Hua walked to the riverside and saw a man wearing a straw hat fishing there. Chen Tao sneaked up behind the man and then boomed,

"Hello, Head Chen!" The man was startled and fell off his stool, his hat dropping on the ground. It was indeed Head Chen. He knelt and kowtowed to Chen Tao, saying,

"I am guilty! I am guilty!"

Chen Tao helped him to his feet and asked him what he had done with the defective steel bars. Head Chen told Chen Tao that it was the warehouse Director Li who had asked him to use these bars. Li said it was safe to mix them with good quality bars because the block was only four storeys high, so the load-bearing precast panels should not be a problem. Li had given him three thousand yuan for accepting these bars. It was just the time when Chen desperately needed money for the dowry for his brother's fiancée, so he agreed and used these bars. He was frightened after the accident, so he hid in his hometown. Chen Tao said to him,

"CEO Zhang and our company have treated you well. How can you do such a thing to damage our company's reputation?"

"Do you know CEO Zhang has been arrested for this accident and he is facing a sentence?" He Hua said angrily.

Head Chen felt fearful and said,

"I will plead guilty. I will go to jail rather than let CEO Zhang suffer."

He agreed to go back with Chen Tao and plead guilty in court and accept his punishment.

After Chen Tao had found Head Chen, Dan Dan and Lin Jianguo were pleased as they had found one of the key links in this investigation. The next step was to find Director Li of the warehouse. Lin Jianguo and Captain Fan went together to search for him. From the local police station, they knew Director Li lived in a poor area that would be redeveloped soon. But Li was not at home. His neighbours said his wife Wu Ying was seriously ill and in hospital, having treatment. Li had also disappeared after the accident. Lin and Fan thought they should find Li's wife first, and then they would know his hiding place. But there were more than ten hospitals in the city, how would they be able to find her quickly? Lin thought Li He would be the person to help them, as he had been working in medical circles for twenty years and was familiar with the system. When they visited Li He's company and told him about the situation, he was willing to help to find the woman. He said Brother Feng was his saviour, and it was an opportunity for him to repay Zhang Feng's kindness. He asked Qing Lian to take over and left with Lin and Fan.

Li He believed Wu Ying was likely to be having treatment in either the cancer or surgical wards. So he tried to contact his close friends in several hospitals. In the end, he narrowed it down to two hospitals. In the first one, they did not find the woman. In the second one, the director of the cancer department said there was indeed a female patient called Wu Ying in the ward after cancer surgery. Fortunately, her cancer had not progressed. Li He, Lin Jianguo and Fan Wei were all pleased and walked to the wards, but they did not find her. The head nurse told them her family members had asked for a cheap, hidden ward for her, so the hospital had placed her in the basement.

Entering the ward, they saw a haggard woman who looked nervous when she saw them. She said she did not know where her husband was and when he would come here to see her. Captain Fan gave Lin and Li a wink and said to Wu Ying,

"In that case, we will not bother you."

Leaving the ward, Fan said he thought it was very likely Director Li would come to see his wife soon as he had not come to see her for the previous three days. He decided to hide and keep watching over this ward, and Lin and Li said they would like to stay with him. They found a small storeroom opposite her ward and hid there, watching and sleeping in turns overnight. Lin Jianguo used to be a scout in the army, so he could remain vigilant at night. At about 2.00 am, he heard soft steps in the corridor. From the small window in the door, he saw a man entering Wu Ying's ward. He woke Fan and Li and the three of them walked to the door of her ward.

They could hear a man inside saying to her that she should relax and recover from her illness. His troubles would finish soon. After ten minutes, the man opened the door and as soon as he stepped out, Fan, Lin and Li grabbed him and took him to their hiding room. Seeing Lin Jianguo, Director Li knew he had to confess what he had done with the bars. He said a man in his fifties had sold these bars to him for peanuts, and asked him to give them to the precast panel factory. For doing this, he gave him 10,000 yuan. Initially, Director Li had refused to accept these bars, but he desperately needed money for his wife's operation at the time, so finally, he bought them. He had also bribed Head Chen in the factory to use these bars. Captain Fan showed him the photo of Cai Wenge. He looked fearful, claiming he did not remember the face of the man. Fan and Lin felt that he did not want to identify this man. To relax him, Fan said to him that if he could help them to find that man, he would get a lighter punishment. They released him and sent him home, but arranged for two policemen to keep a watch over his house in case the man who had sold him the bars contacted him again.

The next few days, Wang Hai was busy searching for the factory that had produced those bars. In the end he found it, but it was already bankrupt. Wang Hai met its boss in a metal equipment shop. The boss recognised Wang Hai and asked him whether he would like to buy something there. Wang Hai asked him quietly what he had done with those defective bars. The boss said,

"I initially wanted to sell them to an iron and steel factory as scrap metal, but a stupid man had approached me, willing to buy these bars. He said he would use them to make metal rails, so I had sold him the bars."

When Wang Hai showed him Cai's photo, he said,

"Yes, that looks just like him, with some grey hair, and he was wearing glasses. Why are you investigating this guy?"

"He owed money to my friends but did not want to repay it." Wang Hai replied.

"If needed, I would be able to identify him." The boss said.

After all these investigations, Dan Dan, Yu Mei, Lin, Fan and Li all felt happy. It was obvious that to cause a building accident and ruin Zhang Feng's company, Cai had bought these bars and sold them to Director Li. But another key piece of evidence was that Director Li would have to identify Cai as the person who had sold him the bars, otherwise, Cai could deny it. So they would need to persuade Director Li to identify Cai, but if Cai had threatened Director Li he would not dare to identify him. Yu Mei said,

"I would try to persuade Li's wife and ask her to cooperate with us."

Everybody agreed to work twenty-four hours a day as Zhang Feng's enemies pushed the court to start the trial soon.

Chapter III

CEO Zhang Has Been Wronged

Sitting in an unmarked car for a whole day, Captain Fan, Lin Jianguo and the other two policemen had not seen anybody entering the house of Director Li. At 9.00 pm, all of them felt tired. Suddenly Fan gasped.

"Look, there's a man coming!"

Lin looked at the man carefully, and his voice betrayed his excitement.

"It is that cunning Cai Wenge. I guess he intends to ask Director Li to keep quiet. It seems he has brought some food to persuade Director Li."

They slipped out of the car and hid behind a tree. They thought Cai might stay in the house for half an hour, and then they would be able to arrest him when he left the house. But only ten minutes later, Cai left the house in a hurry. Lin said,

"Oh no, Cai may have tried to kill Li. You chase and arrest him. I will go into the house to see what happened."

Entering the house, Lin saw Li slumped unconscious on his chair, and it looked like Cai had slipped a drug into his drink. At this moment, Cai was pushed in by Captain Fan. Lin asked Cai what drug he had slipped into Li's drink. Cai said Li was just drunk. Fan was suspicious and called an ambulance straight away to take Li to the same hospital where his wife was. He asked his assistant to lock Cai in their office and not let the others know, as some of Cai's accomplices in the security bureau, like that inspector of the financial crime investigation.

Arriving at the hospital, Li was checked by the doctors. They said he had been poisoned with a special drug that could leave him in a vegetative state. Unfortunately, Western medicine had no way to detoxify him. Fan and Lin started to worry, because if Li could not wake up to identify Cai as the backstage manipulator, Zhang Feng would be in big trouble. Cai quibbled about the situation and said Li was just his drinking fellow. Lin thought of Li He because he used to practise Chinese medicine. Perhaps he knew of special herbs to detoxify this drug.

After receiving Lin's phone call, Li He came quickly with his old supervisor Dr Wang, who was known nationally as a doctor of Chinese medicine. They checked the pulse and tongue of Director Li. Dr Wang said he remembered a secret family herbal formula that could detoxify this poisonous liquor. Li He asked the doctor on duty to open the storeroom to take these herbs. Qing Lian came at this time and offered to boil the herbs for Director Li and administer them to him. Dr Wang and Li He also gave Director Li acupuncture to strengthen his immune system.

Lin Jianguo rang Dan Dan and updated her about their progress with the investigation. Dan Dan asked him how likely it would be for Director Li to wake up before lunchtime the following day, as Zhang Feng's trial would begin at that time. Dan Dan did not ask what would happen if Director Li did not wake up, because she knew it would mean Zhang Feng would have to go to jail. Lin answered they would try their best to wake Li up. Yu Mei said to Dan Dan that she would go to the hospital to talk to Li's wife. Yu Mei had told her a few days before that the company would give her financial support to treat her illness, which had moved her. So Yu Mei would ask her to persuade her husband to identify Cai.

The next morning, Dan Dan visited Zhang Feng in the detention centre and told him the progress of the investigation. He pondered for a while and said,

"Yes, we have a chance of winning, but we have to prepare for the worst to happen. If Director Li is unable to wake up, we will lose the trial." Before she left, she leant on his shoulder to cry. He held her and said,

"My dear Dan Dan, do not worry. This is not our part forever during the Cultural Revolution. After a few years in jail, I will still be a great man."

Governor Shen and his lackey Li Qiu went to the city court quite early. Governor Shen was very pleased his sworn political enemy Zhang Feng would be sentenced today. He also hated Zhang Feng for his success in business, his huge wealth, luxurious villas and prestigious cars. So this time Zhang Feng would face jail and bankruptcy. The judicial system had improved a lot after the Cultural Revolution, but people could still see this was a case of interference. Shen would use his power to push the court to give Zhang Feng a heavy sentence.

In the court, President Liu and the chief judge discussed Zhang Feng's case. They took this case seriously as Zhang Feng was the former mayor and a successful businessman. President Liu had a very good impression of Zhang Feng, so he insisted the trial should be delayed to find more evidence of a possible conspiracy. But Shen kept putting great pressure on the court and said the central government wanted to placate public indignation about jerry-built projects by giving heavy sentences to those businessmen.

Shen asked the chief judge how long the sentence could be. The chief judge said Zhang Feng was only liable for his management error, so five years would be the maximum. Shen disagreed, said that was too light, ten years should be the minimum. President Liu said that was too long, seven years was the longest. Shen said the court should also close Zhang Feng's company and remove his business licence. Liu said it was not good for the economy to close a big company just because of one accident. Shen was unhappy and said he would attend the trial. The chief judge reluctantly gave him and Li Qiu two seats on the side of the court.

It was noon. The observers of the trial had not entered the hall. Zhang Feng was escorted to the defendant's place. He was calm and held his head up. Shen said to him with a smile,

"Mayor Zhang, oh no, CEO Zhang. Do you still feel well today? After fighting against me for so many years, are you pleased to stand for this trial? Ha, ha!"

Zhang Feng sneered,

"I am responsible for the management mistake. But the backstage manipulator who planned this conspiracy should also be tried. I think you are familiar with him."

Shen knew Zhang Feng meant Cai Wenge, as he had guessed the person who had framed Zhang Feng was Cai, even though Cai had not told him. He would definitely support Cai to do this so as to destroy Zhang Feng's future. Li Qiu also mocked Zhang Feng,

"My old classmate, you never listened to my advice in the past, then you must suffer the consequences today."

"Is it good to be your political lapdog?" Zhang Feng replied.

Shen and Li wanted to curse Zhang Feng more, but at this moment the observers entered the hall, including Dan Dan, Chen Tao, Wang Hai, Zhang Lin, Huang Lei and other senior managers from Zhang Feng's company. Chang Zheng had sent his secretary. Present also were Zhang Feng's business friends and previous subordinates when he was the mayor. Journalists from the main media also came as this was a high-profile case.

When the trial began, the prosecutor declared that this was a dangerous case of jerry-building with serious casualties. Although the legal representative of the company, Zhang Feng, did not have a criminal record, he was legally responsible for this accident. Zhang Feng's solicitor defended him and said there was some evidence showing it was a conspiracy to damage his reputation, though more evidence needed to be collected to clear his name. Therefore, the solicitor asked the court for a postponement. His request drew loud applause from the observers. The chief judge said he needed to discuss this with the other judges, but Shen made a gesture to object to this request.

The presiding judge had no choice but to declare,

"Without enough evidence, we cannot postpone the trial. The defendant can appeal from jail if he gets more evidence. We will now have a break for half an hour, and pronounce the sentence after the break."

Sighing over the disappointing declaration was heard in the hall. During the break, Dan Dan, Wang Hai, Chen Tao and other friends made supporting gestures to Zhang Feng. He also tried to comfort them with his gestures.

Then a dramatic scene occurred. After the break, the chief judge intoned,

"For the collapse of the block of flats built by the Song Jiang Real Estate Company, I sentence…"

His announcement was suddenly disrupted by the shrill wail of a police siren. Then the back door of the court burst open. The audience saw Captain Fan and Lin Jianguo push aside the bailiffs who tried to block the entrance. Holding his pistol, Captain Fan shouted to these bailiffs,

"Get out of my way! We are bringing important evidence to the court."

Then the people saw Li He, Qing Lian, Yu Mei entering, followed by Director Li, Head Chen and the boss of the bankrupt steel factory. Cai Wenge was escorted by two policemen. Lin Jianguo said to the chief judge,

"Your Honour, we have arrested Cai Wenge, the criminal who plotted this conspiracy, and also brought all related witnesses and evidence. Please take a break and try this case again!"

Almost all the observers stood up and applauded Lin's report. Journalists kept taking photos. Shen and Li made their escape through the side door. The chief judge announced that the court would take a recess as the details of the case had changed greatly. But the trial would continue and the sentence would be pronounced after two hours. His declaration drew loud applause from the audience. Cai and the witnesses were escorted out of the courtroom and Zhang Feng was taken to a restroom. He waved to his lovers and friends. His solicitor held up his thumb to Zhang Feng, and said,

"We have won!"

Dan Dan, Yu Mei, Qing Lian, Wang Hai, Li He and the other friends all felt very happy and started to embrace each other. Qing Lian also embraced Li He for the first time since they got divorced. They all expressed their gratitude to Captain Fan and Lin Jianguo for their key role in arresting Cai.

Yu Mei told her friends about what had happened the previous night. Dr Wang and Li He continued to treat Director Li with herbs and acupuncture. Yu Mei kept persuading Director Li's wife to cooperate with them. Fortunately, Li had woken up at 6.00 am this morning, but was still groggy. At last, he was able to speak at 9.00 am. Lin Jianguo told him about Cai's attempt to poison him with the drugged liquor, and how Dr Wang and Li He had saved him with Chinese medicine. His wife came in on a wheelchair pushed by Yu Mei. The couple cried on each other's shoulders. His wife told him how Zhang Feng's colleagues had helped her to recover and were supporting her financially. It was also Zhang Feng's friends and colleagues who had saved him. She encouraged him to tell the truth and identify Cai, which would help to clear Zhang Feng's name.

Director Li said it was indeed Cai who had bribed him to buy those defective steel bars and asked him to give them to Head Chen to make panels with them. After the accident happened, Cai threatened to kill his wife to make him keep quiet. Now Cai had even tried to kill him. Director Li said he had got over it now. He preferred to stay in jail for a few years rather than harm CEO Zhang.

When all the evidence and witnesses were ready, it was already noon. They were anxious as they knew the trial had started. Captain Fan sent his assistants to pick up Head Chen and the boss of the bankrupt steel factory. He rang his colleagues to send Cai directly to the court. Then he and other policemen raced to the court in two police cars, sirens blaring. When they arrived at the court, the bailiffs would not allow them in. Then came the scene the people inside had just seen: Captain Fan brandished his pistol to clear the way and enter the courtroom, and shouted to the chief judge asking him to stop pronouncing the sentence. After Yu Mei finished her story, everybody said it was thrilling and could be written in a novel.

After two hours, the court reconvened. Hearing that there had been a development in Zhang Feng's case, more citizens and journalists rushed to the court, even the corridor was crowded. Both Zhang Feng and Cai Wenge were in the dock. Cai also had a temporary solicitor arranged for him. Director Li, Head Chen and the bankrupt steel factory's boss were all in the witness box. Seeing the smiles on the faces of the president and chief judge, the observers guessed the sentence must be in favour of Zhang Feng.

The chief judge declared that, according to the new evidence, this case was a combination of financial and criminal cases. The new defendant Cai Wenge had a criminal record. During the Cultural Revolution, following the Gang of Four, he had been actively involved in a rebellion against the new leaders and was sentenced to eleven years in jail. After he was released, he ran a real estate business, but he was a dishonest trader. Last year, he committed attempted rape and was sentenced to one and half years in prison. But he soon got out on medical grounds. Now he had deliberately plotted to frame his business competitor. Through bribery and threats, he had sold defective steel bars to Song Jiang Estate Company to cause the building to collapse, severely injuring several people. He had also tried to kill the main witness. Therefore, this was a serious criminal case. According to PRC law, he was sentenced to six years in prison.

Director Li, from Song Jiang Real Estate Company, had accepted the bribe and the steel bars that caused this accident. But he showed remorse and exposed Cai's crime. So the court gave him a two-year suspended sentence. Head Chen, from the panel factory, used the defective steel bars to make the precast panels that caused the accident. He confessed and took the initiative to expose other criminal elements. So the court gave him a lighter sentence of one year, also suspended.

Finally, the chief judge declared that the original defendant Zhang Feng had no previous criminal record. He had been an honest official when he worked as the mayor of the city, contributing greatly to the reform movement. He had a good reputation after he started to run his company and made a great contribution to improving the living conditions of the citizens and the construction of public facilities. As for this accident, he had some responsibility as he was the CEO, so he needed to compensate the injured residents and check the other buildings for possible defects. The court then announced that the defendant Zhang Fang was acquitted of all charges.

The observers burst into thunderous applause. A bailiff unlocked Zhang Feng's handcuffs and let him leave the dock, while Cai Wengo was handcuffed and escorted by the bailiffs to the jail.

To the sound of loud cheers, Zhang Feng walked to his friends and colleagues. Everybody shook hands with him or embraced him. Dan Dan, Yu Mei and Qing Lian also kissed him. He Hua wanted to kiss him as well. But seeing Dan Dan and Yu Mei, she stopped, and just embraced him. While embracing Wang Hai and Li He, Zhang Feng said,

"Oh, my good buddies, you have saved me once more."

They replied they were just repaying his great kindness in

saving their lives in the past. Embracing Lin Jianguo, Zhang Feng held back tears and said, "Jianguo, you saved me again."

Lin smiled and said, "No, Brother Feng, you just have extremely good fortune."

Captain Fan had left, and Zhang Feng said to Lin that he must thank him later for his great help.

Surrounded by the excited people, Zhang Feng walked out of the court. The spacious platform outside the court was crowded with journalists who continually took photos. A senior journalist asked Zhang Feng,

"CEO Zhang, you are a really influential man. When you were mayor of the city, you experienced ups and downs on the sea of politics. Now you are battling with the winds and waves on the sea of the business world. Did your ship almost overturn this time?"

Zhang Feng answered with confidence,

"You are absolutely right. You have to face challenges and risks if you want to succeed. The sea of commerce is not calm, but always turbulent. Yet my company will bravely battle with the winds and waves, sailing to a peaceful harbour."

His speech drew loud applause from the audience.

Chapter IV

Reviving the Business

After thanking all the people who had helped to clear his name, Zhang Feng left the court. Dan Dan drove him and Yu Mei back home. His son Dan Feng was waiting for him outside the house. He had been looking forward to seeing his daddy since Zhang Feng was arrested. The negative reports on the media had spread in his school. Some children who did not like him scorned him,

"Your father is an evil businessman doing jerry-building projects!"

His friends also worried he might not be elected as the class monitor again. Dan Dan and Yu Mei tried not to tell him about the case, but he had eavesdropped on their conversation. He knew today was the day of the trial, so he was waiting outside their front garden after school. Seeing his father get out of the car, he ran to him, hugged his daddy and cried. Ruffling his son's hair, Zhang Feng said,

"Dear son, I have been acquitted. Why are you still crying?" Dan Feng smiled and said,

"I know my daddy is an honest Confucian businessman, not a greedy profiteer."

His father and two mothers all laughed. After a rich dinner, everybody felt tired and sleepy. Zhang Feng fell asleep in Dan Dan's bedroom. Yu Mei asked Dan Dan to sleep with him. But Dan Dan asked Yu Mei to sleep with him. In the end, Dan Dan said,

"He is so tired, let him sleep on his own. Both of us can sleep in another bedroom."

The next morning, Dan Dan and Yu Mei asked Zhang Feng to stay at home to rest. But he missed his company and staff. One month had passed since he had been arrested. The three of them drove to the car park of the company. Getting out of the car, they heard a loud noise. Zhang Feng was worried and asked Dan Dan and Yu Mei whether it was the proprietors coming to ask for compensation again. Walking out of the car park, they were surprised to see several hundred company staff lined up on the steps in front of the building, holding flowers and small red flags. A huge banner displayed the words, 'A warm welcome! CEO Zhang returns in triumph!' Many people stood around to watch the fun. Seeing Zhang Feng, Dan Dan and Yu Mei getting closer, Lin Jianguo conducted the company's amateur band to play the lovely music, 'Wish you happiness'. The staff waved their flowers and flags and cheered,

"Welcome CEO Zhang! Welcome CEO Zhang!"

Three young girls walked up to present flowers. This welcome ceremony expressed the care and respect for Zhang Feng from his staff. He was almost moved to tears. He raised the bunch of flowers, paying tribute to his staff. Walking to the highest step, he turned back and spoke to the crowd,

"Staff of Song Jiang Real Estate Company, brothers and sisters, thank you very much for your support and your loyalty to the company. We have survived this crisis. Our enemy attempted to destroy our company, but in vain. But we need to draw a lesson from this accident, improve our monitoring system and avoid loopholes in our management that can be exploited by our enemy. I am confident that our company will go from strength to strength!"

To the cheering of his staff, he entered his company for the first time in over a month.

In the evening, Zhang Feng held a banquet in Song Jiang Hotel for the people who had helped him in this crisis. The hotel manager Wang Li was very pleased that Zhang Feng had survived this crisis, so she had personally arranged this big banquet. She walked to him and said to him jokingly,

"My CEO Hamlet, you suffered from your uncle's conspiracy this time. You should always be careful."

"I will always keep a revenge sword with me," he responded with a smile. He then asked quietly,

"My Ophelia, how are you getting on with the Prince of Norway?"

"It is fine. He will fly here next week and we will have a holiday in Hainan Island, where you can enjoy the tropical climate instead of the cold weather here and in England," she blushed.

Zhang Feng congratulated her on her relationship with Liang Hua, and said he would attend their wedding.

Dan Dan, Yu Mei, Lin Jianguo, Chen Tao and other senior

managers, and his friends Wang Hai, Li He, Qing Lian, and Huang Lei, all sat at the banquet. Captain Fan and Dr Wang were also invited.

When the banquet began, Zhang Feng stood up, holding his cup, and said,

"I am very grateful for all your help in this crisis, otherwise I would be in jail now. During the Cultural Revolution, it was Jianguo and my other friends who saved me on the execution ground. In political circles, it was also because of your help that I survived some political turmoil. I did not realise that doing business could also carry the risk of prison. It seems that if you want to walk ahead of your time, or forge a new path, you will face great challenges and risks. Yet I am a person who likes a challenge. With your help and support, I will work even harder to make our company go from strength to strength, and build our country into a dynamic and prosperous society."

The guests warmly applauded his speech and cheered him and his company. They all sighed with emotion about the existing social issues. Along with the establishment of a commercial society, the political pressure was much less, the living standards were much higher. But the main problem was the corruption spreading in the official and commercial circles. To run a business, you needed not only to be honest but also to be careful about the harm and plotting from those corrupted officials and evil businessmen.

In the next few days, Zhang Feng's company started to rectify the quality control system. There would have to be signatures from three managers in charge of any deal. Two managers would have to sign for purchasing any construction materials. The quality check for finished buildings would also get stricter. Construction had to follow the blueprint and conform to environmental standards. The sales and after-sales service would be honest, they could not exaggerate the size and area of the properties. In addition, they needed to make more parking areas for each residential block, as more and more people were buying private cars now.

Zhang Feng did not forget to visit the injured residents of Block Number Three. The company would pay their hospital bills in full. Zhang Feng wanted to buy some flowers, fruits and supplements for them so he walked into a small supermarket near the hospital. While he was choosing the products, a familiar female voice sounded,

"Brother Zhang, you are ok now."

It was He Hua, standing behind the counter. Zhang Feng said to her with a smile,

"Is this your shop? It looks very nice. Why did you not come to the banquet the other day?"

He Hua said she was too busy that evening, replenishing her stock. Zhang Feng thanked her for her help in finding Head Chen. She said it was not worth mentioning. Zhang Feng said,

"People called you and other businessmen '1984 businessmen' as you all started doing business at the beginning of the reform in the early 1980s. So you are the pioneers of the economic reform."

She replied, "No, no, we were behind you '1992 businessmen' as you were running great businesses such as those in development, communication, finance."

Zhang Feng said to her happily,

"My old friend, we are both businessmen now. So just let me know if you need some help, I will make every effort to help you, just as when I was the mayor of the city."

After leaving He Hua's shop, Zhang Feng visited the injured

residents in hospital. The residents were grateful for his care, especially after they knew the accident had been caused by a wicked man.

Block Number Three was demolished. Zhang Feng and his colleagues discovered the defective steel bars in other units as well. They were surprised but also felt relieved that they had prevented more accidents.

One day, Yu Mei and Dan Dan handed the River City Daily newspaper to Zhang Feng. The front-page headline said 'Trial of a major case, Sentenced at the last minute' and there were photos of Captain Fan rushing into the court, Cai Wenge being escorted into the court and Zhang Feng talking to the journalists. The article gave details of this high-profile case and the outcome. It not only described the details of how Zhang Feng was wronged, but also praised his contribution to the city's construction. It was actually a free advertisement for his business.

Dan Dan said the newspaper was sold out in a couple of hours. Zhang Feng was very pleased. He asked the two ladies why the style of this report was so familiar. They answered with a bit of jealousy,

"It is your sister Qing Lian's writing, isn't it?" He nodded his head and said,

"Yes, it is her style. But she had left the newspaper many years before, how did she get it published?"

"It is easy because Director Lv of the newspaper still has a good relationship with her." Dan Dan said.

Director Lv had always supported Zhang Feng for many years.

Zhang Feng phoned Qing Lian next day and thanked her for publishing the report. She said with a smile,

"It was so easy. Just gave Director Lv a half-price holiday on Hainan Island. " She then added,

"Brother Feng, I suggest you should also have a holiday there. We are having a harsh winter here. But on Hainan Island, you will see white sandy beaches, a blue sea and green palm trees. Also, real estate development is booming there. A lot of developers are planning to build holiday resorts there. You should go and have a look."

After listening to her suggestion, Zhang Feng was interested in the idea of having a holiday on Hainan Island. The recent suffering had made him tired and anxious, so a nice holiday would help to heal him. He asked Dan Dan and Yu Mei to go with him, but both of them said they were too busy with the business, as the reputation of the company had risen greatly after the accident, and more deals had been signed recently. In the end, the two ladies asked Zhang Feng to go with his assistant, a young man who had just graduated from university.

In the first two days on Hainan Island, Zhang Feng and his assistant swam in the sea, sunbathing and eating seafood every day. He felt very energetic and happy. He realised why a lot of his business partners said a holiday could be healing for tired and anxious businessmen. The pity was that Dan Dan and Yu Mei were not here with him. On the beach, many young girls in fashionable swimming costumes looked at his tall, strong body and tried to talk to him, calling him 'handsome old man'. He had to ask his assistant to save him from embarrassment.

On the third day, when he was lying on the deck chair sunbathing, somebody patted his shoulder. Turning around, he was surprised to see Qing Lian standing next to him, in a light green swimming costume. Like Dan Dan and Yu Mei, she looked young, pretty and slim, although she was almost fifty years old. She asked him,

"Brother Feng, may I join you?"

Zhang Feng's assistant noticed the special relationship between them, so he gave her his chair, and left them. She explained to him the reason why she was here. Because wintertime was the peak holiday time here and she had come to inspect the work of her company's branch on this island, as recently there had been quite a few complaints from customers who had been ripped off on the island. She asked him if there were any problems with his holiday here. He said,

"I have had a lovely holiday so far, and thank you for booking such a luxurious five-star hotel for me."

He suddenly realised he was only wearing swimming trunks, so he picked up a towel to cover himself. She smiled and said,

"Brother Feng, you are still so conservative. Don't forget, I have seen your body before." Remembering the accidental sexual encounter between them ten years before, he flushed. Patting his shoulder, she said,

"Don't worry, I am teasing you."

Seeing no acquaintances around them, he relaxed. Having the company of a beautiful woman on holiday would make any man feel happier. Although he did not love her as he did Yu Mei and Dan Dan, he still liked her as a younger sister. He praised her for her beauty and youthful looks, and said she looked like a lotus rising out of water. She was flattered and became lovey-dovey with him. They swam together, sunbathing and drinking fruit juice, which made both of them happier. He recalled that she was his saviour and had given him a lot of support, as well as her efforts to save the witness, which had helped him to survive the crisis. Together with his guilty feeling about their sexual encounter, he felt that he should treat her kindly. So to keep her happy, he held her hand and wandered around with her like a pair of lovers. Noticing a lot of people watching them with envious expressions, she felt very happy. Even though she only had one chance in many years to stay with him, she was satisfied.

His assistant had met some fellow townsmen and Zhang Feng allowed him some time off to see them. He was very pleased, and Qing Lian was also pleased as that meant Zhang Feng would be free for her. She drove him along the coast to find some places suitable for building holiday resorts. Zhang Feng quite liked the climate and environment here and said if his company build a holiday resort here, he would give it to Qing Lian's company to operate. She was pleased not only because she would have an opportunity to make more money, but because she would spend more time with him. Although Huang Lei still tried to woo her and she knew she should have a partner to live with, and her daughter needed a father, she was unable to control her love for Zhang Feng. Some women could have the courage to live if they had a Prince Charming in their hearts, let alone they could see him and help him.

On the last day of Zhang Feng's holiday, Qing Lian invited him to dinner. After dinner, they went back to his room. She asked room service to bring wine and some snacks. Zhang Feng said he loved Qing Lian's daughter Lan Hua, and he felt she looked like his own daughter. He remembered his son Dan Feng also liked to play with Lan Hua, so he said to Qing Lian that they might become relatives by marriage. To his surprise, she said, no, Lan Hua was not a match for Dan Feng. After chatting and drinking, she was blushing and delicately pretty. Holding his hands and sitting on the bed, she said,

"Dear Brother, I wish time would stop at this moment. It is so precious for me as I only have it once in ten years."

Zhang Feng suddenly became sober and remembered the accidental sexual encounter with her. He stood up immediately and said to her,

"You are drunk, Qing Lian."

"No, I am not drunk, it's just I can never forget your caresses when you made love to me ten years ago."

Zhang Feng was embarrassed and said,

"I feel terribly sorry about that. I owe you too much."

She showed him the jade bangle on her wrist which he had given her after that night, and said,

"You have already compensated me."

Seeing the bangle, Zhang Feng sighed with all sorts of feelings. He felt he should treat her more kindly. When he hesitated, she pushed him on the bed and started to kiss him. He felt it very difficult to reject her, but he also did not want the same incident to happen again. Qing Lian read his mind, and said to him,

"Brother, I won't be hard on you. I will never snatch you from Dan Dan and Yu Mei. I would be happy if I could just sleep in your arms tonight."

Then they embraced each other on the bed. Looking at her pretty and innocent face, his heart ached for her. He then held her tight and they soon fell asleep.

The next morning, she saw him off at the airport. After entering the check-in gate, he turned back to say farewell to her. Seeing tears in her eyes, he turned away. He said in his mind, 'Qing Lia, Qing Lian, why can't you find a man to love you.' But then he remembered the three flowers on the fortune-telling picture made by the Taoist monk. It seemed that he was destined to be entangled with the three women in his life.

Part IV

Paying the Price for a Better Society

Chapter I

Should We Follow the Road of Socialism or Capitalism?

Then the 21st century came. Like the people in other countries, Chinese people looked forward to seeing more change for the better in their country. Yet many of them did not realise that the progress they expected was not plain sailing. Some of them could feel confused, bitter and even hopeless. Not wanting to follow in the footsteps of the Eastern European countries, Chinese leaders implemented reforms gradually. After the death of Deng Xiaoping, China became a country with a collective leadership. The political atmosphere was comparatively relaxed. People could think and speak freely. There was an atmosphere of democracy inside and outside the party. But still, only a small number of the social elite dared to talk about a multi-party political system. The free market economy pervaded the whole country and a consumer society was formed. Even the younger generation just wanted to find a good job, earn more money and enjoy life. A lot of them did not care about state affairs, lacking the political enthusiasm of the students on Tiananmen Square in 1989.

After joining the WTO, international trade brought about the rapid development of manufacture in China, especially for private enterprises, joint venture and foreign companies. But the state enterprises were facing great challenges. They had obsolete equipment, were overstaffed and made outdated products. Some of them were on the verge of bankruptcy. Therefore, in the following few years, there was a huge wave of modernization of state enterprises, which was both rewarding and painful.

In April 2002, the early spring put a green cloak on the River City. With an uneasy mind, Wang Hai drove to his factory. Today's meeting of the senior managers of his factory would decide the future of his factory. The previous evening, in Zhang Feng's home, Dan Dan and Yu Mei told him he could adopt a shareholding system with Volkswagen to change his factory into a joint-venture company. The state would give him some help as his factory was still one of the biggest motor vehicle factories in the country. The policy for the modernization of state enterprises was 'Invigorate large enterprises and relax control over small ones'. The central government intended to support about 150 large enterprises, but sacrificed tens of thousands of small enterprises to mergers and acquisitions, privatisation and even bankruptcy. Jili Motor Vehicle Factory was one of the 150 large enterprises, so it would get support from the state.

Drawing a lesson from the purchase from Volkswagen a few years earlier, Wang Hai still worried whether the forthcoming negotiations with Volkswagen would be successful or not.

The Germans sometimes could be too serious and inflexible. Also, he worried about the overstaffing situation in his factory. He remembered that Helen, the Chinese lady working for Volkswagen, had told him the previous time that if one day Volkswagen wanted to form a joint venture with Jili Motor Vehicle Factory, they would ask for some workers to be laid off before they signed the deal.

Entering the meeting room, Wang Hai saw the room was full of people, including his senior colleagues, officials from the Mechanical Engineering Department, and several representatives from Volkswagen. A German representative told him that their deputy CEO in their Asian headquarters would host the negotiations today, but her flight had been delayed for one hour. Wang Hai said they would just wait.

About forty minutes later, a young Asian lady, with her German colleague, rushed into the room, explaining their flight had been delayed and the deputy CEO would come soon. After five minutes, a slim, elegant lady, wearing a hat, appeared at the door of the meeting room. She said in a crisp tone that she was terribly sorry for arriving late. Then she took off her hat, tidied her hair and sat down. Helen! Wang Hai was surprised. It was indeed her who had brought him trouble a few years earlier. Wang Hai could feel his heart beating faster. He was pleased to see the woman he loved. But at the same time, he also worried whether her involvement might affect the negotiation.

Helen did not greet him first. With a formal official manner, she addressed the Chinese side politely,

"Dear leaders from Jili Motor Vehicle Factory and MED, I am Helen, the deputy CEO from Volkswagen's Asian headquarters. I will host these negotiations. After China joined the WTO, exports of manufactured goods have grown rapidly and the inland market is also booming. If we cooperate to form a joint shareholding venture, we will expand the scale of the company, speed up our product development and produce highly needed new makes of motor vehicles."

While talking, she glanced over the Chinese representatives. Wang Hai felt that her gaze lingered on him for one second longer than the others. 'She still remembers me!' He was pleased in his mind.

The negotiations began. Both sides presented their plans for the joint venture. Because the plans of both sides were fairly close to each other, a consensus was reached by lunch time. The Chinese side would keep 51 percent of the shares, acting as the controlling shareholder. The German side had 35 percent of the shares. Ten percent belonged to the factory workers, and the remaining four percent would be sold to private shareholders. The composition of the board of directors was formed according to the proportions of the shares. Wang Hai was appointed as the CEO of the joint venture. The deputy CEO was a German manager.

Both sides were happy because of the smooth progress of the negotiations. The factory had arranged a delicious lunch for the Germans. Helen asked her colleagues to go the dining hall first. She stayed in the room to check the agreement for a few minutes. Wang Hai was still concentrating on the documents as he was very pleased with the progress. But he did not realise that only Helen and he had remained in the room until he heard Helen's tender voice,

"How are you, Brother Hai?"

Wang Hai was startled and raised his head. He saw it was Helen talking to him, with tender feelings. Thinking of the lesson five years earlier, he said quietly,

"I am very well. What about you?"

"I am fine," she said.

During the morning negotiations, the German side agreed the five million dollars invested five years earlier by the Chinese side was part of the shares of the Chinese side, which further proved Wang Hai's action was not treacherous. So Wang Hai felt his private contact with Helen would not cause any problems this time. With solicitude he asked her,

"Have you found a man you love?"

She sighed and said,

"I married a Singaporean businessman two years ago. But I do not feel happy as he lacks manliness, like some Shanghai men."

Then she looked at him with a loving expression. Wang Hai remembered that she had loved him because he had the masculinity of northern Chinese men. Not wanting their private contact to affect the negotiation, she whispered she would contact him after the negotiation. Wang Hai nodded his head. She left the room to have her lunch.

In the next few days, the negotiations were mainly focused on streamlining the management structure. Wang Hai and the officials from MED knew that state enterprises would have to fire some workers. This was a common practice in Western countries, so it was normal for the German side to raise these questions. At the negotiation table, Helen acted totally like a bossy CEO. She demanded that at least 1,000 workers should be laid off, which was ten percent of the total number in the factory. Compared with other state enterprises, ten percent redundancy was much less. But the traditional idea of life-long employment in state factories was still deeply rooted in the workers' minds, so Wang Hai felt it was difficult to lay off such a large number of workers. Over ten years ago, to get rid of even a hundred workers would have given him a headache. He said to the German side that he needed to discuss this issue with his colleagues and MED. Obviously, reducing the size of the workforce could improve the efficiency of the company. But suddenly losing their income or living on a very low income would make these workers suffer. After a discussion with MED, Wang Hai and his colleagues asked Helen whether they could make only 700 workers redundant. She said she needed to get instructions from headquarters.

After one day, she told Wang Hai that her superiors had agreed to reduce the number to 800, otherwise it would weaken the long term competitiveness of the company. After more discussion, the Chinese side had to agree to this number. It then was up to Wang Hai and his colleagues to decide who would be made redundant and how to arrange their future. They discussed this for two days to make a plan.

A few days later, there was a factory assembly. Wang Hai told the workers there was good news and bad news for them. He said the good news was their factory and Volkswagen had successfully formed a joint venture, which meant the production of the factory would be developed rapidly. Hearing this good news, the workers applauded loudly. But after hearing that 800 workers would be made redundant, the audience was very quiet. Taking a sip of water, Wang Hai said,

"I know it is hard to let some of you go. But we have to make this step towards establishing a modern enterprise. We will help the redundant workers find other jobs or encourage them to start a business with their severance pay. They can also find different jobs after having new skill training."

After the assembly, the key workers were happy because they would not be made redundant. But those who were lazy or did not have skills started to worry. Wang Hai and senior managers decided the redundancy list should be drawn up by the branches and workshops through collective discussions.

Getting off work, Wang Hai saw a group of workers gathered in the central square of the factory, cursing and shouting. They looked likely to be made redundant. Hiding, he overheard their complaints.

"Is this still a socialist factory? Make money for foreign capitalists but make us unemployed!"

"That German witch was evil!"

"As Chairman Mao said in the past, we are following the capitalist road now. I hope the Red Guards come back to rebel."

"Are we still the masters of this country? But now we have become slaves!"

After listening to those complaints, Wang Hai felt very uncomfortable. He had not realised that the reaction to the redundancy from the workers would be so fierce. He started to worry about Helen's safety. He rang his secretary and asked him to send some staff to protect her and her team, as he knew these angry workers could do nasty things.

He visited Zhang Feng's home in the evening, wanting to get some advice. It was a Friday evening, and Zhang Feng, Dan Dan, Yu Mei and Dan Feng were all sitting at the table having their dinner. They invited him to take a seat and eat with them. Seeing Wang Hai was stressed, Zhang Feng asked him,

"I heard your factory will have a joint venture with Volkswagen. This is a nice thing, why do you look so unhappy? Because you have to fire some workers?"

"This time it is a large-scale downsizing. The workers who are on the list are very angry. I worry they might make trouble," Wang Hai sighed. Dan Dan said,

"The economic reform has to go through this step. We cannot always do the 'egalitarian practice of everybody eating from the same big pot'. To follow the free market, you have to deal with the overstaffing issue. Prime Minister Zhu Rongji is determined to deal with those half-dead enterprises. There will be millions of workers losing their jobs in the enterprises in Northeast China and Wuhan. The situation is quite similar to that in England in the 1980s. Prime Minister Thatcher privatised vigorously and shut down the old industries in the north of England, with thousands and thousands of workers losing their jobs."

Zhang Feng also remembered his visit to the UK when he was the mayor of the city. He said that fortunately there was a welfare system there that could give these workers a basic allowance to live on. Yu Mei asked Wang Hai,

"Your factory is a big one, with support from the state. Is the downsizing fairly small?"

"Neither big nor small. 800 workers will be made redundant," Wang Hai said.

Dan Dan asked him how he was going to rearrange these workers. Wang Hai told them the measures they planned. Zhang Feng said the redundancy compensation might not be enough for them to start a self-employed business now, as the market was almost saturated now after ten years of business changes in the country. He said,

"For example in the catering trade, you would definitely have been able to make money ten years ago, but not now. My friend's relative opened a Sichuan restaurant last year. Initially, he made some money, but then three other Sichuan restaurants opened in his street, which made him have a big loss, and he had to shut his restaurant recently. The national business wave since 1993 created some loafers with unrealistic expectations of business. They dreamed of getting rich overnight but did not like to do normal hard jobs. Some of them even lived off their parents, becoming 'parasite singles'."

"Brother Feng is right. In the long term, you should help these workers to find new jobs or retrain them to get new jobs. I have an idea. We can help Wang Hai to make a recruitment fair and ask different factories, companies, and village and township enterprises to recruit workers from his factory. Government-subsided training courses can also be run in your factory. I can even ask the Shenzhen Industry and Trading Department to recruit some of your workers as a lot of private and township enterprises are short of workers there." Yu Mei said.

Hearing Yu Mei's suggestion, Wang Hai was very pleased. He picked up the cup and drained it in one gulp. He said,

"It is wonderful. You can always rely on your old friends at the key moment."

During the following week, Zhang Feng and his friends went to a lot of places to get them interested in this recruitment fair. Even Chang Zheng promised to help them.

The atmosphere was tense after the redundancy list was announced. Some of these workers started to make trouble. Wang Hai hid in a temporary office. Helen also returned to Singapore for the time being.

The day before Labour Day on 1st May, several hundred redundant workers were preparing a demonstration for the following day. They wanted to tell the public that they should not be abandoned by society, so they prepared slogans and flags for the protest. Suddenly, a worker from the group ran to them and said to them,

"Ah, the factory announced yesterday that there was a recruitment fair today. We thought they were trying to appease us. But now there are a lot of recruitment stands on the square at the entrance, which have attracted many workers. Shall we also go to have a look?" A leader of the protest group said,

"Do not trust the factory. It might be a trick." But other demonstrators said,

"Let's go and see. If this really is a deception, we can start the demonstration straightaway."

When they walked to the square, they were stunned by the scene in front of their eyes: over fifty long tables lined up and with huge signs behind them with the names of various companies. There was a huge horizontal banner: 'Recruitment and Retraining Fair for Jili Motor Vehicle Factory.' Amazed by this big fair, the demonstrators dropped their slogans and flags and rushed to the tables to find out more. The table of Zhang Feng's company was the most attractive. His group employed over one hundred workers, including mechanical engineers, electric welders, plumbers and electricians. These workers were offered a higher salary than they got at the factory. Wang Hai was very happy and kept thanking his brother-in-law. He Hua recruited twenty female workers for her supermarkets. Other private companies also hired many workers. Shenzhen Industry and Trading Department recruited over fifty workers with skills for some private factories in the city. Yu Mei thanked the officers from SZITD for their help.

Seeing Chang Zheng get out of his car, Zhang Feng and Wang Hai went up to greet him. Wang Hai kept thanking him for his help. Chang Zheng sent quite a few city council service companies to recruit workers there. The city taxi company hired sixty taxi drivers as most of the workers were able to drive. Chang Zheng also mobilised neighbourhood enterprises to recruit workers here. Although their salary was not high, at least, the workers would have some income to live on. Chang Zheng said to Zhang Feng and Wang Hai,

"Jili Motor Vehicle Factory is the first of the state enterprises to be downsized, with a relatively small number of workers. I worry there will be more and more medium and small state enterprises needing to deal with a huge number of redundant workers. At that time the government and society will find it difficult to help them to find jobs."

"The period of social transformation will be very hard. People will have to pay a price to finish it." Zhang Feng said.

Apart from recruitment, the fair also provided re-employment training for many jobs such as catering, security, housekeeping services. For female workers without skills, government organisations and companies employed them as cleaners.

When the fair ended, Wang Hai was very pleased to see over 600 redundant workers had found new jobs or got training places. The remaining over 100 workers could either be helped to find new jobs or given redundancy compensation. It seemed that the biggest obstacle to forming a joint venture had been overcome.

Chapter II

A New Stage to Build a Modern Enterprise System

After solving the issue of redundancy, Wang Hai felt more relaxed. The follow-up negotiations went smoothly. They all agreed on the allotment of shares, the composition of the board of directors, the company going public and the selection of professional managers. Then the Jili Motor Vehicle Factory changed from a state enterprise into the first joint shareholding venture in the Chinese automobile industry. This inspiring story became headline news in the major media and was regarded as a milestone of the economic reform.

In mid-May 2002, a big celebration was held in the main auditorium in Jili Motor Vehicle Factory. Representatives from Volkswagen, officials from MED, leaders from the province and city, business leaders, and journalists from the media, all attended this celebration. Zhang Feng, Dan Dan, Yu Mei, Lin Jianguo, Chen Tao, Li He, Qing Lian, Huang Lei were all invited to the celebration. There was a warm atmosphere. During the celebration the good news came that the company had raised two billion yuan on the stock market which could be used for increasing output, developing new products and opening new branches. Hearing this good news, the audience burst into thunderous applause. Zhang Feng said to Chang Zheng,

"Look at Wang Hai. He jumped up to applaud. Such excitement is not the manner of a CEO."

"He can never lose his style as head of a collective household in the countryside," Chang Zheng said with a smile.

"Is that the German Chinese lady who brought trouble to Wang Hai a few years ago?" Dan Dan said.

Zhang Feng and Chang Zheng looked at the rostrum and confirmed it was her. Wang Hai might have another honey-trap this time. But Yu Mei had told him their private relationship would not affect the cooperation as it had been done successfully.

During the cocktail party after the celebration, Zhang Feng and his friends found Wang Hai, who was having an animated conversation with Helen. Zhang Feng shook hands with Helen, and said,

"I am Zhang Feng, CEO of the Song Jiang Real Estate Company, a good friend of Wang Hai's. If he behaves badly, please let me know, I will punish him for you."

"I will punish him myself," Helen said with a smile. The people around them all laughed.

Helen had a good memory, and she thanked Dan Dan for her help with informing on Wang Hai a few years ago. When Helen saw fairy-like Yu Mei, she inquired,

"Who is this lady?"

"She is CEO Zhang's first lady," Wang Hai joked.

Helen still remembered that Wang Hai told her that Dan Dan was Zhang Feng's wife. So in confusion she pointed to Dan Dan and asked,

"Isn't Dan Dan CEO Zhang's wife?"

Wang Hai jested,

"Dan Dan is his second lady. Because CEO Zhang has made a great contribution to the city, the city council granted him the privilege to have two wives." Seeing Zhang Feng was going to punish him, Wang Hai scuttled away.

As the elite of business circles, Zhang Feng discussed the reform of state enterprises with Helen. Zhang Feng mentioned his visit to England many years ago and his discussion with an English businessman about the privatisations by Prime Minister Thatcher. Dan Dan used to be an economist so she explained that different national conditions would need different ways to manage their economic systems. Privatisation in China would be quite difficult. Helen agreed with her.

Wang Hai brought back a tray and served everyone a glass of champagne. He said he was pleased his dream to have a shareholding company had come true. But he felt great pressure as a CEO and he would have to go if the company did not perform well in the coming years. Helen and Dan Dan agreed. A CEO was after all a wage earner. As a CEO, he or she needed a sensitive nose for business and marketing foresight. Wang Hai said maybe he should do an MBA somewhere. Dan Dan said Qinghua University had a reputable MBA course and she would make an inquiry for him. Wang Hai was happy with her suggestion.

After the joint venture began to work, Helen had to go back to Singapore. The day before she left, she met Wang Hai at the same place on the riverside. Leaning over the railing and watching the flowing water, they had so many things to tell each other, but remained quiet for a while. Helen wanted to break the ice, so she teased him,

"It is interesting that your friends are all handsome men and beautiful ladies. CEO Zhang is already in his fifties, but he looks like a handsome young man in thirties. His two wives are so beautiful."

"Do you mean I am not as handsome as CEO Zhang?" he asked.

"Do I detect jealousy? Yes, yes, you are as handsome as CEO Zhang."

After talking for a while, she said unhappily,

"I am afraid my relationship with my husband will not last long. It is a pity you already have your own family."

Wang Hai also felt depressed. He loved Helen, but he could not betray his family. He tried to comfort her and said life had all sorts of joys and sorrows. She gazed with deep feeling at him, and said,

"Brother Hai, can I be your female confidant?"

"Of course you can. I will miss you all the time." Seeing they were hidden by dense weeping willows, she pleaded,

"Brother Hai, would you mind embracing me?"

He hesitated, then held her in his arms. Helen closed her eyes and enjoyed his caresses. She suddenly stood on tiptoes, with her lip trembling. Wang Hai knew she wanted him to kiss her. He lowered his head to kiss her with passion.

A new look could be seen after the joint venture was established. The management was stricter and incentives were higher, as the workers felt they were also part of the company because they could get a dividend.

But the rigid left-wing leaders were unhappy with the new shareholding system. Governor Shen said to his evil follower Li Qiu,

"These guys are just interested in capitalism. In these foreign, private companies and joint ventures, the bosses exploit their workers and fire them at any time. The workers are no longer the masters of the country, but the slaves of the capitalists."

"A wave of unemployment is coming as more state enterprises are facing bankruptcy. There will be good drama to watch." Li Qiu said. Shen asked how the medical bail for Cai Wenge was going. Li said triumphantly,

"It is easy. I have contacted the prison governor. He said Cai was behaving himself well, so his sentence could be shortened, and he would have an early release."

Hearing this, Shen was happy because Cai was his cash machine. If Cai was released, they could hook up together to make illegal money.

The situation Chang Zheng worried about occurred. The wave of unemployment started after more small and medium state enterprises faced bankruptcy. One morning, his secretary rushed to his office and told him,

"Something bad has happened. The female workers from the City Textile Factory are demonstrating at the entrance of the city council. They are asking the government to help them to get new jobs and make a living."

Coming to the city council, Chang Zheng saw about 500 female workers protesting there, with slogans and flags. They shouted,

"We want work! We need to raise our families! We want to live!"

There were over a thousand onlookers. Some officials tried to persuade these women to stop their demonstration, saying the council would help them to make a living. But these female workers did not trust these officials as they just offered rubber cheques. Chang Zheng was the mayor of the city. Discussing the situation with the deputy mayor, he stood on the platform and spoke to the female workers,

"Dear female workers, sisters, I am Chang Zheng, the mayor of the city. I fully understand your difficult position and anxiety. The reform of the state enterprises is a difficult task, which has brought a lot of social issues. But in the long term, this reform will benefit our country and people. We will make an effort to resolve these redundancy problems. We will try to see whether your factory can be merged with other textile factories or sold to private companies. If your factory has to go bankrupt, we will try to find you new jobs or offer retraining courses for you to gain new skills. If the worst happens, we will sell the land and machines to get money to pay for your compensation or a living allowance. Please give us a little more time to resolve your problems."

Because his speech was reasonable and justified, and he had a good reputation, the demonstration leaders negotiated with him and the deputy mayor for ten minutes. Then they dismissed the demonstrators.

In the following week, Chang Zheng asked his officers to look for any private or foreign textile companies to do mergers and acquisitions. But the result was disappointing, as there were hundreds, maybe thousands of textile factories in Southern China. Their products were good and cheap, sold nationwide and internationally. They were not interested in the old and inefficient factories in the north.

It was also difficult to find new jobs for those female workers. They did not have any special skills and could only work as shop assistants, cleaners, domestic service assistants, etc. They were between forty and fifty years old, and learning new skills was difficult for them. Zhang Feng's company only employed twenty of them as sales assistants. He Hua employed forty of them as shop assistants. Various township enterprises employed another 100 in total. That still left 800 female workers who could not find jobs.

The City Textile Factory was a big factory that was owned by the Provincial Industry and Commerce Bureau. The bureau could decide to sell the site and equipment in case the factory went bankrupt. But the equipment of the factory was very old and nobody wanted to buy it. Therefore the factory could only sell its land. Thinking Zhang Feng could use this land to build properties, Chang Zheng visited him at his home one evening to discuss this with him. His son Jian Jun was a first-year student at Jili Industry University. He said he also wanted to go to Zhang Feng's house, as Dan Feng was going to receive his university admission letter. Jian Jun wanted to know which university Dan Feng would attend.

It was the first time for Chang Zheng to visit Zhang Feng's new home. Entering Zhang Feng's house, Chang Zheng and Jian Jun were amazed by this luxurious villa. Chang Zheng said to Zhang Feng,

"No wonder there are more and more corrupt officials now. They are jealous of businessmen like you, because you live in luxurious villas, drive prestigious cars, play golf and go to exclusive clubs. Then they try to use their power to get illegal money."

Zhang Feng said with a smile,

"Why don't you also give up your power to do business, like me. Or buy a villa from my company, with a discount."

"Oh, no, if I have a villa, people will think I got the money via corruption. The next official who is investigated by the discipline inspection commission will be me."

He said that people in the city knew Governor Shen got his villa through corruption. Zhang Feng said he must have got the villa from Cai Wenge. Cai also got Shen's help many times, with business opportunities and a shortened sentence. One day, if evidence of his corruption appeared, he would definitely be investigated.

When Yu Mei served tea to Chang Zheng, the laughter of two boys was heard in the corridor because Dan Feng had got a place in the Computing Department at Jili University. He had come first in science in the national entrance exam in the province. He could go to Beijing University or Qinghua University, but he decided to study at the local university because he was a filial boy. He was the only son and he would look after his parents when they got old. The Computing Department of Jili University was a nationally famous department, with quite a few members of the Chinese Academy of Science. Jian Jun congratulated Dan Feng and said they would be able to meet each other quite often as their universities were very close to each other.

Jian Jun asked Dan Feng whether he still saw Lan Hua and Bai He. Dan Feng said the two girls studied in high school now and they came to his home sometimes to play with him. Jan Jun was jealous.

"Call me when they are in your home. Do not forget I am the saviour of Lan Hua."

"Yes, but make no mistake, both of us are her saviours," Dan Feng said with a smile.

Dan Dan entered the sitting room and invited Chang Zheng and his son to dinner. Chang Zheng liked the cooking of Yu Mei and Dan Dan, so he accepted the invitation. When only Zhang Feng and he were in the sitting room, he quipped,

"You are so capable, to steal my girlfriend in the past, and still keep your ex-wife with you."

"Dan Dan is just my next-door neighbour. So we can have a meal and other activities together," Zhang Feng quickly explained.

"I am teasing you." Chang Zheng laughed.

After dinner, the two boys played in the gym. Drinking his tea, Chang Zheng told Zhang Feng and the two ladies the purpose of his visit. The City Textile Factory had to declare bankruptcy, and the only way to help the factory was to sell the land. He asked Zhang Feng whether he was interested in this land. Dan Dan said the company had a cash flow problem recently because there were too many projects. Zhang Feng said the funding was indeed tight, but he might consider it as this was a matter of survival for the workers there. Yu Mei asked how much the land cost. Chang Zheng answered about eighty million yuan for the land and another five million yuan for the debt and redundancy compensation. Zhang Feng and the two ladies discussed for a while. They said they would need to borrow some of the money from banks. Before Chang Zheng left, he said he would discuss this with the Provincial Industry and Trading Bureau to see whether Zhang Feng was able to pay half of the cost for redundancy compensation and living allowances for the workers and pay the other half later. Zhang Feng said he would wait for the result of Chang Zheng's discussion.

Chapter III

The Difficult Situation of the Redundant Workers

Over the weekend, Governor Shen met his mistress secretly in the villa Cai Wange had given to him. Like many corrupt officials, he not only greedily made money but also dallied with women. He had a lot of mistresses, including his secretaries, female staff or even the women who asked for his help to get a better job. The secret lover he met today was his new secretary, a pretty young woman with her own family. Shen's wife was already old and she knew he was a satyr, but dared not to confront him.

Somebody was at the door. It was Cai Wenge who had just been released early from prison thanks to Shen's help. Cai nodded and bowed to Shen to thank him for his help. Shen knew there must be some opportunity to make money. As he guessed, Cai said,

"Dear Governor Shen, there is a good chance for us to make money. You know the City Textile Factory is for sale. My previous business partner said we could buy it first, and then resell it to other developers to make money. If you ask the Industry and Trading Bureau to reduce the price for us, we will definitely make a huge profit." Shen was very pleased to know this. Cai handed some big wads of cash to Shen, and said,

"This is half a million yuan for you to start with. After we get the land and resell it, you will have a few millions more."

Shen grinned, "No problem, the director of the bureau has to follow my instructions. It does not matter if the factory gets less money for the female workers. Let them suffer from harder living and see whether they still support the reform or not, ha, ha!"

After a few days, Zhang Feng received a phone call from Chang Zheng. He thought Chang Zheng had got an answer about the sale of the textile factory's land. But Chang Feng could not hide his anger when he told him that the ITB had sold the land cheaply to another buyer. They said they did so because the buyer paid cash to the factory, so the workers would get their redundancy compensation sooner. Chang Zheng thought this must be an illegal deal. Somebody had taken the opportunity of the reform of state enterprises to steal the state-owned property. Zhang Feng said it was very likely this was again a corrupt deal made by Shen and Cai, because somebody told him that Cai and his business partners had visited the factory to see the site there a few days ago. Chang Zheng fumed,

"This is their evil way of killing two birds with one stone. They got a large amount of money, but at the same time, shirked their responsibility to help the workers!"

"It is a pity we are unable to collect evidence to expose

them. In the past, we criticised the desire for money during the primitive accumulation period of capitalism, as Shakespeare described in Timon of Athens, but nowadays we are facing the same problems." Zhang Feng said.

One day, after school, Lan Hua, Bai He and one of the other girls in their class, called Huo Ying, walked through the city centre. They saw a lot of unemployed workers selling things from stands on the pavement because they did not have enough money to live on. Huo Ying suddenly saw her mother at one of the stands. She was selling towels and socks produced by the textile factory. Huo Ying asked her mother,

"Mum, why are you selling these things on such a hot day? Hasn't your factory given you some redundancy compensation?"

Her mother sighed and said,

"The factory only gave us a small amount of money. They also gave us some unsold products as part of the compensation. If we can sell them, we will get some money, if not, we are poor. Your father has developed a severe illness, but we do not have enough money to pay for his treatment."

Then she started to cry. Huo Ying also cried. Holding her mother, she said she did not want to go to school. She would help her mother to sell these products to make a living. Lan Hua and Bai He felt very uncomfortable. They used their pocket money to buy some towels and socks from Huo Ying's mother. Huo Ying and her mother kept thanking them.

Back home, Lan Hua and Bai He told their parents about the situation of Huo Ying's family. Qing Lian and Li He also felt sad for these redundant workers. They realised there was a price to pay for building a better society.

A few days later, Zhang Feng and Lin Jiango drove past the textile factory. They got out of their car to inspect the site and see how much it should be sold for. After looking around, Zhang Feng said the real value of the land was double the price they sold it to Cai Wenge. The illegal deal made by Cai and Shen let the state lose half of this property. Before they left the factory, they saw a group of female workers carrying unsold products as their compensation and chatting.

"We are so unlucky. During the Cultural Revolution we were forced to go the countryside when we should have studied. We did not get a better job when we returned to the city. When we married we could only have one child because of the birth control policy. Now we are unemployed when we have a family to support."

One female worker recognised Zhang Feng and shouted to him,

"Mayor Zhang, CEO Zhang, people say you are going to buy our factory. Please buy our factory as soon as possible. Then the factory will give us severance compensation and unemployment allowance. We will have money to buy food."

Other workers also ran to him as if he was their saviour. Zhang Feng said to them,

"Sisters, I was an educated youth as well during the Cultural Revolution. I fully understand your suffering and hardship. I planned to buy your factory. But the Industry and Trading Bureau sold it cheaply to another buyer, which made your situation even worse."

Heard this, these female workers felt very angry. They knew the issue of the loss of state property. But these deals looked legal and there was no way to stop them. Suddenly a fifty-year-old female worker knelt before Zhang Feng, crying and saying,

"Please help me, CEO Zhang! I am near retirement age, but the factory does not have money to pay a pension for us. My husband also lost his job. Our children need to go to school. We only have a little money left, and soon we won't be able to afford to buy food."

Zhang Feng felt depressed. He helped her up and said,

"Sister, you are really having a difficult time."

He asked Lin Jianguo whether there were any vacancies in the company. Lin said the construction team needed a few labourers, but this was not suitable work for weak women. The company office could use a few cleaners. The woman said she was able to do any hard work, but because she looked thin and weak, Zhang Feng offered her a job as a cleaner. The other female workers said they could do hard work. Zhang Feng asked Lin to write down their names. They could go to his company tomorrow to see whether they were able to do some construction work. These women kept thanking him for his help.

Back home, Dan Dan and Yu Mei told him that they saw redundant workers selling small products everywhere. They felt sad about this. They did not realise that the reform of the state enterprises was so difficult, with such a high price to pay. Yet if the country did not carry on reforms, the economy would not develop, and in the long term, most people would suffer, not just a small number of people. Dan Dan said,

"Learning from the process of industrialisation in the West, a country must establish a welfare system to balance the competitive free market. Then you can protect the interests of the weak and poor people while encouraging the rich to do their business, which would make the society stable. We need to do more about this issue."

Yu Mei said the welfare system in Shenzhen and the south was much better because there were a lot of foreign and private companies there. You must have some insurance to protect the interests of the workers. People called them 'five insurances and one fund' which protected workers' pensions, medical care, unemployment, etc. It had become a compulsory condition for recruitment there. Zhang Feng said,

"There are more state enterprises in the north. So after the reform, these enterprises will have to improve their welfare system. Wang Hai told me that after his factory became a joint venture, Volkswagen asked them to set up this insurance. Our company also needs to set up the 'five insurances and one fund' this year. Only when we have a sound welfare system, can we build a competitive free market economy."

In the next few years, the life of those unemployed workers was improved along with the establishment of the welfare system. The wave of state enterprise reforms basically did not cause big social unrest. Because of the Chinese tradition of hard work and supportive families, these workers survived in different ways. But if they had children at university or a family member with a severe disease, they could suffer from very difficult conditions.

Zhang Feng followed his principles as a Confucian businessman. He preferred to contribute more to society rather than just making money for himself. He tried particularly to help the weak social groups. He was active in charity events and built a dozen schools in remote areas to help the children from poor families to receive an education. He often received thank you letters from the children and teachers in these areas after some of the children went to colleges or universities. He and his lovers always felt very pleased.

Chapter IV

He is Your Biological Brother

The children of Zhang Feng and his friends also experienced and understood the changes of this era. Everything facing them, like work, life, love, marriage, their view of the world and wealth, were all different from that of their parents. They had their own options to choose their way of life. They could work hard to become rich or professionals or fail the competition to become poor and depressed.

Time flew. 2006 quickly came. Dan Feng was twenty-two years old and became a tall and handsome young man like his father. He had started his postgraduate studies. Jian Jun, son of Chang Zheng, had finished his first year of postgraduate study. They came from wealthy families, so the tuition fees were not a problem for them. But for students from poorer families, tuition fees could be a big burden for the families. Chinese universities began to charge tuition fees in 1997.

One weekend, Dan Feng and Jian Jun held a picnic inside a riverside wood. They invited their two childhood friends, Lan Hua, Qing Lian's daughter, and Bai He, Li He's daughter. The two girls had changed from cute little girls into pretty big girls. Lan Hua had just started at Jili University, studying law; and Bai He went to Jili Medical University. The picnic was to celebrate their entering universities.

Hearing clear laughter, the two boys turned back and saw the two pretty girls, with fashionable shoulder-length hair and in becoming dresses. The two boys waved to them. There was a lot of food on the plastic sheet and they started their picnic. The two boys congratulated the girls for entering the universities of their choice and told them about some campus experiences they might face. The two boys stressed to the girls that the situation was different from that of their parents when they were students. Universities nowadays allowed students to have relationships. But they should be careful because they were pretty and attractive to the boys on campus. Most boys were not serious about their relationships, so they should just ignore these boys. The two girls deliberately provoked the boys, saying,

"But what about in case these boys take the relationship seriously?"

Jian Jun could hardy retain his composure, flushing and saying, "Do you know, there are already some boys who love you!"

The two girls knew what he meant, but to tease him they asked,

"Who? Where are they?"

"Think about who has treated you well all these years," Dan Feng said.

Lan Hua twinkled,

"You mean both of you? We only regard you as our brothers."

"It does not matter if you call us brothers. My two mothers also call my father Brother Feng," Dan Feng said.

The two girls were happy that these two boys they loved at last admitted that they loved them. Then they jeered,

"Not ashamed! Not ashamed! You should calm down to see whether you are good enough to love us."

Then they ran away laughing to pick wildflowers. The two boys had noticed that the two girls loved them. So they felt very happy. Jian Jun asked Dan Feng,

"Brother, let's do an allocation to avoid fighting. Whom do you love between the two girls?" Dan Feng said he loved both of them. When Jian Jun asked whom he loved most, Dan Feng said he loved Lan Hua more as she looked like her mother, beautiful and pure. Jian Jun said,

"No, no, you should let me choose first. I also love Lan Hua more."

"In that case, let's compete fairly, to see whom she loves more, you or me." Dan Feng said.

The two girls returned to the picnic and brought back a lot of wildflowers. They asked the two boys to twine the flowers into garlands. The boys quickly made two beautiful garlands. The girls sat on the ground and waited for the boys to put the garlands on their heads. They did not mention anything, but in their mind, they wanted to see which boy loved them. Dan Feng began to walk to Lan Hua, but Jian Jun said,

"No, you should give priority to your elder brother." He then walked to Lan Hua and put the garland on her head. Dan Feng walked to Bai He and put his garland on her head. Seeing both boys loved Lan Hua, Bai He was unhappy and said,

"You are lying to say you take the relationship seriously." Dan Feng tried to comfort her, saying,

"Lan Hua is a few months older than you. She is your elder sister, so she should get the garland first." Jian Jun also gave the same reason. Bai He cheered up again.

Qing Lian had noticed that recently Dan Feng visited her home more frequently to see Lan Hua. He taught her computing and brought her some gifts. Qing Lian liked Dan Feng as he looked like his father, whom Qing Lian had loved for so many years. Dan Feng also liked Qing Lian because she looked after him often when he was a small child. He often wanted to call her 'my third mother' but was stopped by Qing Lian as this awakened an old secret in her mind. Initially, Qing Lian did not mind contact between Dan Feng and her daughter as they always played together like brother and sister.

Studying in the same university, Dan Feng saw Lan Hua more frequently. One evening, it was dark when Qing Lian returned home. Getting closer to her home, she saw a couple embracing and kissing each other. After they said farewell to each other, the girl went into the building. Qing Lian recognised the girl was her daughter Lan Hua, and the boy leaving was tall, like Dan Feng. Her heart suddenly beat faster. 'My God! They are in love.' She realised she had to talk to her daughter. Entering the house, she saw Lan Hua was flushed and still immersed in the happiness of love. Qing Lian understood her daughter. She had also loved Zhang Feng deeply in the past. But how could she explain this to Lan Hua? How painful if she was forced to leave her lover.

After dinner, Qing Lian asked Lan Hua to sit on the sofa and had a chat with her. She asked Lan Hua about her study and activities on campus. Then she calmly said,

"Lan Hua, you are just eighteen years old. You should concentrate on your studies, as law, like medicine, is a difficult subject to study."

"Do not worry, Mum, I study hard and I'm at the top of my class. Some people look down upon children from single-parent families. But I will show them that I am equally excellent." Lan Hua said.

How to get to the main topic? Qing Lian thought a little bit, and said directly that Lan Hua was still too young to have a relationship. Puppy love would affect her studies. Unexpectedly, Lan Hua said,

"Mum, times are changing. You told me that when you studied at university, students were not allowed to have a relationship. But now it is totally different. Not only at universities, even in senior high school, the authorities do not mind if young people have a lover."

Thinking for a minute, Qing Lian asked Lan Hua whether she was chased by any boy. Lan Hua flushed and said even before she went to university, she had a lover in mind. Qing Lian asked who this boy was. Lan Hua answered,

"Mum, you know him. He knows you very well. You like him as well." Qing Lian bluntly asked if it was her brother Jian Jun. Lan Hua said, no, he was more handsome than Jian Jun. Then she lowered her voice and admitted,

"He… he is my brother Dan Feng." Even though this was the answer Qing Lian had guessed, she still felt the blood boiling in her heart. She quickly said,

"My daughter, you should consider carefully. Dan Feng is handsome and talented. But he is more attractive to other girls, which will make your relation unstable."

Lan Hua argued that Dan Feng was not a playboy. Qing Lian wanted to mention Dan Feng's father, who had brought trouble to Dan Dan and Yu Mei. But she was also involved, and she should not put down the man she loved. Then she tried to find other excuses to persuade Lan Hua, but she failed.

In the next few days, Qing Lian talked to Lan Hua a few more times, but was still unable to persuade her. Lan Hua was upset and stayed in the university dormitory. Suffering from anxiety, Qing Lian became sick and was hospitalised. Lan Hua did not know her mother was in hospital as she was also depressed these days. She could not help telling Dan Feng about her mother's disagreement about their relationship. Dan Feng was confused as to why his aunt Qing Lian opposed his relationship with Lan Hua.

Noticing Dan Feng's depression, Zhang Feng, Dan Dan and Yu Mei asked him what had happened. He reluctantly told them that Aunt Qing Lian did not like his relationship with Lan Hua. Zhang Feng and the two ladies did not understand Qing Lian's reaction as they all liked Lan Hua. She was clever and pretty. They would be pleased if they had her as their daughter-in-law. Dan Dan remembered that Qing Lian always kept quiet when they had mentioned the possibility of a relationship between Dan Feng and Lan Hua in the past. Maybe there was some hidden reason for this?

Yu Mei said maybe because Qing Lian did not get Zhang Feng, so her resentment prevented her from allowing her daughter to marry Zhang Feng's son. Dan Dan guessed Qing Lian might worry that like his father, Dan Feng was too handsome to be a faithful husband. Dan Dan's opinion shocked Zhang Feng, as he suddenly remembered his accidental love-making with Qing Lian eighteen years ago. Could this have resulted in the birth of Lan Hua? Yet she had moved to Dalian after the affair and married there to have Lan Hua, unless she hid the truth and she did not marry any man there. That could explain why she never mentioned whom she married there.

Lan Hua rushed to the hospital after she heard her mother was sick, even though she was still unhappy about their disagreement. When she entered the ward, she saw Li He and his wife were there. Seeing Qing Lian's haggard face, Lan Hua held her mother's hand and cried. Li He and his wife tried to comfort them and left the ward as they knew there was a conflict between the mother and daughter. They wanted to give them time to discuss the issue privately.

At this moment, Zhang Feng came to see Qing Lian. Li He met him outside the ward and told him Qing Lian and Lan Hua were talking about their problem. Zhang Feng said in that case, he would wait outside for a while. After stopping crying, Lan Hua asked her mother,

"Mum, are you sick because of my attitude towards my relationship with Dan Feng? I still do not understand why you asked me to leave Dan Feng. He is so excellent and I love him deeply." Qing Lian sighed and said,

"Lan Hua, it is not because I am unkind and unreasonable. I have my own difficulties which I cannot speak of, otherwise I will bring big troubles."

Lan Hua still did not understand why her mother was unable to tell her the secret. Qing Lian's heart was bleeding. She held her aching face, trying to block her tears and thought, 'Should I reveal the secret that has been buried in my heart for eighteen years or not? If I do not, it will cause a tragedy to my daughter.' She knew if she revealed the secret, it could give her daughter a temporary shock and sadness, but it would be better for her in the long term. She could still find another boy who loved her. At least, Jian Jun was a good option for her.

At last, she made up her mind. She lowered her hands, looked intently at Lan Hua and whispered,

"Lan Hua, the reason why you cannot have a relation with Dan Feng is… because he is… he is… your biological brother."

Hearing Qing Lian's words, Lan Hua was shocked. She thought she had not heard clearly, so she asked,

"What did you say? What kind of brother is Dan Feng to me?"

Qing Lian got up the courage to speak louder.

"He is your biological brother!"

Lan Hua was shocked and startled. She ran out of the ward, crying.

Zhang Feng also heard what Qing Lain said and was shocked. He did not know whether he should chase Lan Hua or enter the ward to comfort Qing Lian. After he calmed down, he decided to ask Qing Lian about the details of the incident. Qing Lian was surprised to see Zhang Feng walking in and felt awkward. She realised he must have overheard her. Zhang Feng sat on her bed and tried to comfort her. She suddenly threw herself into his arms and cried,

"Brother Feng, my heart is aching!"

Zhang Feng gently caressed her and let her calm down. He realised that as a real man, he should be responsible for this incident and not let Qing Lian suffer alone. After calming down, she told him the details.

She found she was pregnant after having sex with Zhang Feng that night. She was both surprised and happy. She knew she was unable to have Zhang Feng, but to have his child was a happy ending for her. To avoid any possible trouble for both of them, she moved to Dalian and gave birth to the girl in a relative's home. She found a 'back door' to register the birth of the girl and found a job in a newspaper office there. She returned to the River City in 1993 and ran a travel agency with her ex-husband Li He. She did not want other people to know this secret and just wanted to raise her daughter, as she still loved Zhang Feng deeply. Yet fate always played its role. Lan Hua loved Dan Feng. But they were unable to marry each other as they were biological brother and sister.

After listening to her story, Zhang Feng apologised to her again for the mistake he had made. He said he would take full responsibility for this incident and not let her suffer. Qing Lian was happy and kissed him. She said she could do a DNA test to prove the kinship between Lan Hua and Zhang Feng, which would convince Dan Dan and Yu Mei that she did not deliberately get involved in this family circle. Zhang Feng said, no problem, he would go to do the test.

Lan Hua made a phone call to Dan Feng saying she was waiting for him at the riverside. He rushed to her as he worried she might do something stupid. Seeing the boy she loved deeply, but who could no longer be her boyfriend, Lan Hua threw herself into his arms and cried. She stammered,

"Brother Feng, I… I… feel… very sad. My mother… said… we… cannot be… together… as… as… you… are my… my… biological brother!"

"What?" Dan Feng was surprised after listening to her. 'Does this mean Lan Hua is the daughter of my father and Aunt Qing Lian?' He thought, 'Is it possible? Father is not a playboy. Although his relationship with mother and second mother is another matter.' After comforting Lan Hua, he returned home and decided to tell them this shocking news. They might feel angry but they would be able to judge the authenticity of this matter.

Both Dan Dan and Yu Mei were surprised after listening to Dan Feng's narration. They knew Qing Lian loved Zhang Feng secretly, but they did not believe Zhang Feng would take the initiative to have sex with her.

Zhang Feng returned home in the evening. He knew the two ladies would 'interrogate' him. He would tell them the truth, and he would not shirk his responsibility to Qing Lian. Seeing their unhappy expression, he was aware of their anger. But after he told them the truth, their faces eased because they still remembered the painful situation of their love triangle at that time. Especially for Yu Mei, when she knew Zhang Feng had mistaken Qing Lan for her, so she sympathised with him in her mind. Seeing both ladies relaxed, Zhang Feng told them that Qing Lian had agreed to do a DNA test. Dan Dan said it was necessary as both Dan Feng and Lan Hua could be convinced and Qing Lian could prove that she did not lie.

One week later, the DNA test result came out. It proved that Lan Hua was indeed Zhang Feng's biological daughter. The secret of many years had been revealed. The families' relations needed to be adjusted. It was fate, not caused by any scheming person.

Dan Dan and Yu Mei generously invited Qing Lian to dinner. Seeing how awkward this was for Zhang Feng, Qing Lian insisted that it was her mistake to cause this difficult situation. Although both Dan Dan and Yu Mei knew Qing Lian had loved Zhang Feng for so many years, she was willing to take advantage of his confusion to make love with him. Qing Lian said she wanted to maintain the existing situation. She and her daughter did not intend to force themselves into Zhang Feng's family, otherwise she would have revealed this secret much earlier. She did not ask Zhang Feng to fulfil his duty of supporting her daughter. Although Lan Hua could not have Dan Feng as her boyfriend, she would be pleased to have a brother because children at that time did not have any brothers or sisters under the birth control policy. Qing Lian deliberately did not mention that Lan Hua would be happy to have a father, as she did not want to let the other two ladies feel that she intended to push her way into their family.

PART V

2008, a Year of Great Sadness and Rejoicing

Chapter I

Chaos in the Real Estate Industry

A week later, Dan Dan and Yu Mei invited Qing Lian and Lan Hua to their home, in order to establish the new relationship among Zhang Feng, Dan Feng and Lan Hua. Dan Feng and Lan Hua had accepted their new relationship as brother and sister. The atmosphere during the lunch was fairly relaxed. Lan Hua still called Dan Feng brother, although the meaning of brother was different now. But Lan Hua still felt shy about calling Zhang Feng father.

Zhang Feng went to the mailbox to pick up some letters. When he walked back, he met Lan Hua in the corridor. She still called him Uncle Zhang out of habit. Zhang Feng remembered each time when he met Lan Hua in the past, he always had an unusual intimate feeling. Maybe this was the intuition from their blood relationship. Seeing Zhang Feng was in a trance, she asked what he was thinking. He told her about his intuition for her. Interestingly, she said she had the same intuition for him as she always wanted to have a father like Zhang Feng. Living only with her mother, she envied other children with a father. She was moved to tears. Gathering the courage, she murmured,

"Daddy."

"Lan Hua, my daughter!" Zhang Feng hugged her.

Taking each other's arms, they entered the dining hall. Everybody was pleased to witness this situation. Dan Feng exclaimed,

"Our family gets bigger and bigger now!" Everyone laughed. Zhang Feng, Dan Dan, Yu Mei and Qing Lian were all in their fifties. They had all experienced the hardships of life and joys and sorrows in their emotional experiences. So they were more tolerant and open-minded. The three women around Zhang Feng could get along well like sisters. Qing Lian said she would still live with her daughter, but she and Lan Hua would visit Zhang Feng's home often to let Lan Hua see her father and brother.

The news that Lan Hua was Zhang Feng's daughter spread among friends. Jian Jun was very happy as he was able to woo Lan Hua now. After confessing his love to her, she accepted him. Bai He also accepted Dan Feng. The two boys and two girls still played together, just in a different relationship.

One day, Chang Zheng, Li He, Qing Lian, Wang Hai and Zhang Lin visited Zhang Feng's home. They were all happy that their relations had become closer. Zhang Feng, Chang Zheng and Qing Lian became relatives by marriage. Zhang Feng and Li He also became relatives by marriage.

Having a cigarette on the balcony, Wang Hai said to Zhang Feng,

"Brother Feng, what do you think about the fortune-telling picture by the Taoist monk? It is so accurate. In the past, you always argued that you did not have any relationship with Qing Lian. But now you not only had a relationship with her, but you also have a daughter with her."

Zhang Feng looked awkward and explained,

"It was only by accident. I was drunk and mistook her for someone else."

"Qing Lian was willing to have this accident as she had loved you for so many years. You have had good fortune in your love affairs. Three ladies, one son and one daughter. But I only have one woman. Next time I will also have a drunken accident with Helen. You and your sister cannot blame me," Wang Hai said.

"You should still be careful with my Pili boxing." Zhang Feng patted Wang Hai's shoulder.

"Fate is so unfair to me!" Wang Hai mumbled.

The winter of 2007 came soon. The River City became a white crystal world again. One day, Zhang Feng and Yu Mei drove to their company. Dan Dan normally drove herself to the company, to give the staff the impression that Zhang Feng and his ex-wife only had a working relationship.

Passing the riverside, Zhang Feng and Yu Mei were attracted by the sparkling winter scenery, so they got out of the car to enjoy it. In the mist, the torrential river was flowing into the distance. The water vapour formed crystal rime on the weeping willows, creating a dream-like snow and ice world which was so beautiful! They admired the beautiful scenery. Looking at Zhang Feng, Yu Mei asked him,

"Brother, am I still Snow White in your mind? I am an old woman near sixty now."

Looking at her pretty face and holding her waist, he said,

"Yes, you are still my Snow White. It seems that you, along with Dan Dan and Qing Lian, have taken some longevity elixir and never get old. Although you are fifty-seven years old, you still look like a charming young lady in her thirties, with long black hair. I already have some grey hair."

Leaning on him, she asked, "Am I still your favourite?"

Zhang Feng knew that she wanted to know her place in his heart among the three women around him. Kissing her on her snow-like smooth face, he said,

"Do you still remember I told you before your place in my mind? You are like a surging sea, giving me endless intense emotion. Dan Dan is a peaceful lake, giving me a wife's care and tenderness. Qing Lian? She is more likes a babbling stream, a little sister who wants to play with me."

Moved by his words, she kissed his face.

Arriving at the company, they went to their offices. After about half an hour, Zhang Feng heard a commotion downstairs. Yu Mei and Manager Xiao entered his office. Xiao said,

"CEO Zhang, there is a property speculation group of twenty people from Wenzhou. They went to our sales office yesterday, and said they wanted to buy sixty apartments with a river view. We thought they were boasting and told them that there were only forty apartments with a river view left so they asked to come to our headquarters to negotiate. They have come now and asked to talk to you directly."

Zhang Feng had heard that there were a lot of property speculators from Wenzhou, a famous city in Southern China making small commodities. People there had made a lot of money in recent years, so they wanted to invest in the real estate industry by buying and selling properties as the housing market was booming rapidly. They already made the housing prices rise in Shanghai, Nanjing and Beijing. Now they had come to Northeast China. These speculators had very good business sense. Seeing Jili City was a nice city with beautiful scenery and a place to avoid the summer heat, they intended to buy a large amount of property here and then sell it at a profit.

Zhang Feng asked Manager Xiao to bring these buyers up to his office. Dan Dan came in and said to Zhang Feng and Yu Mei,

"We should be careful. These speculators will give us money. But they will make the housing prices increase rapidly, causing a bubble in the housing market. The collapse in the British housing market in the 1980s was caused by housing speculations."

"You are right. The housing price here and nationwide has doubled in the last five years. Many people buy property to get rich quickly, not for living in." Zhang Feng said.

A few minutes later, Manager Xiao brought in a middle-aged woman. Wearing a gold necklace, bracelet and ring, with a golden perm, she looked like an upstart, following a trend of people who were willing to show off their wealth. Manager Xiao introduced Zhang Feng to her. She arrogantly said,

"I will only talk to CEO Zhang. Other people should not be here." Dan Dan and Yu Mei were unhappy about her arrogance but Zhang Feng waved them away, dismissing them. After Dan Dan and Yu Mei left the room, seeing Zhang Feng was a handsome man, the woman fluttered her eyelashes at him.

"CEO Zhang, you may have heard that our Wenzhou property buyers have a lot of money. We have come here to look after your business. We want to buy sixty apartments with a river view. We will pay cash, so please give us some discount."

Zhang Feng was disgusted by her. But he still politely said,

"We know you Wenzhou residents are talented businessmen. People call you 'the Jews of the East'. You buy large amounts of properties, but you do not stay there and do not let them to tenants, you just wait for housing prices to rise and sell them for profit. But if the price drops, you will make a loss. Also, raising housing prices will make it difficult for ordinary people to buy their homes, which will not benefit society."

Listening to Zhang Feng's talk, the woman was surprised. She said,

"My God, it is the first time I meet a developer trying to persuade us not to buy too many properties. CEO Zhang, you really are a Confucian businessman, putting interest in ordinary people first and profit second. OK, we will buy less, thirty apartments, with a thirty percent discount."

Zhang Feng respected honest businessmen and customers, but he did not like those who made money by any kind of means, especially property speculators. They disturbed the housing market and caused bubbles. He did not want to give in to this woman, so he said,

"The cost of building these apartments has gone up. So I cannot give you even ten percent discount."

The woman was unhappy and said she and her associates would only buy twenty apartments.

Sending her away, Zhang Feng told the two ladies and other colleagues of his deal with the Wenzhou group. They all agreed with him. Next day, Yu Mei called Lin Jianguo urgently from the sales office. She said the Wenzhou group had paid six million yuan in cash from their travel bags for the apartments they had bought. She asked Lin to come with a solid van and a couple of strong men to send the cash safely to the bank. Lin told this to Dan Dan and Yu Mei. They said, "These Wenzhou upstarts really had a lot of money."

Zhang Feng and his team had not realised that the purchase by the Wenzhou property speculation group would cause panic buying in the city. A few days after the Wenzhou group had bought the apartments, Zhang Feng and Yu Mei saw a very long queue of several hundred buyers outside their sales office before opening time. The security guards told Zhang Feng that some people had started coming from the previous evening. It meant they had spent the whole night queuing in the chilly weather. Yu Mei said,

"The reason why so many people came here to buy property is that our properties prices have remained the same, but other companies have all increased their prices. But the problem is we only have about a hundred properties, not enough for all the buyers here. Brother Feng, should we also increase the price a little bit?" Zhang Feng said he needed to see how many people were in the queue.

He got out of the office and walked along the queue to count them, and also to see what kind of people these buyers were. When he passed a few young men, their talk attracted his attention. One of them said,

"It is so difficult to be a young man now. When you try to find a girlfriend, the girls always ask you, 'Do you have a house or apartment? Do you have a car?' If your answer is no, they leave you straight away. I have to borrow money from my parents as a deposit."

Zhang Feng sympathised with these young men. He also sighed with emotion. Social practices and attitudes changed so rapidly. Young women were so materialistic. Money and wealth were more important than emotions and love.

Passing by a few middle-aged men, Zhang Feng overheard that their reason for buying property was to let it out to get the rent money to supplement their pension when they grew old. Zhang Feng could understand them, as in the West people did the same thing.

Passing by a few upstarts, Zhang Feng heard them boasting. One of them said he already had five properties and he was going to buy some more. He would sell some of them in one year or even a few months' time at a large profit, because housing prices were always going up. To invest in the housing market would earn more than investing in the stock market, with much less risk. Zhang Feng did not like these upstarts. But the free market would produce such people. They were able to earn money in different or even dirty ways, but still legally.

Back at the sales office, Zhang Feng said to Yu Mei,

"We should help those buyers who need properties to live, but not those who speculated with property to turn a quick profit. The government should make a law to control these speculators who kept pushing the housing prices up and making it difficult for ordinary citizens to buy their own property."

"Although as developers, we need to make a profit, selling property to the people who really need to have their own accommodation would make our society equal and better. I quite like the idea of some think tank that 'property is for living but not for speculation'. The government should have some control policy if a bubble occurs in the housing market." Yu Mei agreed.

After some discussion, Zhang Feng and Yu Mei decided to keep the original price for these hundred apartments and try to sell them to those who really needed their own accommodation, but not to the speculators. Manager Xiao announced this decision to the people in the queue and they all cheered up.

In Jili City, recently people could see long queues outside many property sales offices. The most popular topics among people were, 'Have you bought a property?' 'Try to borrow money to buy a property, the housing prices are up again!' Unlike Zhang Feng, other developers tried to make more profit by any kinds of means. Some hoarded properties, some placed misleading advertisements to attract buyers.

One day, Wang Hai and Li He were walking past Cai's sales department and saw a long queue there. Wang Hai was curious, as the price of Cai's properties was much higher than the other companies. Wang Hai messed up his hair and pretended to be a worker from the countryside. He asked a foreman-like person,

"Big brother, do people in the city all have so much money to buy property?" The man looked at Wang Hai and said,

"From the countryside? Want to earn some quick money? You will earn 200 yuan just to stand in the queue for a day."

"I do not have enough money to buy property," Wang Hai answered. The man whispered in his ear,

"You do not need to buy anything, just stand in the queue. Other buyers will think the properties here are in high demand. We will get a commission after the boss here has made a profit."

Wang Hai pretended to be happy and said,

"Oh, how wonderful to have easy money. I will go to change my clothes, then come back." Then he left with Li He.

In the evening, Wang Hai visited Zhang Feng's home and told him and the two ladies about Cai's deceit with the fake customers. Zhang Feng said angrily that Cai used to be a political swindler, but now he was a business swindler. He had already got the dirty money through buying the land of the textile factory. Now he was cheating the property buyers again. Dan Dan said,

"I am quite worried that a bubble in the housing market might appear soon. We should be careful."

A few days later, Zhang Feng met Chang Zheng at a party. He told Chang Zheng about the panic buying of property. Chang Zheng said he was also worried. Nationwide, the local governments were selling land to developers and got money to build infrastructure like train stations, airports, and motorways. But the developers tended to add the land price to their business costs, which also pushed housing prices up. In addition to this, there were some mad purchases by the property speculators. Both caused the housing prices to rise. In big cities, young people could not afford to buy properties. Housing demolitions and relocations also caused resentment from the people. He hoped the central government would make a policy to control the housing market, stopping the speculations and allowing ordinary people to buy a home easily.

In 2008, the Spring Festival came. Zhang Feng and his family celebrated together. But they felt both happy and worried, as there were signs of a crisis in the housing market.

Chapter II

Facing Bankruptcy in the Crisis

The approaching financial and housing market crisis was not noticed initially by the people in China. Facing the soaring housing prices and property speculation at the end of 2007, the central government had started to make policies to control the housing market, such as only the local residents could buy the property in their city, and no more than two properties. Deposits increased from ten percent to forty or even fifty percent. The interest rates of mortgages also went up.

Zhang Feng and his colleagues were pleased and thought the new policies would prevent further rises in housing prices and even reduce prices and make properties more affordable.

But just when Zhang Feng thought things were getting better, he received an email from Wang Li, who was married and living in London. In her email, she warned Zhang Feng that the American subprime mortgage crisis had started to affect the global economy, and many banks in the West had gone bankrupt. The housing markets there also showed a slump or had even collapsed. She advised him to prepare for the crisis as it began to hit Asian markets now.

But Zhang Feng did not realise that the impact would come so soon. Two weeks later, Yu Mei called him urgently and told him that the sales office was very quiet, nobody was coming to buy property. She asked other companies' sales departments, they all told her that their business was also very quiet, and the housing prices kept falling.

Zhang Feng held a senior management meeting to discuss how to cope with the crisis. Dan Dan said the latest situation was that housing prices in all big cities, like Beijing, Shanghai, Guangzhou and Shenzhen, had fallen ruinously low. The stock market crashed, exports declined and many manufacturing companies were facing bankruptcy.

Zhang Feng said,

"We are facing a major crisis. The problem is that people are reluctant to buy property when the price drops. They think the price might go down further. Also, affected by the bad economy, people have less money in their hands, and cannot afford to buy property."

"We have to follow the austerity policy, lowering our property prices to sell them quickly to avoid loss." Yu Mei said.

Lin Jianguo suggested stopping work on planned projects both in the city and outside provinces.

The most terrible part of the situation was broken capital chains. Not only did the unfinished projects need funds, but they also had to repay the interest of their loans from the banks. Most of the banks now had started to squeeze credit. Zhang

Feng admitted that avoiding a broken funding chain was the most critical issue. He would approach the financial institutes with a good relationship with the company to get funding. But his colleagues all knew that if the company really had funding problems, the situation could be devastating.

Like other cities in the country, the housing market in the River City was chaotic and dismal. A lot of buyers tried to return their properties, with various excuses, even if they had already started the legal procedures. One day, the woman from the Wenzhou group found Yu Mei, and said they wanted to return the twenty river view apartments to the company because they had found quality problems with these properties. Yu Mei knew they were trying to find some excuse to get their money back, because these apartments were in very good condition when they bought them. The woman said the ventilation was not good so mould had appeared on the walls. Yu Mei and Manager Xiao went to the apartments. Luckily she had taken photos of the inside of the rooms before the properties were sold, showing the walls were very clean and smooth. Looking at the mould on the walls, she realised that the Wenzhou woman had deliberately spread water on the walls and shut the windows to produce mould. She exposed the fraud on the spot. The Wenzhou woman was very embarrassed and stopped asking to return the properties.

Manager Xiao felt relieved. He praised Yu Mei's foresight in taking the photos, and said,

"Fortunately you saw through her fraud, otherwise we would lose six million yuan."

Yu Mei sighed and said,

"We still have thirty to fifty buyers, who had not paid a deposit, cancelling their orders every day. The future is not optimistic."

Hearing of Zhang Feng's company's plight, his friends including Wang Hai, Li He, Qing Lian and Huang Lei all came to comfort him. Wang Hai said the recession had affected his company as well. Some workers could not repay their mortgages on time and had to give their properties back to the banks. The banks tried to sell these properties at auctions, so they made a loss as well. Li He said the recession had hit the tourist industry, his business was bad as well. Qing Lian asked Zhang Feng why there were so many unfinished buildings on street. Zhang Feng told her that because the developers had started too many projects before the crisis and most of them had broken the capital chains, they had to stop these projects halfway. So there were so many unfinished buildings on the street.

Heaving a sigh, he said his company also had several hundred unfinished apartments. Wang Hai and the other friends intended to help Zhang Feng, but his working capital was over ten million yuan. It was very hard for any individual person to help him. The only hope was a possible rescue from the government. But facing such a worldwide crisis, nobody knew when the recovery would come.

The next day, Zhang Feng and Lin Jianguo went to the construction sites and saw a lot of buildings were only half-finished because there were not enough materials and funds to finish them. Zhang Feng and Lin decided to use the remaining materials to complete the nearly finished properties, and leave the rest waiting for funding to come.

In the next few days, Zhang Feng and his two ladies went to many banks and financial institutes to raise funds. But they were told that because of the impact of the recession, the housing market was very bad, so if they lent money to Zhang Feng's company, the loan would turn into bad debts. Zhang Feng tried to contact some banks with good relations with his company, but they said they needed to think about it, as the financial situation was not optimistic. They asked Zhang Feng to come back in a few days' time.

In his villa, Governor Shen was chatting with Cai Wenge. The last time they met, he had got several million yuan for selling the land of the textile factory to Cai cheaply. This recession was again a good opportunity for him to get dirty money. He did not forget his enemy Zhang Feng and asked Cai how Zhang Feng's company was doing. Cai said with a smile,

"He is just waiting for bankruptcy! He has several hundred unfinished properties and is anxious to raise funds." Shen slapped his thigh and gloated,

"Excellent! He will become a beggar soon. I will notify all the banks not to lend money to him, as the government has a policy of financial austerity."

After a few days, Zhang Feng went back to the banks that had a good relationship with him. But their attitude had changed. They told him there was a mandate from the provincial government saying they were not allowed to lend money to developers. Zhang Feng guessed this was spite from Shen, his way of kicking a man when he was down. He knew he could bribe some of the bank directors, but he was unwilling to do this.

Chang Zheng rang him in the evening and said that he had tried to persuade some city banks to lend money to Zhang Feng's company, but the directors said they dared not to do it as the provincial government had given them a strict mandate not to lend funds to developers. Chang Zheng also guessed Shen was involved in this.

Two weeks had passed, no funds were coming. Seeing the other real estate companies close down one by one, Zhang Feng and his colleagues were very anxious. If they were determined to delay the worst, they would have to repay interests to some banks, pay salaries to some of the staff and workers, and lay off others, paying them redundancy compensation. Having no alternative, they decided to sell their villas and cars and rent a small flat to live in until things improved. Both Dan Dan and Yu Mei agreed. Like the time during the Cultural Revolution, his two lovers supported him without hesitation. With tears in his eyes, Zhang Feng embraced them with deep emotion. After knowing the decision of Zhang Feng, Qing Lian was also very sad. She suggested that Dan Dan and Dan Feng could live with her and her daughter. Zhang Feng and Yu Mei could live in Wang Hai's house. Zhang Feng thanked her for her offer, but said they could rent a three-bedroom apartment for themselves as they still had some savings.

Zhang Feng sent information about his villas to an estate agent he knew well. He told the manager that he would like a quick sale, even if it meant getting less than the asking price. The manager sympathised with his situation and said he would try to sell them as soon as possible.

Two days later, the manager telephoned Zhang Feng and said there was a buyer wanting to view the villas at lunchtime that day. Zhang Feng was pleased to have a viewing so soon because it was not a good time to sell luxury villas. At noon, somebody knocked and Yu Mei walked to the door to open it. But suddenly she cried out in fear. Zhang Feng was surprised to see the viewer was his sworn enemy Cai Wenge. Seeing the surprised expression on Zhang Feng and Yu Mei, Cai triumphed,

"Oh, my old classmate, you never thought it would end like today, facing bankruptcy and selling your villas. Ok, I will buy them to help you." He looked at Yu Mei lasciviously and said,

"Especially since one of you is my ex-wife and one is my old classmate, ha, ha!"

Clenching his fist, Zhang Feng almost wanted to say, 'Get out! I will sell to anybody but you!' Yu Mei took his arm, asking him for patience, because the company would face bankruptcy straight away if they were unable to sell the villas. She asked the sales assistant from the agency to accompany Cai to view the villas. Then she took Zhang Feng to the back garden and they sat on the bench to wait. Zhang Feng was angry and anxious.

Suddenly, Yu Mei clutched his arm and asked him if there were any important things in their bedroom, as Cai seemed to be searching for something in the room. Zhang Feng turned back to look into their bedroom through the French window. Cai was snooping in the room. He suddenly picked up the velvet quilt and kissed it. Obviously he was fantasising about Yu Mei sexually. Yu Mei turned her head away and said, "Disgusting!" Zhang Feng was so angry that he stood up, about to go into the room to beat Cai up. But Yu Mei held him back and soothed, "Brother, be patient, Cai is just a lascivious man." Yu Mei then rang Dan Dan to tell her Cai had come to view the villa, and advised her to stay in the summer house in the back garden.

After Cai left, Zhang Feng telephoned the manager of the agent and asked him not to accept the possible offer from Cai straight away, but wait for a few more days to see whether other buyers would come, because he preferred not to sell the villas to his enemy Cai. The manager readily agreed, and suggested to Zhang Feng to move his furniture and other belongings out soon, to make the villas look more spacious and attractive. Zhang Feng agreed.

In the next few days, Zhang Feng and his family packed the furniture and cleaned their villas. Wang Hai sent a big lorry to move the furniture to their small three-bedroom flat. When they left their villas, Dan Feng could not help crying. Dan Dan and Yu Mei also had tears in their eyes. Zhang Feng tried to comfort them and said,

"We will come back!"

Compared to their villas, their rented flat was so small. The sitting room, kitchen and bedrooms were all small, with only one bathroom, which made Dan Feng unhappy. Dan Dan told him that in the past, his father, second mother and herself had only lived in straw and mud houses in the countryside during the Cultural Revolution, with nothing inside. So compared with those poor living conditions, this flat was good enough. Zhang Feng also calmly told his son that a great man knew when to yield and when not. Only if you could endure hardship could you make great achievements. Listening to his father's lecture, Dan Feng understood how he should cope with hardship.

Qing Lian and Lan Hua visited the flat and brought nice food as they knew Zhang Feng and his family had just finished moving and did not have time to cook. Lan Hua tried to comfort her father and brother, saying things would get better soon. She also invited Dan Feng to stay with them if he felt the flat was too crowded. Li He and Bai He came and gave Zhang Feng fifty thousand yuan. He said the money was part of his repayment of Zhang Feng's financial support when he faced bankruptcy after his disastrous losses in the stock market. The money could help Zhang Feng to pay his rent and living costs. Zhang Feng and the two ladies thanked him for his help. Bai He asked Dan Feng to visit her home to play with her.

He Hua also came to see them. She felt sad when she heard Zhang Feng had sold his villas and cars. She gave thirty thousand yuan to Zhang Feng. Dan Dan and Yu Mei asked her to keep the money for herself as the recession might also affect her business. But she insisted on giving the money to them. Zhang Feng accepted the money and promised he would repay her after the situation got better.

One week later, the manager of the estate agent told Zhang Feng the two villas had been sold to a different buyer who kindly paid the asking price. Cai had only given quite a low offer. Zhang Feng and his two lovers were all relieved. They would have felt aggrieved if the villas had been bought by their sworn enemy, Cai. Their cars were also sold with Wang Hai's help. He lent them two second-hand Volkswagen cars for them to still be able to drive around.

With the money from the sale of the villas and the cars, Zhang Feng was able to pay his staff and workers and prepare for the worst to happen. Zhang Feng and his colleagues held an assembly of staff and workers. On behalf of the board of directors, Zhang Feng explained the difficult situation of the company, which was caused by the recession. Sadly, if the government did not rescue the housing market, the company would face bankruptcy. So he announced that all the projects under construction had to be stopped. The workers would still receive their salary for this month. For those who wanted to quit their jobs, the company would give them severance pay. Finishing his announcement, he stood up, bowed three times to the assembly, and said,

"I apologise to everybody in our company."

Because Zhang Feng and his company had always looked after the staff and workers, they respected and loved him and his senior managers. Some of them had tears in their eyes and some shouted,

"CEO Zhang, we will not leave; we will stay with our company, life or death!"

Zhang Feng was moved by their reaction, and said,

"Thank you for your understanding and support. But the situation is serious. If we cannot get extra funding within three weeks, we will face bankruptcy. Our enemies have tried to ruin us and have plotted to make us bankrupt. Let's do in this way: If you want to quit, you can claim severance pay after the meeting. For those who intend to stay, wait for another three weeks." Almost all of the staff and workers said they preferred to stay, which moved Zhang Feng and his senior managers.

Back in their apartment in the evening, Dan Dan and Yu Mei rushed to cook. They wanted to cook something that Zhang Feng liked. In the kitchen, Yu Mei said to Dan Dan,

"Sister Dan Dan, I recall the time during the Cultural Revolution when we tried to rescue Brother Feng from the jail where he faced the death sentence. When he was punished politically after the event of 4 June 1989, we tried to find some way to mitigate his punishment. Two years ago, when he was sabotaged by the building collapse, we also rescued him. So this time, maybe we can still find some way to avoid bankruptcy."

Dan Dan stopped her cooking and said,

"Yes, Sister Yu Mei, we should think about it."

She held Yu Mei's hand, and together they walked into the sitting room. Drinking tea with Zhang Feng, they began to think about alternative ways to rescue the company. Yu Mei said,

"What about Mr Du, who built the five-star hotel for our city and helped us to open this company. Do you think he might help us again?"

"I have also been thinking about this possibility. Mr Du sold his shares to us after our company was on the right track, and he returned to Shenzhen to operate his own company. But this recession might have affected his business as well and he might be facing difficulties now." Zhang Feng said.

Yu Mei said it was worth trying anyway. She would travel to Shenzhen the next day to visit Mr Du and the other directors in his company with whom Yu Mei was also on good terms. Yu Mei's idea inspired Dan Dan. She said she could travel to Hong Kong to visit Liang Hua's brother Lian Fu, who used to help Wang Hai to expand business in overseas markets. Although she had broken up with Liang Hua, the two brothers still respected her. To help their beloved man, the two ladies were always brave and determined. They were going to travel to Shenzhen and Hong Kong the next day.

2008 was a disastrous year in China. There was a heavy snowstorm at the beginning of the year. There was a magnitude eight earthquake in Sichuan in May, with over 400,000 casualties, which shocked the whole country. Premier Wen Jaibao travelled to the site to take command of the disaster relief. People all around the country offered aid to the earthquake area. Chinese people have a characteristic. Normally they only look after themselves, but when the nation is facing a major disaster, they will show solidarity and help each other.

One day, Zhang Feng and his son were walking home together. On the way, they saw some students collecting donations for the earthquake area. In the past, Zhang Feng would have donated several million yuan to the quake victims. But now he could only put a couple of hundred into the donation box held by a little girl. Dan Feng also put all his pocket money into the box. Patting his son's shoulder, Zhang Feng said to Dan Feng,

"You are a good boy, Dan Feng, you must be a righteous Confucian man concerned about our country and our people."

The deadline for the official bankrupt liquidation was approaching. Originally, the government had given Zhang Feng's company three weeks to do something to avoid it. But Shen and Li did not want to see a rescue policy from the government coming. They kept pushing the Industry and Trading Bureau and the city court to start the procedure sooner, to deliver a vital blow to Zhang Feng's company. Yu Mei and Dan Dan contacted Zhang Feng every day to inform him of their progress to get possible financial support. Yu Mei told Zhang Feng that Mr Du was still in Taiwan. He would go back to Shenzhen in the next few days. Dan Dan told him that Liang Fu needed to discuss this matter with the other directors, as some of them were hesitant to give money to another business in this difficult time.

Two days later, when Zhang Feng was discussing with Lin and Chen how to finish the last few projects, Manager Xiao rushed in and said to Zhang Feng,

"The fat is in the fire! The liquidation team has come."

"What?" Lin and Chen almost jumped out of their chairs.

Zhang Feng said to Manager Xiao calmly,

"Let them wait for ten minutes, then take them to the meeting room."

After Manager Xiao left, Zhang Feng stood up and said to Lin and Chen,

"My two brothers, I have been expecting this day. I'm sorry I let you down. I should not have asked you to do business with me fifteen years ago. The sea of commerce is not peaceful, it is turbulent. Even a big ship can sink in the storm."

With tears in their eyes, Lin and Chen said to Zhang Feng,

"Brother Feng, we were willing to join you to sail on the sea of commerce. This financial crisis is beyond anyone's control. Do not worry, even if we have to beg on the street, we will go with you!" Zhang Feng shook hands with them and embraced them tightly.

Entering the meeting room, Zhang Feng and his colleagues saw six men sitting at the table. They came from the Provincial

Industry and Trading Bureau and the city court. The head of the team was a subordinate of Shen. He said arrogantly to Zhang Feng,

"CEO Zhang, I can still call you by this title, but not tomorrow." Lin Jianguo angrily said,

"There are still another ten days to the deadline. Why did you come earlier?" The head brayed,

"The banks cannot wait. The bankruptcy liquidation process takes a long time and there are a lot of companies in the queue. The state will have a greater loss if we delay the process."

"I think it is not the banks that are unable to wait. It is your Governor Shen who cannot wait," Zhang Feng sneered. The head wanted to refute him. But a voice was heard at the door,

"Yes, I just cannot wait anymore!" Turning around, the people in the room saw Shen and his flunkey Li Qiu walking in to enjoy Zhang Feng's embarrassing situation. Sitting down uninvited, Shen mocked Zhang Feng,

"Ha! Ha! My previous Mayor Zhang, my CEO Zhang now and my Beggar Zhang tomorrow. At last, you have your end today. In the past, you always fought against me in the official circles. You are still against me after you have done business. You were lucky to survive the building collapse, but this time let me watch you falling into the abyss of bankruptcy."

Li Qiu also gloated,

"My old classmate, you never listened to my advice in the past and you are unlucky now. You should kowtow to Governor Shen and plead guilty. Maybe he can give you a bit of money to buy some food."

Zhang Feng stood up and spoke to them in a calm voice,

"It seems the two of you came to kick me when I'm down. But unfortunately I won't bow to you. I may fall today, but I will stand up tomorrow!"

Shen was very angry. He made a gesture to the head of the team head to start the liquidation procedure. The head stood up with a sneer and trumpeted,

"I announce that the bankruptcy liquidation procedure for Song Jiang Real Estate Company has begun now!"

But surprising everybody in the room, a clear female voice was heard in the corridor,

"Hang on! You are too impatient!"

Chapter III

Business Is Booming Again

At this moment, the door opened. Beautiful and smart Yu Mei, together with Mr Du, walked in. Yu Mei addressed the people in the room,

"Let me introduce Mr Du, CEO of Taiwan International Travel Company. He built our five-star hotel twenty years ago and helped us to start our company as well. This time, he has decided to invest eighty million yuan to help us to overcome our difficult situation. Gentlemen from the bankruptcy liquidation team, Governor Shen and Director Li, sorry if you feel disappointed."

Lin Jianguo, Chen Tao and Manager Xiao all jumped up from their chairs. Other senior managers and assistants also applauded. Looking at the gloomy face of Shen, the head of the team thought for a while, and said,

"Do not be too happy! Although you have eighty million yuan, after you repay the bank interest, pay the salaries of your staff and workers and buy materials for some of your projects, there will not be any money left." When Yu Mei and Mr Du tried to argue with him, another silvery voice was heard at the door.

"You do not need to worry, we will have more funding." What a coincidence, smart and graceful Dan Dan was entering the room. She said to Zhang Feng with a smile.

"CEO Zhang, the Hong Kong businessman Liang Fu has decided to invest fifty million yuan in our business; the amount will reach our account tomorrow." Then she said to Shen, Li and their team. "I am terribly sorry to see you are disappointed, as you seem so keen to see our company bankrupt."

Shen, Li and the team members all stood up in dejection and started to leave. Zhang Feng said to them loudly,

"Governor Shen, Director Li, you cheerfully came today to see how I would collapse, facing bankruptcy. Instead, you have seen another good drama. But one side effect of the free market economy is that it has also produced a lot of corrupt officials. I suggest you restrain your greedy desire for money. Otherwise, the person going to jail next time will be you!" Shen and Li hung their heads in shame and left the room.

The atmosphere in the room was electric. Everybody stood up to applaud the two ladies and Mr Du. Zhang Feng stood up to shake hands with Mr Du. Then he embraced Yu Mei and kissed her. After that he wanted to do the same thing with Dan Dan, but she looked very shy. Zhang Feng embraced her anyhow and said,

"Do not feel embarrassed. We are still an old couple." People around them all laughed.

Zhang Feng gave Mr Du a seat and asked Manager Xiao to serve Tie Guanyin tea to him. Yu Mei and Dan Dan started to describe their fundraising experiences. Yu Mei said Mr Du had just returned from Taiwan to Shenzhen the previous morning. After listening to Yu Mei's description of the urgent situation at her company, Mr Du immediately discussed it with the other directors and decided to give financial aid to Zhang Feng's company. He not only trusted Zhang Feng, but also he predicted that the Chinese government would have to try to rescue the depressed economy. The real estate industry was involved in many different industries, so the collapse of the housing market would affect the whole economy. Thus the government would have to rescue the housing market as well. Before Yu Mei finished her speaking, a senior manager rushed into the room and shouted,

"Good news! Good news! China Central Television just broadcast an important report. The state council will give 4,000 billion yuan to stimulate the economy and shore up the markets against the impact of the subprime mortgage crisis."

Everybody cheered up and praised Mr Du as a business prophet.

Dan Dan also told them about her trip to find Mr Liang Fu. She said Liang Hua was very helpful this time. He tried to persuade his brother to help Zhang Feng. Liang Fu was a businessman with foresight. He also predicted that the government would do something to boost the economy. Therefore, he decided to give Zhang Feng's company financial support.

Listening to both Yu Mei and Dan Dan's descriptions, all the people in the room said they had been very lucky to get help from these two kind businessmen at the critical moment. Zhang Feng invited Mr Du to dinner. Du said he had already booked a room in Song Jiang five-star hotel, and asked Zhang Feng to come to the hotel, have some drinks and stay with him overnight, because they were good friends and had not seen each other for a few years.

Zhang Feng and Mr Du kept drinking and chatting until midnight. It was already 10.00 in the morning when Zhang Feng got up. Not wanting to wake Mr Du up, Zhang Feng told the reception that he was going to his company, and left a message for Mr Du saying that he hoped Mr Du could stay a few more days to enjoy the pleasant summer climate, and he would drive him to the airport when he left. Then Zhang Feng rang his secretary to tell him he would be there in half an hour, called a taxi and left the hotel.

Near his company, he heard loud voices. He was surprised, was the liquidation team back again? He got out of the taxi near the wood in front of his company. Watching behind the trees, he saw a lot of people on the steps of the entrance. Looking more carefully, he was relieved to recognise the staff and workers of his company. He walked towards the building and the people saw him. Suddenly a band vigorously played the popular song 'Going from victory to victory'. Zhang Feng knew this was the company's amateur band playing. The staff and workers on the steps applauded him loudly. He waved his hand to greet them. He saw Dan Dan, Yu Mei, Lin Jianguo, Chen Tao and the other senior managers standing in front of the crowd.. Obviously, the good news had spread among his staff and workers. The people who had left or were preparing to leave all returned or stayed. Walking to the top of the steps, with tears in his eyes, Zhang Feng spoke to the crowd,

"All the staff and workers of the company, my brothers and sisters, I am too excited today. At last, we have escaped this critical disaster!" People around him applauded warmly. He continued to speak,

"We owe a great debt of gratitude to Mr Du and Mr Liang for their generous help. I thank you all for your trust in me and my senior managers. We will make a great effort to complete the unfinished properties and sell them. We will steadily take on new projects, overcome this economic crisis and make our company larger and stronger!" The crowd burst into thunderous applause.

After the welcome ceremony, Zhang Feng and Dan Dan held an administrative meeting, assigning tasks to different departments. Everybody was eager to get into action. Lin Jianguo led his construction department to complete the unfinished properties. Yu Mei and her sales department began to sell finished properties and to presell the planned properties. They tried to spread the positive news that the state stimulus of the economy would boost the housing market and the rescue policy would come soon. So now would be a good time to buy property, as housing prices would increase very soon. Their promotional activities seemed to be working, as more and more people came to the sales department to inquire, book viewings and sign sales contracts.

What made Zhang Feng even happier was Chang Zheng's visit. He told Zhang Feng that the central government had given financial support to the housing market, making it easy for real estate companies to raise funds for their business. With his influence, some city banks were willing to lend money again to these companies. His talk made Zhang Feng very excited, as if he could borrow money from the banks, he would then be able to buy unfinished properties from other companies cheaply, complete them and sell them.

Chang Zheng asked Zhang Feng whether he felt it was not easy to do business after this crisis. Zhang Feng smiled and said he did have this idea. When he used to work in political circles, he was bullied by those left-wing leaders, so he preferred to leave politics and entered the business world. But after this crisis, he had also learned some lessons. He should not expand his business too fast and too widely. He needed to proceed steadily. Then it would be easier to cope with another recession. Chang Zheng also told Zhang Feng that the central government and the party had started to fight against corruption seriously. So some corrupt officials like Shen and Li would soon be punished. Hearing this, Zhang Feng was very pleased.

Before Chang Zheng left, he did not forget to tell Dan Dan and Yu Mei that his son Jian Jun and Lan Hua were in a nice relationship now. He did not realise that the two families could become relatives by marriage. Zhang Feng looked a bit embarrassed, as Lan Hua was his daughter through that accidental love affair with Qing Lian. Dan Dan and Yu Mei came to his rescue and said, yes, we did not realise that we were enemies forty years ago, but have become relatives by marriage now. Zhang Feng thought, that's true. Forty years ago, he and Chang Zheng were rivals, as both of them loved Yu Mei. He and Qing Lian were political enemies forty years ago, but now the three of them had become relatives by marriage. Fate sometimes played jokes on people.

Soon, Zhang Feng's company completed those unfinished properties and bought several hundred unfinished properties from other companies. The government rescue policy came, lifting the limits on purchases and relaxing the mortgage restrictions. The housing priced started to increase. Zhang Feng's company sold over 1,000 properties for a good price. All the staff and workers were very happy. Only Shen and Li were disappointed, because they thought they would make a lot of money in this crisis, but they got nothing. Their plot to attack Zhang Feng and destroy his company had fizzled.

Zhang Feng's company quickly earned back the loans from Mr Du and Mr Liang. He wrote to them, telling them that he was able to repay their loans, plus interest. But they said they would like to use that money to buy shares in his company, and become shareholders as they felt confident in his business. Zhang Feng was also happy as he was able to start new projects with these funds.

It was midsummer in July, the country and the people had recovered from the shock of the Wenchuan earthquake and rebuilding work had begun in that area. The economy, manufacturing industries, finance and real estate were all getting better. Society looked promising again. The most exciting event was that the country would host the 29th Olympic Games in Beijing. In modern Chinese history, the country suffered from civil wars, poverty, famine, foreign invasion. The world regarded China as a weak and ailing giant, the 'Sick Man of Asia'.

But now, after thirty years of hard reforms, China had the world's third-largest economy, after the USA and Japan. Taking this opportunity to hold the Olympic Games, the country was able to show its new face to the world. Although the country still had a lot of social issues to resolve, it was no longer a poor country with old shabby cities, poor farmers and uneducated people with long braids.

When the family was in a good mood, Dan Feng asked whether they could buy and move back to their previous villas before they got dearer, as he missed them. Yu Mei also said,

"Yes, it was so lovely living there. In our flat now, we have to line up to go to the toilet."

Zhang Feng asked Dan Dan whether there was enough money to buy the villas back. She said,

"Yes, we have enough money to buy back them now. But it depends on whether the owner is willing to sell them to us, and how high the price will be."

The next day, Zhang Feng phoned the manager of the estate agent, who told him something interesting. The new owner had not yet moved into the properties so the two villas were still empty. The manager also told him that a friend of Zhang Feng called Qing Lian knew the new owner. He suggested that Zhang Feng should get Qing Lian to ask the new owner whether he would like to sell the villas back to them. Zhang Feng told Dan Dan and Yu Mei about what the manager told him. They also felt strange and asked him to contact Qing Lian.

Qing Lian told him that the two villas had been bought by her friend's friend living abroad. The owner had not returned to the River City since he bought the properties, but he was coming back this weekend and would stay there for a few days. She suggested bringing Zhang Feng's family members to the villas at the weekend and asking the owner to sell the villas back to them. If he refused, Zhang Feng could look at other villas nearby to see whether any were on sale.

The weekend was a nice day with warm sunshine and a blue sky. Zhang Feng and his family drove to the villas. Qing Lian was still on her way because the appointment was at 10.00 am and it was just 9.50. Admiring the beautiful front garden, Dan Feng gushed that after living in the small flat, the villas looked so big and nice, with trees around and a river view. He sighed and said, it was so nice to be rich. Zhang Feng immediately said to him,

"You must work hard to get rich. Do not follow those

corrupted officials or profiteers, they are contemptible even if they have millions."

Qing Lian drove there. She said the good weather today was a good omen. She pushed the doorbell but there was no response. Dan Feng looked disappointed. Qing Lian said to him with a smile,

"Do not worry." Then she pulled out a set of keys from her handbag and opened the door. Zhang Feng and the others were surprised and asked Qing Lian why she had the keys. She said,

"My friend gave me the keys this morning and said, if the owner was not there, I could open the door for Zhang Feng's family to view them. The owner gave my friend a set of keys and asked her to look after the villas while he was abroad."

Zhang Feng and the others were all happy. Even if they did not know whether the owner would sell the villas to them or not, at least they were able to view the villas they missed. They had a tour inside the villas and said with emotion that they really appreciated how comfortable, spacious and luxurious the villas were after living in the small apartment. Dan Feng particularly stayed in his room for a while. After viewing the two villas and gathering in the hallway in Zhang Feng's previous villa, they looked a bit disappointed as the villas were still not theirs. Surprisingly, Qing Lian said to them,

"Attention please, I will make an important announcement." Then she jangled the two sets of keys in her hand and continued,

"Can you see these two sets of keys? Now…" She paused for a dramatic second, "They are yours!"

"What? What do you mean?" Zhang Feng and his family were all confused. Qing Lian smiled and said,

"I mean, you can take these keys with you, as you are the owners of these two villas again!"

"Are you joking?" Zhang Feng, Dan Dan, Yu Mei and Dan Feng were even more confused. Qing Lian laughed out loud. She asked them to sit down, and told them the story about that secret new owner.

The truth was, when Qing Lian knew Zhang Feng had to sell their villas, she felt very sad. She visited Huang Lei and told him about the possible bankruptcy faced by Zhang Feng. Huang Lei also felt uncomfortable. Because Zhang Feng was his friend and had helped him financially when he opened his chemical company, he felt he should help Zhang Feng now. But he did not have enough funds available, only a fairly small amount of money, just enough to buy the villas. Knowing Zhang Feng's sworn enemy Cai Wenge intended to buy the villas cheaply, he decided to buy the two villas secretly. Then Zhang Feng could use the money to pay the salaries for his staff and workers. Huang Lei did not want to live in the villas, but to leave them for Zhang Feng and his family after they survived the crisis and were able to buy back the villas.

When he heard from Qing Lian that Zhang Feng wanted to buy back the villas he was very pleased and gave the keys to Qing Lian to pass on to Zhang Feng. He said Zhang Feng did not need to give him all the money straight away, just move in and stay at first, and repay him slowly.

Listening to Qing Lian's account, everybody felt surprised and happy. Zhang Feng jumped up and wanted to embrace Qing Lian. But when he noticed Dan Dan and Yu Mei were at his sides, he hesitated. With smiles, Dan Dan and Yu Mei pushed him from behind, encouraging him to embrace her. Zhang Feng then embraced her gently. Dan Dan, Yu Mei and Dan Feng applauded them.

They would move back into the villas immediately as the lease term for the apartment would expire very soon. When they left the villas, Zhang Feng asked Qing Lian to convey his thanks to Huang Lei, and said he would finish the transaction procedure very soon for Huang Lei to get his money back. Dan Dan and Yu Mei made a point of inviting Qing Lian, with Lan Hua, to visit them and stay in the villas for some days. They were all in a good mood, so they stayed at the riverside to enjoy the beautiful scenery for a while.

Chapter IV

The Inspiring Olympic Games

One week later, Zhang Feng and his family moved back into the villas. The two families still lived like one family. They had each other's keys. They had dinner, chatted and watched TV together. Zhang Feng would stay in Dan Dan's villa two or three days each week. Now grown up, Dan Feng began to understand sexual relations between men and women. He knew his father would go into his mother's bedroom after he went to bed and fell asleep. But his father would return to his own bedroom before Dan Feng got up. 'That is so inconvenient,' he thought. He had noticed the changing attitudes of people towards love and sex in the country now, which were much more flexible than in the past. People did not care about sexual affairs outside the marriage as long as they did not destroy the family. 'But mother and second mother do not care about this special relationship, as both of them love my father deeply' he thought.

One evening, when Zhang Feng was staying in their villa, Zhang Feng asked Dan Feng about his postgraduate study. Dan Feng said he liked computing and information technology. The internet service was developing very rapidly in China, with the largest number of internet users in the world. E-commerce was also a new revolution of technology. He would help Zhang Feng to set up the website for his company, which could attract more clients.

He suddenly changed the topic when his parents listened to him with interest. He said one of his classmate's parents were divorced. But they still loved each other and occasionally stayed together even after he was remarried. His second wife could understand, so this did not cause their family any problems. Dan Feng said, like his classmates, he could fully understand this matter. Normal human desire should not be suppressed. He actually hinted to his parents about their relationship, which made them a bit embarrassed. After this they did not avoid being seen by their son in the same room, which made Dan Feng feel happy.

In order to repay Huang Lei for his help, Zhang Feng invited Huang Lei, Qing Lian and Lan Hua to his home for dinner. Apart from Northeast cuisine, Zhang Feng also bought a lot of seafood from a popular seafood restaurant. They enjoyed eating and chatting. Yu Mei asked them whether they regretted having left academic circles. Both Zhang Feng and Huang Lei said they did not regret it. Their contributions to society now were far more than just publishing articles of research. Huang Lei said,

"Zhang Feng's business gives people spacious and comfortable houses. Chinese people have a traditional idea of their homes which is similar to the English one, 'your home is your castle'. You will feel at ease when you have your own house.

It is also part of your wealth. In the past, people had to wait for many years to have a rented council house, which you had to give back to the government when you left."

"Huang Lei's fine chemical products not only sell well nationwide, but are also exported abroad and earn large sums of foreign exchange," Zhang Feng said. Dan Dan interrupted them and said,

"Do you know, people call you Group 92 businessmen as you are all members of the social elite with a good education and began your business in 1992. The businessmen at the very beginning of the reform in the 1980s are mostly farmers and self-employed vendors without a good education. People call them Group 84 businessmen. Some of them have already quit the market because of the high competition. Some of them still survive, like He Hua with her supermarkets and Song Ping with his electrical products chain stores."

Zhang Feng asked Qing Lian how her business with Li He was. She said their business had improved because of the economic stimulus policy from the government, and also the approaching Olympic Games. More people liked to have a holiday inland and abroad now. Zhang Feng asked Huang Lei and Qing Lian when they would marry. Huang Lei said he and Qing Lian would not bother to marry, as this would involve legal and financial bondage. They planned to just live together, which was much simpler. Zhang Feng and his two ladies agreed with them. Yu Mei said,

"That is fine, like Western people. You go with the trend."

Actually, Huang Lei knew of Qing Lian's old relationship with Zhang Feng, and that Lan Hua was their daughter. But he did not care as he regarded him as his good brother. He also knew Qing Lian still loved Zhang Feng. But Zhang Feng only regarded her as a little sister. Huang Lei was happy to live with Qing Lian as their personalities were complementary to each other. People needed to have a good living partner, even if their partners still fancied other lovers.

It was a hot August, and the Olympic Games would be held very soon. The Olympic Games organising committee recruited nearly two million volunteers. They particularly recruited university students, as this was the time of their summer vacation. Luckily, Dan Feng, Jian Jun, Lan Hua and Bai He were all recruited as traffic information, interpretation and urgent help volunteers. Their parents were all proud. They saw them off at the train station. Zhang Feng asked Dan Feng not to do something to offend Bai He, hinting that he should not have sex with her before they got married. Chang Zheng also said the same thing to Jian Jun. The two boys appeared to agree, but inside they thought that the old generation was too conservative. The younger generation was more liberal on sexuality.

Arriving in Beijing, they wandered around, filled with wonder and excitement. They had come here six years before, but they could not recognise a lot of the places they had visited then. Except for the ancient cultural sites like Tiananmen Square and Beihai Park, most other spaces were occupied by modern high buildings with glass walls. The ring motorways had increased from four to six. The underground also radiated in all directions. They lost their way quite often. Dan Feng said that since the reform had started thirty years earlier, urbanisation had developed very rapidly. All the cities had become bigger and higher.

After they reported to the volunteer centre, they were posted to an information stand near Tiananmen Square. It was a stand with a tent. There were leaflets and free beverages on the table.

Their work was to give direction to the people who would go to the venues of the games. There were so many foreigners travelling to Beijing to watch the matches but also wanted to see the culture and new face of the country.

On the second day, a few foreigners came to their stand. Pointing on a Beijing city map, they asked how to go the Heaven Temple Park. In English, Dan Feng told them the bus route and tube lines to get there. They thanked him for his help and told him that they came from Australia and were interested in Chinese culture. They also told the two boys and two girls that Australian people welcomed them to visit their country.

An old American asked them, stuttering in Chinese, where to find the Hu Tongs (traditional small alleys in Beijing). Dan Feng and his friends were surprised not only because this old man was able to speak a little bit of Chinese, but also that he knew Hu Tongs were a feature of Beijing culture. Jian Jun gave him a city map and showed him the area with typical Hu Tong architecture. Bai He asked the old man where he studied Chinese. The old man told her he came from California and he had been very interested in Chinese culture since his childhood. The rise of China started to attract more and more people around the world. A lot of adult education centres offered Chinese language classes, and he had studied the language for one year in his city. These Olympic Games were a good opportunity for him to see Chinese culture. He had heard that the Hu Tongs in Beijing were worth visiting, so he asked them where to find them.

Dan Feng and his friends felt their volunteer work was very rewarding, with a good chance to practise their English and to learn the impression foreigners had of China.

One day, there was a couple from Canada. The gentleman looked unwell. As a medical student, Bai He asked the lady what was wrong with her husband. The lady told Bai He that her husband felt dizzy. Bai He asked the gentleman to sit down and drink a cup of tea. After checking him, Bai He believed this man had a heatstroke and gave him some Chinese herbal medicine. He felt much better after ten minutes, and the couple kept thanking Bai He for her help.

The most interesting thing was the day there was an English middle-aged man asking them the way. He stopped to chat with them. He said he was surprised that China had become a totally modern society. His father was a missionary in China in the 1940s and brought back a lot of photos he had taken in China. From these photos, he thought China was still a poor country with narrow roads, decrepit houses, rickshaws and uneducated people with long braids. But he was very surprised that the country now had wide roads, skyscrapers, brand new cars on the street, huge airports and train stations, motorways, lively and clever people in colourful dresses and mobiles in their hands. It was a thoroughly modern country.

After listening to his speech, Dan Feng and his friends were very pleased. They told this man that the Chinese people had also experienced hardships and setbacks in modern times, but in the last thirty years, after the Cultural Revolution, the country drew political and economic lessons from the past and learned from the Western developed countries, carrying out great political and economic reforms. Therefore China now had become a more dynamic and prosperous society, although it still had some social issues to resolve. The English man praised their good English and said he welcomed them to visit his no longer glorious country which used to be 'the empire on which the sun never sets'. Dan Feng and his friends were amused by his English humour.

On 8 August, 2008, the opening ceremony of the 29th modern Olympic Games was held in Beijing. The attention of the country and the whole world was focused on Beijing. Zhang Feng, Chang Zheng, Wang Hai, Huang Lei used to love sports, so they all gathered in Zhang Feng's big sitting room to watch the live broadcast of the games on Zhang Feng's newly purchased big HD screen TV. Chinese athletes kept winning more and more medals. Chinese people hoped they would get the most medals this time, as China was the host of the games. Dan Dan, Yu Mei and Qing Lian became servants, providing a steady stream of beverages and snacks. If there were some finals, they needed to cook dinner for them as well.

At the opening ceremony, they all felt amazed by the performance directed by the famous director Zhang Yimo. At the very beginning of the ceremony, people saw huge footprints magically formed in the sky by fireworks, one after another moving to the central stadium, When the last one appeared in the sky above the stadium, it was the 29th, representing the 29th modern Olympic Games. The famous gymnast Li Ning flew to the torch tower to fire the torch. The performance with the background of Chinese culture pleasantly surprised the audiences around the world. Zhang Feng and his friends believed this ceremony was the most amazing performed in the history of the Olympic Games.

During the two weeks of the games, Zhang Feng and his friends were bursting with excitement every day, especially when Chinese sportsmen won medals. In the end, for the first time ever, Chinese athletes won the most gold medals and came second in the list of total number of medals. Zhang Feng and his friends leapt from their chairs and cheered. All the people in the whole country were also excited, because it showed to the world that Chinese people were no longer the 'Sick Men of Asia'. This was a successful Olympic games, with nearly forty world records broken. The American swimmer Phelps and the Jamaican sprinter Bolt were brilliant stars. Both Zhang Feng and Chang Zheng had been athletes in middle school and competed against each other in a competition. In the end, Zhang Feng won both the high jump and the 100 metres race, winning the heart of Yu Mei.

Chang Zheng teased Yu Mei by asking her whether she felt sorry then because he had lost to Zhang Feng. Yu Mei smiled and said, quite the opposite, as she only regarded him as her brother but not a lover. Everyone started to laugh at him, and said it was his wishful thinking that Yu Mei was his girlfriend. But Wang Hai and Huang Lei said it was very interesting that the two rivals in the past were the previous mayor and the incumbent. Chang Zheng sighed and said he envied Zhang Feng because he had left the sea of politics. Yet he still fought against corrupt officials like Shen and Li, which made him feel tired.

Seeing the CCP chairman Hu Jintao at the opening ceremony, Zhang Feng and his friends also talked about their impressions of the two top leaders, Chairman Hu Jintao and Premier Wen Jianbao. Because they were not the 'red younger generation' of the old communist leaders, they did not have bureaucratic airs and were closer to the people, especially Wen Jiaobao, who emphasised political reforms to make the country more democratic. But some old leaders and left-wing elements did not like him as they did not want to lose their privileges. Possibly because of the Olympic Games, the Chinese Communist Party wanted to give the world an impression of openness and freedom, so the political atmosphere was very relaxed in 2008. Some scholars dared to speak openly about a constitutional society and multi-party rule in China. Liu Xiaobo and 300 other celebrities even drafted Charter 08, asking the communist party to give up single-party rule and adopt the Western-style democratic political system. Zhang Feng, Chang Zheng and Wang Hai thought Charter 08 represented the wishes of the Western-oriented elites and liberal groups inside the party. Taiwan was an example that Chinese society was able to establish a democratic political system. Some old leaders and left-wing leaders inside the party believed the single-party rule in Singapore was their example. But the democratic groups inside and outside the part insisted Singapore was only a city, not a big country, with totally different social conditions.

Chang Zheng said one of the problems was that people worried the minority regions might want to leave China if the country became a democratic one. In the end, everyone thought the country should at least allow people to discuss their social structure freely without punishment. The flexible atmosphere now was a good thing, meaning they no longer had a similar situation as during the Cultural Revolution.

On New Year's Eve of 2009, Zhang Feng held a party at home with his friends and colleagues. Apart from Wang Hai, Li He, Chang Zheng, Huang Lei and Qing Lian, he also invited Lin Jianguo, Chen Tao, Liang Hua, Wang Li and He Hua. There were also some children at the party. During his toast, Zhang Feng said,

"2008 is really a year of great joys and sorrows. Our country suffered from natural and man-made disasters. Our company also experienced a business crisis. But the government stimulus policy rescued our economy, and we survived the crisis. We also successfully held the Olympic Games."

"Another happy event was our astronaut who walked in

space for the first time in history. The sad events also included the poisoned milk powder, making a lot of children sick," Wang Hai said.

Dan Dan said, yes, we should draw lessons and carry on the reform. All of the people at the party made a toast to friendship and cooperation.

During the party, Zhang Feng and Dan Dan came to Liang Hua and Wang Li and congratulated them on their marriage. Dan Dan said to Liang Hua with an apology that she had delayed his marriage for too long. Still showing love in his eyes, Liang politely said it did not matter as life was changing.

Zhang Feng teased Wang Li,

"How are things going now, Ophelia, are you happy to live with the Prince of Norway?"

She quipped,

"Oh, CEO Hamlet, after giving Ophelia to others, you can enjoy your life with your two queens."

Liang Hua said he did not understand what they were talking about. Zhang Feng laughed and told him to ask his wife.

Toasting He Hua, he said he was happy to know that she had just opened her sixth supermarket in the city. She was a successful Group 84 businesswoman. He Hua said her business was very small, could not compare with Zhang Feng's at all.

After drinking a lot of alcohol, Zhang Feng felt a bit hot, so he walked into the back garden to enjoy the winter scenery. Suddenly he heard Qing Lian's voice behind him,

"Brother Feng, I am very pleased you have survived the crisis and have a double harvest in love and career."

Zhang Feng noticed a bitter tone in her voice, so he asked her,

"Having a happy life with Huang Lei?"

She realised he was trying to comfort her, so she said,

"He is a good partner. I like and respect him. But…" she looked at Zhang Feng, "I really only love one man." Then she quickly kissed him on his face and ran back to the villa, leaving Zhang Feng trying to wipe the lipstick off his face.

Part VI

A Golden Age with Some Social Issues

Chapter I

The Big Development of Urbanisation

Two years passed in the blink of an eye. 2010 came. Like the real estate industry around the country, Zhang Feng's company entered the fast track of development. Because of the economic reforms, private developers' companies were able to enter the market, replacing the slow and inefficient state companies. In the last thirty years, they made the cities in the country bigger, higher, and modern.

On a warm day in spring, Zhang Feng was sitting in his office. Although he was sixty years old now, he still looked strong and sturdy, with only a bit of grey hair at his temples. Dan Dan and Yu Mei sat on the sofa. They still looked like mature beautiful women in their forties. When they went shopping with Lan Hua and Bai He, people could regard them as the elder sisters of the two girls.

Zhang Feng was discussing advanced modern city architecture with them. This huge complex was not only used for shopping, but also provided catering, entertainment and leisure services. Yu Mei said it looked similar to some shopping malls in Singapore. Zhang Feng said,

"This complex will provide more services to people than they expected. So we could call it 'Happy City', as it can let people, especially young people, stay there the whole day without feeling bored."

"This project is very advanced. This could be the direction of city development in the future. We should give the plan to our staff and get their opinions and suggestions." Dan Dan and Yu Mei said.

After the plan was given to the staff and workers, their response was very enthusiastic. They believed this project was a very advanced modern city project and made many suggestions. Zhang Feng gave the plan to Chang Zheng, who also liked it. He said the city council would support it, but it needed approval from the provincial department because it was a huge project.

After handing in the plan to the Provincial Construction Bureau, Zhang Feng, Dan Dan and Yu Mei were worried as their enemy Governor Shen could oppose this project. As they expected, the bureau turned down the plan and said it was too big and would occupy too much land. Obviously, Shen was behind the rejection of this project, because he could use his position to take revenge on a personal enemy. Zhang Feng and his staff felt disappointed.

Chang Zheng called Zhang Feng, saying he had expected this result. But there was an opportunity for Zhang Feng to get his project approved. There would be a visit by a minister from the Commercial Development Department from Beijing to inspect the situation of commercial developments in Northeast cities. Chang Zheng would recommend Zhang Feng's project to him. If this minister was interested in this project, Shen would not be able to block the plan.

One week later, the minister from CDD visited Jili City. Chang Zheng introduced Zhang Feng to him and showed him the plan. He was very interested in the project and said there were similar shopping malls in the South and they attracted many people. These shopping malls recouped their costs in just a few years. He said he would ask the provincial government to accept Zhang Feng's plan. At the end of the talk, the minister said to Zhang Feng with a smile that it was no wonder that Zhang Feng's project was well considered, because he was the previous mayor.

Not daring to defy the minister's request, Shen had to approve Zhang Feng's plan. Zhang Feng and his staff were very pleased. They mobilised all the staff and workers to construct this huge 'city inside a city' and tried to finish it in one year.

After one year, the spring breeze turned the River City green again. Dan Feng found a job in a foreign electronics company after he finished his postgraduate study. Jian Jun worked in an architectural design academy. One day, Dan Feng told his lover and friends that his father had finished his huge project, the Happy City. At the weekend, he asked them to wander around this huge complex with him.

They met at the entrance of the complex. Looking up at this huge building with glass walls, they were amazed.

They entered the complex and saw the huge hall and eight storeys of service areas, which left them feeling dazzled. The two girls preferred to go shopping and wanted to go to some famous brand shops first. Dan Feng winked at Jian Jun and said to the girls that they would go the electronics shops. They would meet the girls after two hours in the catering section.

The two boys actually went to the jewellery shops because they planned to buy rings and propose to the girls that day. The Western style of marriage proposal was more fashionable among the younger generation in China nowadays. It took them almost one hour to choose nice rings. In the end, they followed the recommendations of the female assistant and bought two rings they thought the girls would like.

They met the girls at noon, so Jian Jun suggested having something to eat. They moved up to the catering level but were overwhelmed after they looked at the signboard, because there were almost a hundred restaurants there, including famous Chinese cuisines such as Guangdong, Sichuan, Hong Kong, Taiwan as well as foreign cuisines including French, Italian, English, Mexican, Japanese, Korean. Lan Hua said,

"Let's choose among Japanese, Korean or Taiwanese."

Dan Feng said he wanted to try three-cup chicken in a Taiwanese restaurant as Mr Du had recommended this dish to his father. They went over to the Taiwanese restaurant but there was a long queue outside and they waited for half an hour before getting a table. They liked the three-cup chicken very much as it was so tasty, and said they would recommend the dish to their friends.

After lunch, they wanted some entertainment. They went to the cinema at the rear of the complex. The boys liked James Bond films, so they watched the latest 007 adventure together. Leaving the cinema, Lan Hua said, "I have really enjoyed myself, do we really need to go home yet?"

Dan Feng said, "Sister, Father told me that people could stay here the whole day without feeling bored. Let's find something else to do."

They found a beautiful indoor garden with exotic plants and flowers. There were some coffee bars, a tea house and a karaoke bar inside. A few couples were dancing inside a coffee bar that had a marble dance floor in the middle. Dan Feng danced with Bai He and Jian Jun danced with Lan Hua. The two girl were flushed with happiness. After the music stopped, Dan Feng winked at Jian Jun. Then he asked the girls to stand in the middle of the dance floor, saying he wanted to see which one was taller. When the girls were confused, the boys knelt down on one knee in front of them and raised their hands with the rings, saying in unison,

"Will you marry me?"

The people inside the coffee bar all stood up to watch them. Feeling so many people's eyes on them, the two girls were shy. They covered their faces with one hand and offered their other hand to the boys for them to put the rings on. The people around them burst into warm applause.

Another big city construction project was to rebuild the shanty areas where Wang Hai's family used to live. Many poor people lived in these areas, including the redundant workers. These areas blighted the modern face of the city, so the city council planned to demolish these shabby houses and build better accommodation for these people. The local government contracted developers for this work. The developers paid a demolition fee to compensate the residents or gave them new apartments after these areas were rebuilt. But the problem was some developers did not give enough compensation to the residents there, so they refused to move out and became a 'nail household'.

One morning, Lin Jianguo entered Zhang Feng's office and told him one of the households was in serious conflict with a developer because he had offered them very low demolition compensation and the household refused to move out. The developer was prepared to use force to push out the people living there, which might have serious consequences.

Zhang Feng and his colleagues decided to see the place as his company was about to accept some rebuilding projects. As they got closer they heard noise, curses and crying. The spot was surrounded by a lot of onlookers. Zhang Feng and his colleagues pushed their way through the crowd and saw a shocking scene: two bulldozers were facing an old house. A dozen people were standing in front of the house, shouting at the developers and a group of police,

"Three generations of our family all live here. The demolition compensation you have offered us is not enough to buy a one-bedroom flat. How we can find a proper property to stay in?"

A developer with grey hair roared at the residents,

"I have already given you enough money. You just need to add a little bit of your savings to buy a house. You cannot rely only on the public funds!"

Cai Wenge! Zhang Feng and Yu Mei recognised this villain straightaway. It seemed that again it was Shen who had helped him to get this project. A resident next to Zhang Feng told him that the compensation given by Cai was much lower than that of other developers. He then used force to drive away those who did not want to move.

Cai shouted at the residents that they had five minutes to leave, otherwise the police would use force to drive them away and the bulldozers would knock down the house. Zhang Feng knew these policemen were corrupt and received bribes from Cai. When Cai started to count down, an old woman inside the house came out and poured gasoline on her clothes and shouted,

"If you dare to knock down my house, I will burn myself in front of you!"

Cai thought the old lady was just bluffing, so he shouted to the bulldozer drivers,

"Do not listen to her! Go ahead and knock down the house. What she poured on herself is not gasoline but water!"

But when the two bulldozers started to move forward, the old lady lit the gasoline with a lighter, and her small body was surrounded by flames.

"She will die!" the onlookers screamed. Some of them ran to the old lady and tried to put out the flames on her body. Cai Wenge, the policemen and the bulldozer drivers were all scared. Somebody called an ambulance. By the time it arrived, the fire had been put out but the old woman was severely burnt. People around all berated Cai as a corrupt, evil businessman. Scared by the old woman's action, Cai and his accomplices ran away, but some journalists with a deep sense of justice had taken photos of the accident. Zhang Feng and his colleagues stormed off the site.

Back at the company, Dan Dan said there had been other cases of violence and protests caused by these demolition projects. A lot of them were caused by collusion between corrupt officials and greedy businessmen, like this incident caused by Cai and Shen. Yu Mei said,

"If we had been contracted for the project to rebuild the shanty area, we would rather make less profit than exploit poor residents. They should be the beneficiaries of the reform, not its victims."

The photos of this tragedy in the newspaper aroused people's anger. On behalf of the city council, Chang Zheng gave Cai Wenge a heavy fine. His contract to develop this area was also annulled. Cai was made responsible for the costs of the victim's medical treatment and he was ordered to pay her a sizeable compensation. Zhang Feng and Chang Zheng knew Cai was backed by Shen. But without evidence, there was no way to inform against him.

Before they knew it, 2012 had come. Zhang Feng and his colleagues realised that urbanisation meant not only the expansion of the main cities, but also towns and rural communities. Some migrant workers in his company told him that their hometowns in the countryside had now become medium-sized cities. Zhang Feng considered that developing village and county towns was a big potential market. He decided to go to Hua Dan County, where he had spent eight years farming during the Cultural Revolution, and helped He Hua to carry out the Land Contract Scheme when he was the mayor of the city. In the past, it took many hours to get there by train and bus. But now the motorway network had connected most large and medium-sized cities. Zhang Feng had bought a new Audi made by Wang Hai's car company, and he was keen to try it out on the motorway. With Lin Jianguo and Chen Tao in his car, he drove about two hours to arrive in Hua Dan County.

Entering the town, they could not recognise it. In the past, it only had twenty to thirty old, low buildings. But now they could see over a hundred six or seven-storey buildings and a few thirty to forty-storey high buildings. The streets were very wide, with willows and poplars on both sides. There were also some wide squares surrounded by high commercial buildings. The county town now looked like a medium-sized city. Zhang Feng and his colleagues were really amazed. It seemed that urbanisation development had spread all over the country and the farmers also had an opportunity to work in cities now.

Walking around the town, they visited some estate agents

to find out the price of houses, which was about half that in Jili City. They started to understand why a lot of workers migrated to the main cities to earn money, and then bought houses in their hometowns. The properties in county towns were more spacious, brighter and warmer than their mud and straw houses in the village.

At noon, they found a dumpling restaurant to have lunch. Entering the restaurant, they heard a familiar voice,

"Brother Zhang, it is very nice to see you here!" They saw smartly dressed He Hua sitting at a table with a man in his sixties. The elderly man stood up and greeted them with warmth,

"Mayor Zhang, Director Lin, Director Chen, haven't seen you for many years." The elderly man was the previous county Secretary He, who had supported Zhang Feng to carry out the Land Contract Scheme with He Hua and also helped them to do the village-township enterprises. They shook hands with each other, then they sat down to chat.

He Hua told Zhang Feng that she already had six supermarkets in Jili City and she would also like to open some in county towns, because they had become medium-sized cities and the citizens here needed supermarkets to provide them with good quality food. Organic food had become popular in China in recent years, and He Hua and her village team had established an organic food cooperative with one-stop production and sales. Her village team grew organic vegetables and sold them directly in her supermarkets. This business was booming as there were no other competitors. Zhang Feng praised her for her clever business sense.

Secretary He said he was retired, but was still concerned about the development of the county. He met He Hua often to discuss possible new projects. He knew Zhang Feng had left the political circles and now had a business with real estate development. He asked Zhang Feng whether he was interested in building a shopping centre in the county town.

Discussing it with Lin and Chen, Zhang Feng said, yes, his company was able to do it as the land here was cheap and the market demand was high enough. His colleagues would draw a detailed plan to submit to the county Industry and Trading Bureau. Secretary He was very pleased. They then enjoyed the tasty dumplings and drank local beers.

After lunch, Zhang Feng said he missed He Hua's village as he had not visited it in twenty years. He regarded the village as his second hometown because he had worked there as an educated youth for eight years during the Cultural Revolution. In the 1980s he helped He Hua carry out the Land Contract Scheme to improve their grain output and also helped her to establish village-township enterprises. He Hua said she also wanted to go back to her village to see how the business of their organic vegetable cooperative was going. She told Zhang Feng there was a guest house in her village and Zhang Feng and his colleagues could stay there. Lin Jianguo and Chen Tao were also very happy to see He Hua's modern village again.

Bidding farewell to Secretary He, Zhang Feng, He Hua, Lin and Chen drove to He Hua's village. What leapt into their eyes were endless plastic greenhouses, with all sorts of fresh vegetables inside. From a distance, they could see tractors and other machines working on the fields. At the entrance of a greenhouse, Zhang Feng and his colleagues met He Hua's brother, the grey-haired team head Pan. He greeted Zhang Feng and told him about the great changes in the last twenty years since the Land Contract Scheme. Head Pan said that because more and more farmers had moved to big cities and worked there, a new scheme of 'land transfer' had begun. A large amount of land was transferred to big grain growers, cooperative farms and agriculture parks, which strove to improve efficiency and increase output by using machines and advanced technology. Zhang Feng thought they sounded like the family farms in the USA. Chen Tao said they were very similar, but the ownership was still collective.

Entering the greenhouse and seeing the lovely fresh vegetables, Zhang Feng asked Head Pan about the sales and profit of their business. Pan proudly told Zhang Feng that demand exceeded supply. He also told Zhang Feng that they grew organic crops without using any chemical fertilisers, and their price was twice that of normal crops.

In the evening, Head Pan and his team members cooked a farmhouse meal for Zhang Feng and his colleagues. They stayed in the comfortable village guesthouse for one night. He Hua told Zhang Feng that she planned to promote agricultural tourism to attract the city dwellers. Here there were mountains, rivers and fresh air, which could be enjoyed by the people from crowded cities.

He Hua's plan reminded Zhang Feng of a longstanding wish. He asked He Hua whether she still remembered what he had said twenty years ago. He wished to build a farmhouse and retire here. He Hua smiled and said she remembered, but she thought he was joking at the time. Zhang Feng said he would turn sixty-five in a few years and was looking forward to quitting the stressful business and enjoying a relaxing rural life. He asked her if there was any place nearby suitable for retirement life. He Hua thought for a while and said there happened to be a good place not far from here.

The next day, He Hua led Zhang Feng to a place about ten

kilometres from her village, where there was a peaceful lake surrounded by hills and woods, with green grassland, many flowers, fish swimming in the crystal clear lake and the singing of colourful birds in the woods. This beautiful scenery was completed by the blue sky, white clouds and bright sunshine.

Sighing in admiration, Zhang Feng said it was almost a Utopian land of peace and happiness away from the turmoil of the world. Lin Jianguo said,

"You could build a bungalow on the lakeside, grow vegetables in the back garden and raise chickens and ducks."

Chen Tao suggested installing solar power and a marsh gas tank for the house. He Hua asked if it would be similar to the ecological park in England and Zhang Feng said he hoped so.

Zhang Feng said it was really an ideal place to spend his retirement, but he would need planning permission to build a house here. He Hua said it should be easy to get planning permission from the county. But she still believed Zhang Feng would spend his retirement in the city as he had children and a big family there, and she was surprised when Zhang Feng really moved there a few years later.

Chapter II

A Life-and-Death Struggle against Corruption

The spring of 2013 came. The new leaders of the CCP realised the uncontrolled corruption could damage the party and the country. So they launched a vigorous movement against corruption in the name of 'slap the tiger and swat the flies'. The party set up a discipline commission at various levels and sent inspection teams to the local authorities.

After the second inspection team came to Jili City, the team called on people to report corrupt actions, which made Governor Shen and his followers panic, as he had made a lot of money illegally for many years and had sex with a lot of women. He was also worried that his political enemies, including Chang Zheng and Zhang Feng, might use this opportunity to knock him down politically. He planned to strike first to gain the upper hand. He needed to fabricate a charge against Chang Zheng to distract the attention of the inspectors.

Chang Zheng's secretary was a single middle-aged woman with average looks. He did not want a pretty, young woman to work as his secretary, to avoid trouble as people said pretty, young women were usually their superior's mistress. One day, his secretary left the office late. On the street, she was sexually harassed by some hooligans. When she called for help, a young man rushed out to rescue her. She was grateful to him and invited him to a meal. Since then they started dating. This young man said his name was Huang Hong, a manager in a company, and still single. He praised her mature looks. She was flattered and started to take the relationship seriously.

One day, Huang Hong rang her to invite her to dinner. She said she could finish her work earlier as Mayor Chang Zheng was in a meeting in another department. Huang said he would drive to her office to pick her up. At 5.00pm, Huang came to her office. He said he was curious to see how luxurious the offices of the city leaders were. The secretary let him in, but when they had just started to talk, a person who claimed to be a policeman telephoned her and told her that some criminal had stolen her money from her bank card and asked her to check her card. Because her bank card was in her bag in her office, she asked Huang to wait for her, and went her own office. In that one minute, Huang quickly put a big envelope into a drawer of Chang Zheng's desk. The secretary returned to the office and told Huang that the police had made a mistake, her money had not been stolen. Then they went to dinner.

In the evening, the inspectors received an anonymous phone call, saying the city mayor Chang Zheng had accepted a bribe from somebody. If the team searched his office, they would find the illicit money. The team needed to check whether this accusation was true, even though they knew Chang Zheng was an honest official from the feedback of the citizens.

The next day, when Chang Zheng went to his office, he saw several inspection team members standing outside his office. He thought they had come to discuss the corruption cases with him. But he was surprised when they said somebody had informed them of his corruption and they had to search his office. Chang Zheng calmly let them in because he had not received any illegal money. The team members asked him to wait outside and started to search his office. He was surprised when, after two minutes, the team members asked him to enter the office, and showed him a big envelope on his desk. They told him they had found this envelope in a drawer of his desk, and asked what was inside. Chang Zheng said he had never seen this envelope before and did not know what was inside. They opened the envelope and found a wad of cash inside. There was also an advertisement leaflet of Zhang Feng's company inside.

Chang Zheng realised that somebody planned to frame him, and tried to kill two birds with one stone by also implicating Zhang Feng. It seemed a typical case of collusion between officials and businessmen. Chang Zheng told the team that somebody had tried to frame him and Zhang Feng. He and Zhang Feng were good friends so if he wanted to bribe him, he could give him the money at home and did not need to send the money to his office. He asked the team to investigate this case. The team members told him that Chang Zheng would be supervised during the investigation. He was also suspended from his post temporarily and could not return home.

Zhang Feng was also interviewed by the inspection team the following day. Zhang Feng said it was obviously a conspiracy to frame him and Chang Zheng. He suggested to the team to check who had the key to Chang Zheng's office. They said only Chang Zheng's female secretary had the key, but the inspector of the city's economic investigation team had already asked her about this, and she said she had not brought anybody to the office. Zhang Feng knew this inspector was Shen's lackey. During the incident with the building collapse, he had tried to press criminal charges against Zhang Feng. When this inspector questioned the secretary, he hinted to her that as long as she could confirm she did not bring anybody to the office, she would not be punished, otherwise, she would be put in jail. She was scared and immediately said she did not bring anybody to the office.

The supervision team did not detain Zhang Feng, but only asked him to stay in the city waiting for further questions.

Zhang Feng discussed the situation with his ladies and colleagues. Dan Dan said the inspection team did not have any direct evidence to prove the money had been sent by Zhang Feng. But if they were unable to find who was behind this, the case would remain unresolved and Chang Zheng would not keep his post.

Lin Jianguo said the key person was the female secretary. He would visit her with his friend Captain Fan of the city's detective team. Captain Fan had helped them in the building collapse incident. Zhang Feng agreed.

Lin Jianguo and Captain Fan found the female secretary and persuaded her to tell the truth, which would help to clear Chang Zheng's name. She quite respected Chang Zheng and regarded him as an honest official. In the end, she told them about the suspicious young man Huang Hong who tried to seduce her and went into the office. After Chang Zheng was detained, she tried to contact him, but his mobile was always switched off. He had not given her his home address or told her where he worked. Lin and Fan asked her to try hard to recall anything he had mentioned to her. Thinking for a while, she remembered that he said his home was near North Bank Bridge and he quite often went jogging on the bridge. She said Huang was about six feet high, thin, with a mole under his left ear. Lin and Fan were pleased to get this information.

Starting the next day, Lin and Fan went running on the North Bank Bridge and tried to find any runner who looked like Huang Hong. But they did not find any runner like him. On the third day, they waited on the bridge until 9.00 when people started to work. Just when they felt disappointed and prepared to leave, they suddenly saw a tall man running slowly from the other end of the bridge. Lin and Fan leaned on the rail and pretended to view the scenery. When the man got closer, they held out their cigarettes and asked him,

"Brother, a light, please."

The man stopped and responded, "I do not smoke."

In those few seconds, both Fan and Lin noticed a mole under his left ear. Fan showed the man his police badge and said to him,

"I am the police. You are under investigation!"

Huang was a coward, he immediately knelt down and said,

"I will confess everything."

He was brought back to the police station, where the female secretary identified him as Huang Hong. Huang admitted that he was asked to seduce the secretary and leave the envelope in Chang Feng's office. He got fifty thousand yuan in advance and would get another fifty thousand after completing the job. He told Fan the physical characteristics of the person who gave him this task.

Captain Fan quickly found the man behind Huang Hong. He was the secretary of Director Li, Shen's flunkey. Obviously it had been a set-up. Both Captain Fan and Lin Jianguo were very happy. The names of Chang Zheng and Zhang Feng would be cleared. Lin Jianguo rang Zhang Feng, telling him the good news. Then he and Captain Fan rushed to the inspection team to rescue Chang Zheng. In these few days, Shen used the media he controlled to give enormous publicity to this case and said it was an extraordinary case of collusion between officials and businessmen, and the inspection team would punish Chang Zheng and Zhang Feng severely.

Entering the office of the second inspection team, Captain Fan and Lin Jianguo told the head of the team the truth of this case. The head said they also had doubts about the case as they had received many reports about the corrupt activities of Shen and Li. It seemed they planned to distract the attention of the team with Chang Zheng's case. Yet the feedback the team received about Chang Zheng and Zhang Feng were all very positive. Almost all the citizens said Chang Feng was an honest leader, and Zhang Feng was a Confucian style businessman.

The team head led Fan and Lin to the room where Chang Zheng was detained. In the corridor outside the room, they heard somebody rebuking Chang Zheng. The voice came from Governor Shen,

"Chang Zheng, you should see the situation clearly and confess your crime. Then you might get a lighter punishment. Otherwise even your retired admiral father cannot save you."

When Chang Zheng tried to argue with him, the head of the team opened the door. Seeing the head, Shen said to him,

"Chang Zheng is very stubborn. You must give him a heavy sentence to calm the public anger!"

But he was surprised when he saw Lin and Fan behind the team head. The team head said to him,

"Deputy Governor Shen, you are so impatient. Mayor Chang Zheng was framed. We have found the perpetrator and plotter."

Hearing these words from the head, Shen said immediately, "I need to leave for a meeting." Then he left, dejected.

Chang Zheng knew it was Captain Fan and Lin Jianguo who had solved the case. He stood up and embraced Fan and Lin. He shook hands with the team head and said he would work hard to cooperate with the team to carry out the anti-corruption campaign.

While Chang Zheng and Zhang Feng celebrated their escape from Shen's frame-up, Shen was preparing his escape. He knew he was hated by a lot of people as he had done so many corrupt things: he had obtained several hundred million yuan of illegal money, he had sold posts to his subordinates, he had over twenty mistresses. Like a lot of corrupt officials, his wife and son had already immigrated to Canada. He also had several passports with visas. His followers Li and Cai disappeared to avoid punishment. He got a secret message that the inspection team would detain him soon, so he went to the airport in the middle of the night. He planned to fly to Beijing first, then fly to Canada to meet his family and have a fairytale happy life there.

He was on board the aeroplane, waiting for it to take off. He was starting to feel relief when somebody touched him on the shoulder,

"Deputy Governor Shen, you are charged with extorting a large amount of money and other crimes. Please come with us." With a deep sigh, Shen said to himself, 'God does not bless me.'

After hiding for a few days, Li Qiu was arrested at the train station when he planned to run away to another province. Cai Wenge surrendered himself to the police, trying to get a lighter punishment. Over twenty officials at city and province level were prosecuted for their corruption. People called it 'landslide corruption', which perhaps was the result of the free market or was caused by defects of the political system.

During the celebration party, Chang Zheng and Zhang Feng thanked Captain Fan and Lin Jianguo again for their great help. Sighing with emotion, Chang Zheng said,

"It is so difficult to be an honest official as the temptation of money and women is great. If you cannot control yourself, you will fall in the trap. Yet, if you do not take illegal money, you only have a property allocated by the government, a small living allowance and special wards for high-ranking officers in hospital after retirement. But those corrupt officials can emigrate to the West to have a luxurious life like millionaires."

"If we only depend on the Singapore style anti-corruption bureau, we are unable to eliminate corruption completely. We must improve our political system to control power. Chinese people now also know the wise saying by Lord Acton, 'Power tends to corrupt, and absolute power corrupts absolutely.'" Zhang Feng said.

"You can find corruption in many countries to different degrees. If we do not control the spread of corruption, our country will be in danger, like the end of many dynasties in our history," Dan Dan said.

A few weeks later, the provincial court sentenced Shen to twelve years in prison. Li Qiu was sentenced to ten years. Other corrupt officials got similar sentences. Cai only got four years as he surrendered himself and voluntarily returned the illegal money. After an investigation, Chang Zheng was exonerated as an honest officer, and he was promoted to Shen's post as a deputy provincial governor. Zhang Feng and friends were pleased as their sworn enemies were punished and their good friend was promoted. Yet they were sure that corruption would not be controlled totally if the country did not have further political reforms.

Our characters had joy in worry and worry in joy. Their younger generation had married late because these boys and girls concentrated on their education and careers and were keen to create their own futures without relying on their rich and powerful parents. Dan Feng was twenty-nine years old and had his own website design company. Jian Jun was thirty years old and had an architect design studio. Dan Feng's fiancée Bai He was a gynaecologist. Lan Hua, Jian Jun's fiancée and the daughter of Zhang Feng and Qing Lian, was a commercial solicitor.

Urged by their parents, the two boys and two girls started to prepare for their wedding. They did not like the popular ostentatious, expensive weddings. They preferred a Western-style wedding with a relaxed and happy atmosphere. So they arranged an open wedding in a nice garden on the riverside. Their parents all agreed.

One day in summer, the popular River City wedding garden was full of laughter and joy. The joint wedding of Dan Feng, Bai He, Jian Jun and Lan Hua was held here. It was a private wedding, without government officials and business partners. Wang Hai, Zhang Lin, Li He, Qing Lian, and Huang Lei arrived first, then Lin Jianguo, Chen Tao, Captain Fan and He Hua came. Five minutes before the wedding, Wang Li and Liang Hua also came.

The wedding started with lively music. In their formal suits, Dan Feng and Jian Jun stood on the platform. The brides were in their beautiful white wedding dresses. Zhang Feng held Lan Hua's arm, Li He held Bai He's arm, and they walked slowly towards the platform. Then led by the host, the brides and grooms swore their marriage vows. The grooms kissed the brides to the applause of the guests. The wedding was full of laughter and cheers. The participants all felt that the Western-style wedding was more interesting and relaxing, with a human touch.

After the wedding, the two couples did not want properties from their parents. They would rent first, and then buy their own properties after they had saved enough. Zhang Feng and Chang Zheng were pleased that their children were independent and did not rely on their parents.

Chapter III

A Golden Age with Worries

Another year had passed rapidly. Zhang Feng's company developed steadily in a fiercely competitive market. It had become one of the top ten real estate companies in the country. Zhang Feng kept in mind the lessons from the last crisis, avoiding over-borrowing and unreasonable business expansion. At the same time, he still needed to carefully fight against corruption.

Nearing the official retirement age, he started to consider his business successor. He, together with Dan Dan and Yu Mei, persuaded Dan Feng to leave his business to his partner and travel to the UK to study for an MBA degree. Then he would have mastery of company management skills. Dan Feng agreed to this arrangement.

Being busy with his business for so many years, Zhang Feng did not have time to travel around the country. He wanted to relax and also to see the great changes in the country since the reform movement had started three decades earlier. Dan Dan said she would stay to look after the business of the company and asked Yu Mei to travel with Zhang Feng.

Zhang Feng chose Shanghai as his first stop as it was the largest city in China and the financial centre of the country. The high-speed railway was being built rapidly in recent years and the national network had expanded. Zhang Feng wanted to experience what it felt like to travel by high-speed train, so he flew to Beijing first with Yu Mei, and then took the train from there to Shanghai. At the railway station, they saw the beautiful Harmony train, with shining carriages and a bullet-like engine. The seats were very comfortable, especially the first class and business class seats.

After the train left Beijing, it speeded up. The outside scenery was rapidly moving backwards. The travelling speed on the screen quickly changed: 100, 150, 200, 250, 300, at last, the figure stopped at 350 km per hour. Zhang Feng and Yu Mei felt it was almost like sitting in an aeroplane. Magically, they felt very stable, without shaking. When they looked at their teacups, the tea inside was motionless. Zhang Feng said to Yu Mei that Chinese engineers were amazing. Initially, they had learned from Japanese and German engineers. But now they had overtaken them. The total length of the high-speed rail in China was number one in the world now. Zhang Feng still remembered when he had travelled by normal train from Beijing to Shanghai in 1984, the journey took more than half a day. But this trip by high-speed train took less than five hours.

Arriving in Shanghai, Zhang Feng could not recognise the city. Thirty years before, he remembered some European style buildings and low, dull-coloured buildings on the western bank of the river. The eastern side of the river was a wild field. But now the city was a magnificent metropolis with so many skyscrapers. The eastern side of the river looked like New York City. Apart from the East Pearl TV Tower, you could see the 632-metre high Shanghai Centre, which was the second-highest building in the world. You could also see the 421-metre high Jinmao Tower and the 492-metre Global Finance Centre.

Zhang Feng admired Chinese engineering, as building one-hundred-storey buildings in such a narrow space in the city was a very difficult task. The cityscape of Shanghai was very modern now. There were so many huge bridges flying over the Huangpu River. There were wide streets, the underground going in all directions, motorways surrounding the city. The previous slum areas were replaced by tall modern buildings. Both Zhang Feng and Yu Mei sighed with emotion. It seemed that when the wisdom and capability of Chinese people were released, they would produce surprising creativity. Fortunately, the economic reform succeeded.

After the sightseeing, Zhang Feng and Yu Mei went to the seaside. Sitting on the beach and enjoying the blue sea view, they felt relaxed. Seeing the other couples embracing and kissing each other, Yu Mei leaned on Zhang Feng's shoulder and said to him,

"Brother Feng, I have been with you for over forty years. Do you still love me? As I am old and not pretty now."

Holding her tightly, Zhang Feng said with emotion,

"Why do you say this? You are a fairy and never get old. You look like a woman only in her mid-thirties, with exceeding beauty. Remember how many times when we have meals in restaurants, the waiters tell me I can sit at that table with my daughter. It means we look like we are from different generations."

"You do not look old. Yesterday there were a few young girls who called you handsome brother," Yu Mei gushed.

"They just flattered me," he said.

"Many Shanghai men lack masculinity, so you are attractive to Shanghai women." Yu Mei said.

Watching the surging sea, Yu Mei asked him,

"Brother, am I still a turbulent sea in your mind?"

"Yes, unless one day the sea is totally calm. To you, my emotions are always in a constant turbulent riot." He said.

Yu Mei held his neck and kissed him.

Returning from South China, Yu Mei asked Zhang Feng to travel to the Southwest with Dan Dan, especially to Sichuan Province as it was a very popular holiday resort with beautiful scenery and delicious food. Zhang Feng was a bit hesitant. Yu Mei said,

"You should calm down in the lake after coming back from the sea. I will look after the business here. Feel free to go with Dan Dan."

Dan Dan was pleased to travel with Zhang Feng, as she had heard the Jiuzhai Valley was the best place in the world to enjoy aquatic scenery. They travelled again by high-speed rail. As they approached Sichuan, they saw the train was speeding in the mountains. Some railway bridges between the two mountains were several hundred metres high. There were so many tunnels, some even over ten kilometres long. Zhang Feng said with emotion, no wonder the foreigners called China 'an infrastructure giant'. Chinese engineers and workers could finish such a huge railway project in just a few years.

They visited the panda park in Chengdu and tasted the hot pot there. Then they flew to the famous Jiuzhai Valley national park. In this beautiful and peaceful park, people could see all kinds of scenery formed by water: rushing rivers, screen-like waterfalls, green-blue lakes. They sat on a lakeside grass field surrounded by dense forest. Gazing at the blue-green crystal clear lake, Zhang Feng said.

"I have seen pictures of the lakes in the Rocky Mountains in Canada. The colour of the lakes there is the same as the lakes here, as the water is the melted water flowing down from the high mountains covered with snow and ice. Because there were different minerals in the water, the colour is so unusually beautiful."

Dan Dan said she had once travelled to the Rocky Mountains with Liang Hua. She was amazed by the beauty of Lake Louisa, which was facing a huge glacier and surrounded by dense pine forest. The colour of the lake water was the same as the lake in front of them. Zhang Feng asked,

"You must have enjoyed that time. Liang Hua is a nice man." Attentive Dan Dan noticed a hint of jealousy in Zhang Feng's words. She said with a smile,

"What are you talking about? We always stayed in separate rooms. I feel sorry for him, that I have kept him waiting for many years, just because I was unable to forget my childhood sweetheart."

Zhang Feng understood the reason why Dan Dan could not marry Liang Hua was that she still loved him. Although Dan Dan was no longer legally his wife now, in his mind, she was still his wife. Seeing nobody nearby, he held her in his arms. Looking at the crystal lake, Dan Dan asked him,

"After seeing the sea and looking at the lake now, do you have some different feelings?" Her words surprised him. 'Does Dan Dan know that I compare Yu Mei to the sea and her to a lake?' he thought. Noticing the surprised expression on his face, she said to him with a smile,

"Are you trying to hide this secret from me? Yu Mei has told me about your comparisons. We regard each other as sisters and are willing to share any secret."

Listening to Dan Dan's explanation, he felt relaxed and said half in jest,

"Looking at this tranquil, crystal clear lake, makes me feel so peaceful. Yes, I like the sea, but I also like the lake that is like a virtuous and beautiful wife, letting me feel happy."

Dan Dan patted him and said,

"You do have a sweet mouth!" They kissed each other.

Zhang Feng did not realise that in one month's time, he could see the three ladies who loved him separately. Back from Sichuan, he received an invitation from an international city development forum held in Paris. He travelled to France and attended the forum. After the forum finished, he planned to tour the city. In the evening when he looked at the map to find the main attractions in Paris, somebody knocked on the door. He thought it was the hotel waiter. But he was surprised to see Qing Lian was at the door. She wore a white skirt and looked pretty and slim. Like Dan Dan and Yu Mei, she was beautiful and did not look her age.

She told Zhang Feng that she had come to France to research the tourism there. She and Li He planned to offer a new holiday itinerary in Europe because Chinese people had more money and they could afford international holidays now. Recalling their holiday on Hainan Island last time, Zhang Feng realised that actually, she had tried to find a chance to get together with him, although it seemed so difficult for her. Feeling he owed it to her in the past, he agreed to explore the city with her for a few days. She was very pleased.

The next day, they visited the Eifel Tower, Notre Dame

and some famous museums. Qing Lian always held his hand and he accepted this as they were abroad and no acquaintance would see them. Qing Lian said she wanted to go to the famous department store Galleries Lafayette to buy something for her daughter Lan Hua. What surprised them was there were so many Chinese tourists in the shop, 'panic buying'. They bought a lot of designer brand clothes, bags and shoes. Zhang Feng said to Qing Lian that Chinese people were richer now. An overseas Chinese beside them told them that thirty years ago, he only saw Japanese tourists here, and the leaflets were only in Japanese. But in recent years, there were more and more Chinese tourists here. The shop had not only added Chinese to their leaflets but also employed Chinese assistants to serve the Chinese customers.

Qing Lian took a fancy to a famous brand handbag and said she would like to buy one for Lan Hua, but was hesitant after looking at the price tag. Zhang Feng called the shop assistant and asked for two of the bags that Qing Lian liked. Qing Lian said to him,

"I did not ask you to buy the bag."

"Lan Hua is my daughter as well," he said.

"But why did you buy two? Is the other one for Yu Mei?" she asked.

"No, no, the other one is for my daughter's mother," he answered with a smile.

She patted him to show she was very happy.

The next day, they visited the Palace of Versailles. After the tour inside the palace, they sat on a bench at the side of a clear stream. Seeing nobody nearby, Qing Lian learned on his shoulder. Watching the clear stream water, Zhang Feng thought, 'Yu Mei is like a sea, Dan Dan is like a lake, Qing Lian is more like this gurgling stream that gives me a different feeling of relaxation and cosiness.' Looking at him, Qing Lian quietly asked him,

"Brother Feng, do you love me?"

He smiled and asked,

"Why do women always like to ask this question? Is it so much more important than other things?"

Qing Lian pretended to be unhappy and said,

"You will tell me again, you only treat me as a little sister."

"Oh, no, my feeling for you is more than a sister."

"In that case, am I your lover? I am satisfied."

He remembered that Qing Lian used to be his political enemy during the Cultural Revolution, and then became his saviour. She was reluctant to marry Li He and divorced him later because she still loved Zhang Feng secretly. After an accidental meeting, she conceived their daughter Lan Hua. Thinking of all these twists and turns, Zhang Feng's heart was full of guilt and love. He could not help embracing and kissing her. She was moved to tears.

After forming the joint venture, Wang Hai's business was booming. One day he was attending a forum in Beijing to discuss the developments in the manufacturing industry after the reform. He met many business tycoons and heard their optimistic expectations about the manufacturing development of the country. He was amused by these exciting facts: The economic aggregate of China had overtaken that of Japan, becoming No 2 in the world, after the USA. The manufacturing industry was No 1 in the world. Steel production, total trade of import and export, foreign exchange reserves were all No1 in the world.

The truth was one century ago the only industries China had were clothes, towels and soaps. But now the country could make motor vehicles, high-speed trains, power equipment, aeroplanes, electrical appliances, and more. The change was enormous.

When he applauded the report, a tender little white hand patted his shoulder. Turning back, he was surprised to see Helen, the woman he missed from time to time. During the break, they sat on the bench in the front garden outside the building. They had not met for five years. Helen was in her fifties, but still looked young and charming. She told Wang Hai that she had divorced her husband as she was fed up with his effeminate character. He was not masculine like Wang Hai. After saying this, she looked at him with deep emotion. Her story made Wang Hai's heart ache. He tried to comfort her.

She asked Wang Hai to look around Beijing with her for a few days. Wan Hai agreed to her request because here he was far away from Jili City. They visited the Forbidden City, Beihai Park, Heaven Temple and the modern CBD district. Helen said the city construction in the capital had developed so rapidly. Beijing was a metropolis now, a mixture of ancient culture and modern architecture.

On the evening of their last day in Beijing, they drank and chatted in Wang Hai's hotel room until very late. Helen showed no sign of leaving and Wang Hai also wanted to stay with her longer. Maybe because of the alcohol, they did not restrain themselves. Helen leant on Wang Hai's shoulder and whispered,

"Brother Hai, you said you regard me as your female intimate. But… can I… can I be more than a female intimate?"

Wang Hai understood she wanted to have physical contact with him. He could feel his libido was also higher with the power of alcohol. But he still hesitated as he felt guilty about betraying his wife. Helen understood his dilemma and said to him,

"Brother Hai, do not worry. I will not destroy your family. I am not the 'other woman'. I have to confess to you my private secret. For many years, I have fantasised about your body since I saw the picture in the newspaper which was taken after you won the cross-river swimming championship. Can… you… let me…" Wang Hai was moved by her words and thought, 'Why can't we do it, since she just loves me without any strings attached. Chinese people now tolerate sexual openness more and even have 'one night stands', not to mention we love each other.' Then he picked her up and walked towards the bed. She stroked his strong chest muscles and closed her eyes in anticipation.

Unlike the love affairs of Zhang Feng and Wang Hai, Li He was very busy with his travel agent work, as Qing Lian was still in Europe. With their better standard of living, more and more people started to take holidays, not only inland but also worldwide, especially to Egypt and Greece, as Chinese people liked ancient civilisations.

One day, during lunchtime, an old man walked in and asked Li He to book an inland holiday for a group of retired people. He said most retired people did not need to work and their children had their own family and careers. So having time and money, they should enjoy their own life now. Li He agreed with him and suggested to him and his friends to have a package tour to the Three Gorges on Yangzi River and Emei Mountain. The man liked this suggestion and booked the tour.

Comparing the life of old people before the reform with that after the reform, Li He saw a huge difference. Before the reform, old people could only squeeze in with their children in the same house, looking after their grandchildren without entertainment or holidays. But thirty years after the reform, the standard of living had risen considerably, old people and their children were able to live separately in different properties and enjoyed their own life, without the trouble caused by the generation gap.

Li He's home was close to Zhang Feng and Wang Hai's home. In the morning, he and his wife would go to the nearby park to practise Tai Chi. He could also watch Zhang Feng and Dan Dan's father doing martial arts. Wang Hai also tried to learn a few movements with them. Dan Dan, Yu Mei and Qing Lian practised Tai Chi Fan with a group of women. After their morning exercise, people would buy deep-fried dough sticks and soymilk in the morning market for breakfast. The retired people would remain in the park, playing chess and cards, flying kites and dancing. In the evening, women would do square dancing and Yanko dance. Liang Hua once said old Chinese people enjoyed a richer retirement life. Yet in the West, old people only walked with their dogs, lonely, in the morning. During the daytime, some of them might play golf. But most of them had much fewer social activities. That was why some old Chinese people returned to their country after visiting their children in the West as they felt retirement there was too dull.

By coincidence, Lan Hua and Bai He gave birth to two big boys on the same day, which made both families very happy. They had a get-together to celebrate the birth of their third generation. At the party, Zhang Feng said he was amazed by the great social and economic changes during his trips to Shanghai and Sichuan. China had become a dynamic and prosperous modern country. Compared with the past country with its poverty, famines, civil wars before the liberation and during the dictatorship, persecution and chaos of the Cultural Revolution, it was a golden age now in modern Chinese history.

Wang Hai said he heard the exciting report in his meeting in Beijing that China had become the second-largest economic giant in the world. Manufacturing, exports and imports, infrastructure and foreign exchange reserves were all first in the world. Li He said even old people could afford to have holidays. Yu Mei said,

"If we look at the changes in the valuable items in a family, we can see the changing times. In the 1970s the most common four big items in a family were bicycles, watches, radios and sewing machines. In the 1980s, the new four items became washing machines, fridge freezers, black and white TV and tape recorders. In the 1990s, they were upgraded to air conditioners, audio equipment, colour TV and video recorders. By 2000, the new four big items were apartments, cars, mobiles and computers."

"The living condition in big cities are very similar to those in the West. People with good jobs own their homes, having cars and going on holidays. This better life is due to the reform movement which released the creativity and business talent of Chinese people, plus their hard-working tradition. The changes do not come from the leadership of those left-wing and corrupt leaders. On the contrary, the less their involvement, the faster the economy would develop." Dan Dan said.

Yu Mei smiled and said to Chang Zheng,

"Do not worry, Dan Dan does not mention you. You are an honest leader. People need you."

Chang Zheng said he did not worry as he would retire in a few years' time, and would be an ordinary citizen. Zhang Feng said,

"As Dickens said in A Tale of Two Cities, this is the best time, but also a time with a lot of serious social issues. A society is like a wall under the sunshine. It has the bright side and a dark side. You need to see both sides, otherwise you bowdlerise history. On the dark side we mainly see the corruption and the difference between the rich and poor. Although the anti-corruption movement is being implemented, the corruption is still spreading. The solution is the improvement of the political system to control the power, like the previous open-minded leaders Hu Yaobang, Zhao Ziyang and Wen Jiabao. But those left-wing leaders still strongly oppose political reform as they do not want to lose their power and privileges. The difference between the rich and poor is also a serious social issue. Although there are more and more wealthy and middle-class citizens, a lot of people in remote areas and weak groups of people living in the slums of the city still live a hard life."

"Young people in the city are still under great pressure, struggling with paying for their mortgages and cars, looking after their children and old parents at the same time as they are all the only child in their family after the birth control policy implemented since the 1980s." Li He agreed.

"Moral bankruptcy is a serious problem. In order to earn more money, some people dare to do anything, such as drug trafficking, internet fraud, using waste oil, even selling poisoned milk powder." Huang Lei added.

Zhang Feng pointed out, "Timon's curse of money used to be our criticism of decadent capitalism. Yet it has become a mirror of a part of our society. A lot of our social issues are very similar to those that occurred in the period of capitalist primitive accumulation."

Chang Zheng worried, "If we do not resolve these serious social issues, our progress towards democracy will be blocked. Like some middle-income countries, our economy will fall into the trap of stagnation."

Not wanting to affect the happy atmosphere of the party, Wang Hai said,

"Ai, Ai, do not forget today is a celebration of the birth of my two nephews. Please talk about something happier, and leave serious topics to other days!"

Everybody laughed and agreed. Zhang Feng and Chang Zheng whispered to Wang Hai, "Did you meet Helen again in Beijing? That is why you looked so happy recently. But remember, a one night stand is fine, but damaging your family relationship is not allowed!"

Wang Hai looked at Zhang Feng's fist, and asked, "Brother Feng, tell me, when you will stop practising your Pili boxing?"

"I will never stop!" Zhang Feng answered. Chang Zheng could not help laughing loudly.

Chapter IV

Following Taoism in His Retirement Life

Life was a dream. Time was flying. 2015 had come. Zhang Feng had reached retirement age, although he could carry on as a CEO of a private company. His mood had changed from active Confucianism to quieter Taoism. Unlike the Confucian scholars in ancient times, his main concern was that human development had damaged the natural environment. Another concern was that political reform had almost stopped, and even moved backwards. The excessive centralisation of power and the strict control of freedom of speech indicated a return to the Cultural Revolution. Even some retired top leaders were also worried about this. If a person could not follow the political activity of Confucianism, he would follow the natural outlook of Taoism.

Noticing Zhang Feng reading Laozi's Tao De Jing every evening, Yu Mei started to worry, and asked him,

"Brother Feng, why are you interested in Taoism now? Do you want to be a Taoist monk?"

"Will you accompany me if I go to the Taoist temple? You may teach me some Taoist true meanings as you were a Taoist nun before," he said.

She looked worried and said to him,

"Brother, do not go too deep into their belief. I went to the Taoist temple because I was hopeless at that time. But you are successful, belong to the elite, with a happy family, and… and three women who love you deeply. Are you willing to give up all of this? The days in the Taoist temple are not pleasant for ordinary people."

Pulling her to his side and stroking her hair, he said,

"My dear little fairy, I am teasing you. How can I leave my beloved ones, especially you, the sea in my mind? I just want to give the business to my children and leave the noisy city, build a farmhouse in a remote area and enjoy a relaxing rural life there."

Yu Mei was pleased to hear his words and said,

"That is very good. I will go with you. Like Tao Yuanming, the famous ancient Chinese poet, we will spend our happy remaining years in a peaceful rural area."

Zhang Feng also told Dan Dan about his wish to have a rural retirement life. Dan Dan said she supported his idea. She would like to assist Dang Feng for a while and then join Zhang Feng and Yu Mei after Dan Feng could operate the company by himself.

Zhang Feng held a family meeting. His son, daughter, son-in-law and daughter-in-law all came. Dan Feng had finished his MBA course and had a basic knowledge of business management, plus his IT training, so he felt confident about running the business. Zhang Feng told the children his retirement plan. He said he would resign from his position as chairman of the board. Dan Dan would be the acting chairman of the board. Dan Feng would be the CEO. Lan Hua worked as their legal representative, Jian Jun was the manager of the architect design department. Lin Jianguo and Chen Tao would continue to assist Dan Feng and the other young people until they retired. Dan Feng and his friends felt sad about Zhang Feng's retirement plan but they were happy that he would have a peaceful retirement.

A few days later, Zhang Feng, Yu Mei, Dan Dan, Lin Jianguo, Chen Tao and two other construction engineers came to the small lake area which He Hua had recommended to Zhang Feng on his previous visit. Zhang Feng had bought the land there. Yu Mei, Dan Dan and the two engineers all liked the beautiful and quiet environment. The engineers said they could build a four-bedroom bungalow with a two-bedroom annex, in case friends with their families were visiting and staying here.

Dan Dan suggested the front of the house would have a garden, and there could be a vegetable garden at the back of the house as the rural life should have the fun of farming. The engineers asked whether Zhang Feng was interested in growing grain. Lin Jianguo said,

"Did you know that CEO Zhang earned 3,000 working points when he did farming as an educated youth during the Cultural Revolution?"

"I would like to build a farm to grow organic vegetables and crops which would make the people in the city envy me." Zhang Feng said, everybody laughed.

Zhang Feng added, "I also want to follow the idea of the ecological parks in England, using solar power, underground water, biogas, and so on."

Chen Tao agreed, "Green energy is the future direction. The pollution in the city is quite serious. But here you will have fresh air, pure water, organic food, and farm work as exercise. CEO Zhang will definitely live to one hundred." Everybody laughed.

It was very convenient for Zhang Feng to have his own construction team. After the engineers finished the design of the bungalow, Lin Jainguo led a construction team to build it, and finished it in one month. In the summer, his family and friends were all keen to see this farmhouse. Arriving at the bungalow, they saw the front garden was full of flowers and fruit trees. Seeing the peony in the garden, Dan Dan was happy as her name meant peony. Lan Hua and Bai He also saw their flowers (Lan Hua meant orchid, Bai He meant lily). Zhang Feng told them he had planted some plum trees in the garden, which would blossom in wintertime, and Yu Mei smiled because her name meant plum flower. Noticing Qing Lian looked unhappy, Zhang Feng told her that he had planted a lot of lotus in the lake, which made her happy as her name meant lotus. Zheng Feng told them it was He Hua who had helped him to plant the front garden and the vegetable garden at the back of the house.

Entering the house, the visitors saw modern decoration and appliances including a washing machine, fridge-freezer, TV and electric heaters. Zhang Feng said the power was all generated by the solar panels on the roof. The water for the house came from a deep well. The construction team had laid an optical fibre cable in the house to provide telephone and internet. Zhang Feng said the internet was mainly for Dan Dan and Yu Mei, as they still wanted to socialise and entertain themselves online. He himself preferred a quiet environment without phone calls and emails. Everybody said they could fully understand. Li He said,

"The internet helps us to not be cut off from the world. Like ancient Confucian scholars, although Brother Feng is a hermit, he still misses the court and is concerned about national affairs and the people. It means he follows Taoism to have a secluded life, but he still has Confucianism in his mind." People around Zhang Feng all laughed.

Zhang Feng's secluded life began. Dan Dan would join them later, so at first, it was a two-person world for Zhang Feng and Yu Mei. Every morning, they ran along the lake. He practised martial arts and sang facing the mountains, enjoying the echo of his voice. Yu Mei was impressed and applauded him. After breakfast, they started reading. Apart from Taoist classics, Zhang Feng read some English novels. He recommended some English and French novels to Yu Mei. Yu Mei suggested that he should write a personal memoir or a novel based on his experience, as his experience was so complex and colourful. He had been a handsome and talented young man, a counter-revolutionary, a death-row prisoner, a famous scholar, a brave politician, a successful businessman and a modern Taoist.

Zhang Feng smiled and said,

"Should I add my love story to it?"

"Can you create a better image of me? Do not write about my miserable story with Cai," she said.

"My little fairy, my turbulent sea, I will describe you as my glorious goddess," he said.

After lunch, they started their farm work. In their greenhouse, they watered the various vegetables. They fed the chickens and ducks and tended the crops. They even had a rice field to grow tasty northeast rice.

In the evening, when the sun was setting in the west, on the grass field at the side of the lake, Yu Mei gracefully danced the traditional Chinese dance 'A Moonlit Night on the Spring

River' to the accompaniment of Zhang Feng's violin. Sometimes they enjoyed ballroom dancing, or he sang an aria from an Italian opera. Their singing and dancing attracted a lot of small animals, birds, rabbits, squirrels, and even deer, standing on the trees or in the wood to enjoy their performance. Zhang Feng said to Yu Mei,

"We live in harmony with nature now."

Dan Dan would visit them every weekend, telling them how the business was performing. She would stay overnight. Then Yu Mei would stay in the annexe and let Dan Dan sleep with Zhang Feng. Dan Dan accepted this arrangement. It was like the situation in the past when two sisters married the same man.

Qing Lian visited them once a month. Each time she asked to stay in a guest room, but Yu Mei insisted on staying in the annexe to let Zhang Feng and Qing Lian sleep together. Both Yu Mei and Dan Dan accepted the fact that Qing Lian was the third woman who loved Zhang Feng deeply, and also had a daughter with him. So they did not mind that she visited Zhang Feng occasionally. Dan Feng and Bai He, Jian Jun and Lan Hua, with their boys, also visited them from time to time.

Autumn came, and friends wanted to see the harvest in Zhang Feng's 'farm'. One weekend, Wang Hai, Li He and Chang Zheng came to the bungalow. They were surprised to see the fruit trees were full of fruit, and various vegetables grew lushly in the vegetable garden and greenhouse. In the field, corn grew on the cobs and golden rice swayed in the wind. Zhang Feng said to them that today was their farmhouse holiday. They could enjoy tasty organic food and go swimming, hunting, fishing and mountain climbing.

Wang Hai enthused, "It is so lovely"

They swam in the warm lake for an hour, and then started fishing. Wang Hai was impatient, pulling up the fishing rod too often and getting nothing. Chang Zheng and Li He were more patient. Chang Zheng caught a big carp, and shouted with excitement.

Wang Hai asked him,

"You are the deputy governor and so busy with the leadership work. Why do you still have such great patience?"

"Ask Brother Feng, he will tell you that as an official, you have to be very patient to deal with the bureaucracy there," Chang Zheng said.

Li He also caught a grass carp. They announced that they would have fresh fish to eat that evening.

They enjoyed an abundant farm banquet in the evening: braised carp with soy sauce, stewed grass carp, mushroom with chicken, various fresh vegetables, fresh sweetcorn pancakes, fresh rice, rice wine and more. Everybody got very full and said they would never have such nice organic food in the city.

The next day, they went to the mountain to hunt. Both Chang Zheng and Zhang Feng had good marksmanship. Chang Zheng hit two wild rabbits. Zhang Feng hit an Eastern roe deer. But Wang Hai hit nothing. He said he would go to the shooting club to practise and come back in the wintertime to go hunting again.

Zhang Feng told them it was good fun in the wintertime here. You could go skating on the lake and go skiing on the mountain. Wintertime was also a good season for hunting. Li He said he would really like to set up a four-season farmhouse holiday programme in this area, which would definitely attract many holidaymakers. Zhang Feng said he would ask He Hua to see whether her team could open a farmhouse resort in this area.

On Monday morning, when Wang Hai, Chang Zheng and Li He left, they took with them bags and bags of organic vegetables and grains that Yu Mei prepared for them. Wang Hai said to Zhang Feng emotionally,

"Brother Feng, you live a fairytale life now."

"True, here there are no political struggles, no business competition, I live in harmony with nature and enjoy fresh air and green food. I have a better life than Tao Yuanming, who was keen to follow Taoism in the Jin Dynasty," Zhang Feng said.

"Your life is the 5.0 version of the Land of Peach Blossoms by Tao Yuanming," Chang Zheng said. Everyone laughed.

During a weekend when both Dan Dan and Yu Mei were in the bungalow, somebody rang the doorbell. Zhang Feng thought it must be He Hua, but it turned out to be Wang Li and Liang Hua. They all greeted each other warmly. Wang Li told them that she and Liang Hua had travelled back from the UK for a holiday. They heard that Zhang Feng had retired and lived in a farmhouse, so they came here to visit him and his family. Liang Hua said he also wanted to find a farmhouse in Cornwall to live in after he retired. Zhang Feng, Dan Dan and Yu Mei showed them the house, garden, field and surroundings. Both Wang Li and Liang Hua praised the place for its beauty, saying it was really a Utopia.

At lunchtime, Yu Mei prepared lunch while Dan Dan walked around the lake with Liang Hua. Zhang Feng had tea with Wang Li, who said to him with a smile,

"My dear Hamlet, I had not realised that after your careers as a scholar, politician, Confucian businessman, you have become a Taoist hermit. Will your father not feel disappointed in Heaven?"

"He would feel pleased for me as I did so many good things

for the Chinese people. I saw him in the wood last night, and he said he also wanted to learn Taoism to ease his resentment," Zhang Feng joked. Then he whispered,

"Having a happy life with the Prince of Norway?"

"Fine, just still miss my Prince of Denmark," she said.

"Hamlet is old now. Ophelia would not bother to look at him," he said. Both of them laughed.

At the lakeside, Dan Dan and Liang Hua were chatting. Noticing the loving expression in his eyes, Dan Dan said,

"I am sorry I kept you waiting for so many years." Liang Hua said he could understand the love between her and Zhang Feng. Wang Li was not as good as Dan Dan, but she was capable and careful. He was pleased with her. Dan Dan smiled and said that was good.

When they said goodbye to each other, Wang Li and Liang Hua said they would invite Zhang Feng and his ladies to visit their English-style farmhouse after they made it ready. Zhang Feng and his ladies accepted their invitation.

EPILOGUE

A few weeks after the visit of Wang Hai, Li He and Chang Zheng, Yu Mei suggested,

"Shall we go back to see our children and grandchildren?" Zhang Feng agreed. Then they travelled back to the River City for a weekend to see their family. Dan Feng, Bai He, their son and Dan Dan lived in Dan Dan's villa. Jian Jun, Lan Hua and their son lived in the villa that belonged to Zhang Feng and Yu Mei. Seeing Zhang Feng and Yu Mei, all their children and grandchildren were very happy. They had a delicious dinner together. The organic food brought back by Zhang Feng and Yu Mei was particularly welcomed.

After the dinner, Zhang Feng received a phone call from Wang Hai, who mysteriously told Zhang Feng that he had invited Zhang Feng, Yu Mei and Dan Dan to the North

Mountain to enjoy the autumn scenery the following day, and not to bring the children with them. Zhang Feng asked if there was any special event there, but Wang Hai said they would find out when they got there.

The next day was Sunday. Following Wang Hai's request, Zhang Feng, Yu Mei and Dan Dan arrived at the park at 10.00 am, and Wang Hai, Li He and Qing Lian also came a few minutes later. They all asked Wang Hai,

"What are you playing at today?"

"Although we all are elderly in our sixties, we can still have an autumn outing. Autumn is a season of maturity. We are also in the autumn period of our lives. We can consider today as a class reunion to enjoy ourselves." Wang Hai grinned.

Because business and family were all going well, everybody was in a good mood to follow Wang Hai.

Close to the entrance, they saw a lamb kebab stand. Wang Hai said he had not tasted lamb kebabs in a long time, so he asked the ladies to wait at the entrance, and brought Zhang Feng and Li He to the stand. The seller had bent over to sprinkle salt and cumin on the lamb kebabs. But when he lifted up his head, Zhang Feng, Wang Hai and Li He were all surprised. This thin man with grey hair was Cai Wenge, the life-long sworn enemy of Zhang Feng. Seeing Zhang Feng and his friends, he looked very fearful, trembling and dropping his iron tongs on the ground.

Wang Hai asked him, "CEO Cai, have you been released from jail? Are you not in the real estate business now?"

Cai Wenge had been sentenced to three years in jail two years before, but there had been a possibility he might get a medical release again to get out earlier. Li He asked him,

"Was it your backstage supporter Shen who helped you again? But he still has another nine years in prison."

"No, no, I am really sick this time and received compassionate release. You can see, I am very weak. A gust of wind can blow me over," Cai hastily explained.

Seeing this vicious enemy who had ferociously competed with Zhang Feng all his life, Zhang Feng was full of hatred. Cai had sent Zhang Feng to the execution ground during the Cultural Revolution, ruining Yu Mei's future, and had framed Zhang Feng many times in commercial circles. Zhang Feng could not help saying to him,

"The saying goes, 'good will be rewarded with good and evil with evil' and this is fulfilled in you. You have done all kinds of evil. You deserve this retribution."

Unlike his previous wild arrogance, Cai was humble, lowering his head. He admitted his defeat for the first time in his life, saying,

"I admit defeat. I have fought you for fifty years. I lost to you in love, officialdom and business. Now my only wish is to have enough food and live a few more years."

Seeing this poisonous snake, Zhang Feng and his friends all lost their appetite. Before they left Cai's stand, Wang Hai warned Cai,

"You have always cheated and harmed people in whatever you do. Is the lamb you are selling rotten? If you do that, we will inform on you to the city management office." Cai Wenge was scared and said, no, no, the lamb he used was all fresh.

Zhang Feng, Wang Hai and Li He went back to the ladies. Noticing Yu Mei was upset, Zhang Feng realised that she and the other two ladies recognised Cai selling the lamb kebabs. Patting her shoulder, Zhang Feng comforted her and told her that Cai was a frozen snake now and was unable to bite people. Li He said he heard Cai's wife had divorced him. He was very poor and could only afford to live in a migrant worker's shed. He could only earn a little bit of money by selling lamb kababs, almost like a beggar. Dan Dan and Qing Lian said he was in the situation of the proverb, 'He who is unjust is doomed to destruction.'

Not wanting this snake to spoil the happy feeling of the group, Wang Hai said,

"The evil person has been punished, which will make decent people pleased. Let's ignore him and enjoy our tour."

Then they climbed the mountain. The good weather had attracted a lot of tourists. Zhang Feng and his group were in good mood. They sat on a big rock to enjoy the autumn scenery in front of them: the surging river flowing eastward, hazy lofty mountains, colourful trees vivid against the blue sky and white clouds. The sound of dashing waves and the whistling of the wind in the pines played a duet of nature. What a picturesque landscape!

As before, the ladies were interested in picking the wild vegetables. There were even more of them in autumn. They walked to the back of the temple to search for them. When they left, Wang Hai mysteriously said to Zhang Feng and Li He,

"Buddies, do you know why I asked you to come here today?"

Zhang Feng and Li He guessed that Wang Hai knew Cai was selling lamb kebabs there and wanted them to see his miserable image. Wang Hai said, no, it was not because of him. Li He thought for a while, and said it was because of that fortune-telling picture for Brother Feng. Wang Hai said,

"Good! Li He, although you are not as clever as Brother Feng, sometimes you can have mortal wisdom. Brother Feng, can you still remember the year when you got the fortune-telling picture from the old Taoist monk?"

"I think a year before the Cultural Revolution, so it must have been 1965," Zhang Feng said.

"1965? This year is 2015. It means fifty years have passed," Li He said, surprising them.

"Yes, half a century has passed. We should be able to conclude whether the prediction of the Taoist monk was accurate or not. I am going to find the picture now," Wang Hai said.

Zhang Feng said the picture would be damaged after such a long time. Wang Hai said it might be fine. Then he walked to the wall of the temple to search the picture. But both Zhang Feng and Li He felt the chance of finding the picture was very small. As they expected, Wang Hai searched in vain for about ten minutes. At this point, the three ladies came back, carrying a few bags of wild vegetables. Zhang Feng called Wang Hai to stop his search. The three ladies asked Li He what Wang Hai was looking for. At this moment, waving a picture in his hand, Wang Hai shouted,

"I found it! I found it!"

Zhang Feng gestured to Wang Hai, telling him to keep quiet. But he walked to the ladies and announced loudly,

"I will tell you a secret concealed for fifty years."

Zhang Feng did not want to tell the secret to the ladies, so he made a few more gestures to Wang Hai, asking him to stop. Wang Hai said to him,

"Brother Feng, half a century has passed, you should let the people involved know the secret."

Li He also felt it was time to tell the secret to the three ladies. Zhang Feng helplessly waved his hand, giving his permission to Wang Hai to tell the story.

Wang Hai deliberately made things look mysterious. He opened the old picture and showed it to the ladies. They looked at it with great curiosity. Dan Dan said,

"It looks like a rough drawing by a child. These are three mountains, one is tall, and the other two on its sides are lower. Is this a garden at the foot of the mountain? Why are there only a few flowers? There is a coil of rope as well."

"I do not understand what secret lies in this picture." Yu Mei said.

Wang Hai smiled and said,

"I guessed you would not understand. Let me tell you the background story of this picture."

Then he told the three ladies about what happened in 1965. He said in that year, Zhang Feng, Li He and he had gone on a spring outing here. They heard there was an old monk would could tell people's fortunes. Then they asked the monk to predict Zhang Feng's future. The monk drew this picture for him. But he did not tell Zhang Feng the meaning of the picture, asking him to think about it. Because Wang Hai was very interested in fortune-telling, so he guessed: the high peak was Zhang Feng, the other peaks were his two friends, Wang Hai and Li He. The three flowers indicated his love affairs, meaning he would have three women loving him. About the rope, Wang Hai guessed it looked like a snake as it was wrapped around the high peak at the time. So the conclusion was: in his life, Brother Feng would have one enemy, two friends and three lovers. Wang Hai said,

"At the time Brother Feng argued with me that he was a decent and honest young man, president of the student union, but not a playboy, how could he have three women in his life? Li He also said Brother Feng was a people person so it was unlikely he would have any enemies. Zhang Feng was not superstitious, so he thought the monk just blindly drew this picture, and was about to throw it away. I tried to persuade him to keep it for future verification. Then I hid it in a gap of the wall. In the end, after fifty years, we found the picture really told the truth."

The picture predicted Zhang Feng would have three lovers! Dan Dan, Yu Mei and Qing Lian looked at each other. It was true! Noticing the surprised expression of the ladies, Wang Hai exultingly said,

"There are more incredible things to see in the picture. Please look at the flowers carefully." The three ladies lowered their heads to inspect the flowers.

"My god, this is a plum blossom." (matching her name) Yu Mei exclaimed.

"This is a peony," Dan Dan said. (matching her name)

Qing Lian looked even more surprised,

"What? There is a lotus as well." (matching her name).

Wang Hai said proudly,

"Isn't it incredible? Do not forget, Brother Feng had not met Yu Mei at that time. Dan Dan was only his 'sister'. What about Qing Lian? She hated Brother Feng at that time because she thought Brother Feng had put her love letter to him on the notice board. Sorry Qing Lian, it was me who put your letter on the board, which made you hate him for so many years. The snake? You all know that it is the evil Cai Wenge."

Wang Hai said, the most magical thing was, after certain periods of time, whenever they met in the North Mountain, the seven persons in the picture were always all there. The three ladies expressed surprise. Then they started to recall together. They remembered after the end of the Cultural Revolution, there was one gathering in spring 1980, Zhang Feng, Wang Hai, Qing Lian and Dan Dan were all on the top of the mountain. Cai Wenge was a prisoner, digging a ditch at the foot of the mountain with a team of prisoners. Only Yu Mei was not there on the day. Wang Hai thought the monk's prediction was not very accurate. But afterwards, they found out that Yu Mei was actually worshipping in the temple on the day and she had asked Zhang Feng not to tell anybody else. Fifteen years later, one day in spring 1995, after Brother Feng established his company, the six of us were all on the top of the mountain, without Cai Wenge. Wang Hai thought the monk's fortune-telling was not that accurate. But Cai suddenly appeared in front of them and challenged Brother Feng again. Then in springtime, 1997, the seven persons in the picture were all here again, with Cai promoting his business at the entrance of the park. This time was fifty years after the monk drew this picture for Brother Feng. What happened? The seven persons were here again!

Seeing the ladies were bemused by the monk's fortune telling, Wang Hai said,

"I have told Brother Feng many times that I would like to be a fortune teller after I retire. I would have some training in the Taoist temple and then go into the fortune-telling business. I think I would earn more than I do now, working for the company as a CEO."

Listening to his talk, Yu Mei asked him whether he could bear the vegetarian food, without meat, and the dull worship and meditation in the temple. Everybody laughed.

They all sat on the rock to discuss the meaning of the fortune-telling picture. The three ladies said to Zhang Feng,

"Brother Feng. We are meant to be your lovers. That is why we have always stayed with you, no matter how much hardship we have experienced."

Seeing Zhang Feng look embarrassed, Li He said,

"The fortune-telling picture indeed predicted Brother Feng's fortune. But it also shows that it is fate that has brought us together. Remember? He has saved every one of us and we have also tried to save him when he was in dangerous situations. Our fate is closely connected with his."

Everybody agreed with Li He.

Watching the grand scenery in front of them, Zhang Feng said with emotion,

"We have experienced our life of ups and downs and the upheaval of the past half century. I used to be a young man intending to serve our country. But unfortunately I became a counter-revolutionary and death-row prisoner during the Cultural Revolution. I was saved at the last second on the execution ground, and was lucky to be in the first batch of university students to graduate after the Cultural Revolution. Then I was a famous scholar, and a brave politician pushing the reform movement. Finally, I entered the commercial world to devote myself to building a modern and prosperous China. The ship of my destiny sailed the red storm of the disastrous Cultural Revolution, sailing through the turbulent sea of politics during the reform time, then sailing against the wind and waves on the sea of commerce and finally sailed into the peaceful Taoist harbour."

His friends and lovers all said he had made an excellent summary of his life. His personal destiny was closely linked to that of the country. Our country's historical ship also suffered from the red storm during the Cultural Revolution, sailing the turbulent sea and treacherous shoals during the periods of economic and political reforms. Hopefully, like your ship, our country's ship will also sail into a happy and peaceful harbour.

Gazing at the colourful autumn scenery, Zhang Feng said,

"The historical changes of our country in this half century are more like the changes of the seasons. The Cultural Revolution in the 1960s and 1970s was like a harsh winter, devoid of life and vitality; the reform in the 1980s was like springtime, full of hope and life; the commercial wave from the 1990s until now is like a hot summer, with all things growing profusely, but with tigers, snakes, flies and bacteria. We hope the future of our country will be a colourful autumn, mature and harmonious, with freedom, democracy and prosperity."

His friends and lovers all agreed with him and said this half century was a historical chapter of sailings, and of seasons as well.

The sun was setting. Facing the golden sunshine, Zhang Feng, his friends and lovers walked confidently into the colourful autumn scenery.

This book is printed on paper from sustainable sources managed under the Forest Stewardship Council (FSC) scheme.

It has been printed in the UK to reduce transportation miles and their impact upon the environment.

For every new title that Matador publishes, we plant a tree to offset CO_2, partnering with the More Trees scheme.

For more about how Matador offsets its environmental impact, see www.troubador.co.uk/about/

For more information about the author and his work, or to get in touch, please visit his website:

http://johnxiaozhang.co.uk